SHADOW WEB

SHADOW WEB

N. M. Browne

BLOOMSBURY

I would like to thank my test readers, Will Browne, Laura Matthews, Deborah Lane and Beth Oddy for their helpful comments, my agent Mic Cheetham for her support, my editors at Bloomsbury for their patience and insight, and my family for putting up with my absent-mindedness and uncertain temper.

First published in Great Britain in 2008 by Bloomsbury Publishing Plc
36 Soho Square, London, W1D 3QY

A CIP catalogue record of this book is available from the British Library

ISBN 978 0 7475 9345 4

All papers used by Bloomsbury Publishing are natural,
recyclable products made from wood grown in well-managed
forests. The manufacturing processes conform to the
environmental regulations of the country of origin.

Typeset by Hewer Text UK Ltd, Edinburgh
Printed in Great Britain by Clays Ltd, St Ives Plc

1 3 5 7 9 10 8 6 4 2

www.bloomsbury.com

*For Paul, husband and history freak
without whom nothing much would happen*

ONE

It began when I was not doing my history essay – same old story. I needed a break and I decided to google for my name. Sad I know, but don't tell me you haven't done it. I had to be a bit furtive because Mum didn't like me going on MSN all the time. She saw some of my messages and freaked out a bit – it was just a friend talking about her and her boyfriend but, you know, my mum's a bit protective – so she was forever popping in and out, offering me cups of tea and 'just looking for something' whenever I was online. To say it was annoying would be an understatement, but I was quick at flicking back to my work screen at the sound of her heels on the kitchen tiles heading in my direction. I was listening out for her that evening while I flicked between various sites when the essay got too dull, then I typed in 'Jessica Allendon' and changed the world. Oh OK, that's melodramatic, but it isn't a lie.

Nothing much happened that night – I found one Jessica Allendon who researched old churches, one who won the hundred-metre breaststroke at some school in Virginia, and her, the one that was to cause all the

1

trouble: sixteen-year-old Jessica Allendon from some-where in London.

That added a bit of intrigue to my evening because I'm sixteen too and live somewhere in London. I clicked on the link – well you would, wouldn't you? Anything is more interesting than the cold war. And there it was – just a line of pale pink text on a black background.

'Bore da. Lighten my darkness. I would be heartened if you could choose to correspond.'

That was it and then her email address – it wasn't hotmail either, but something foreign I'd not seen before. I flicked back to my essay as Mum walked in and then back to my inbox with my heart beating like I'd just run upstairs and back or spotted Josh Heron with his shirt off in the gym. She sounded a bit geeky, but that was all right; I have my moments too and the girl had a certain style, even if pink text on black background was a bit over the top.

I typed quickly. 'Hi! Weird or wot? I'm a Jessica Allendon from Lndn. Get in touch. Mayb we're related? Do u live nywhere nr Sheen?'

I signed it 'Jess', which is what I'm called mostly, and spent the rest of the evening checking my mail – in case she replied.

I didn't get a reply for a couple of hours, and when I did it wasn't what I expected.

'Bore da. I originate from Sheen. I'm a lone wolf seeking a pack. Communication opportunities are limited. Could we perhaps meet on the steps at the first class entrance to Waterloo Station on Sunday 8th at 4.00 p.m.? I will be wearing black gloves. There is no necessity to reply. I will be there until 5.00 p.m. Be safe. Sincerely, Jessica.'

I didn't know what to make of that. It was Wednesday and I hadn't started my weekend waitressing job because Mum wouldn't let me until after my GCSEs, so I was free on Sunday, but this Jessica sounded less odd than borderline psycho and I wanted a second opinion. There was only one person I'd trust with this and that was Jonno, my best friend since for ever.

I printed the email out and hid it in the back of my Oyster card. It was exciting – wondering if I'd go or not. I'm not an idiot and I knew that 'Jessica' could be a fifty-year-old bloke with a thing for young girls, but I thought that if he was, he'd probably have tried to sound more normal – and 'Jessica' didn't sound that. Oh, and I asked Mum and found out that 'Bore da' – pronounced 'borra da' – was Welsh and meant hello. So maybe he was a fifty-year-old Welsh child molester.

Jonno was dead against me going. He isn't very adventurous and he didn't much like going up town anyway – he thought he was likely to get mugged or shot the second he stepped off the train. His dad was in the army and got killed in Northern Ireland so I suppose Jonno had his reasons for being paranoid and it never bothered me. To be honest I think he kept quiet with his mates and never let on that he would rather chew off his own foot than go out alone after dark. He didn't look like anything would bother him. He looked like he could have been in the army himself – six foot three, skinhead haircut, fit body – but I knew him when he was weedy and cried all the time so I never fell for his hard man routine.

To get back to the email – Jonno kicked up a big fuss and said if I didn't take him with me he'd tell Mum, and he would've too. He knows Mum well because he was always round our house after his dad died and his mum got depression. She's better now – his mum that is – and she remarried last year and has a new baby. My mum thinks the sun shines out of Jonno's backside. She trusts him as much as I do.

Jonno and I argued right up until we got on the train. He even left a note in his bedroom for his mum to find in case he didn't come back – typical Jonno. I was angry about that, in case she found the note before we'd even gone, but Jonno had worked it all out – she was taking the baby to see her sister and wouldn't be back until six. We stopped arguing on the train because we didn't want everyone staring at us.

I was listening to some songs I'd just downloaded on my Ipod and Jonno was on edge and pretending to read a paper; he thought I should have left my Ipod at home and knew that I was only listening to it to annoy him. It was an uneventful journey until we got to Vauxhall, when there was this amazing flash of lightning – a great white sheet of light that seemed to come from nowhere and a rumble of thunder so loud that the train began to shake. I gripped Jonno's arm and put my Ipod in his pocket so he knew I wanted a truce. I hate storms and he knew that. I've always been scared of being electrocuted – don't ask me why – and I wasn't the only person who was scared, I can tell you that: the big guy with tattoos sitting opposite me went white and took his watch off. It had a metal strap so I suppose he thought it would be safer. We stopped for about twenty minutes at Vauxhall by which time it was almost twenty to five – a stupid time to go into town as the shops shut early on Sunday.

It wasn't that busy when we got off at Waterloo. It still hadn't rained like it usually does when there's a storm, and there was a strange feeling in the air, an ominous stillness. The air smelled hot and burnt. Not smoky burnt – it's hard to describe; it smelled like a matchhead at the moment the flame ignites. I gripped Jonno's arm even tighter.

'Don't worry,' he said. 'I'm here. I won't let the nasty lightning get you.' He laughed and I almost believed him. There is something about Jonno that inspires trust. It isn't just his size because I still trusted him when I was nearly a foot taller back in nursery when we used to play Spider-Man together.

We got off at Platform 19 and walked past the Eurostar entrance towards the exit. I didn't know what she'd meant about the first class entrance, but I guessed she must mean the grandest one, the original main entrance. I was nervous as we walked along the concourse. Everything felt strange, almost muffled. The sounds of the station were muted. My trainers seemed to make no sound as we walked across the polished floor. I felt sick and I was getting the headache I often get before a storm. It felt like something big was going to happen. I wished it would rain. There should be rain. I looked up at Jonno.

'We can turn back, Jess. I won't care if you don't want to meet her.' He looked around the station for inspiration. There was a sculpture of some guy called Cuneo and an uninspiring café and then his eyes lit up. 'I knew there was an Upper Crust here. We could go get a pie – they're well tasty. We could go and eat it on the South Bank and pretend that's what we meant to do all along.'

I was quite tempted and might have agreed if he hadn't suggested a pie. I didn't want a pie. If he'd suggested we get an ice cream or even a hot chocolate, I'd have gone along with it. He didn't though. I think he thought I'd made my mind up, but I hadn't – not completely. Strange to think that if I'd been hungrier, none of what happened next would have happened.

Outside, the sky was not the dark grey I had expected, but a washed-out shade of blue. I could barely hear the traffic. I felt like my ears were blocked, like they get sometimes in a plane or up a mountain. My heart was beating very fast with something more than excitement – a kind of instinctive fear. I probably should have taken more notice of that.

'Wait here!' I said to Jonno, and he was about to argue, I know, when he saw her and his jaw dropped – as if he was a cartoon. I followed his eyes.

She was standing next to the war memorial halfway down the steps. I could see the brass plaque and the words '1914 Roll of Honour 1918' just above her head. She was wearing long trousers, more like culottes, cut so that they looked like a skirt, in some dark green cotton. She wore a crimson linen jacket in an unfamiliar cut and her dark hair was up in a bun under a small red hat. She was, as advertised, also wearing short black gloves. She looked good in an outlandish, modern retro kind of way. It wasn't the clothes that had startled either of us though, it was the fact that, apart from her scarlet slash of lipstick, she was exactly like me.

I didn't look back to check that Jonno had waited as I'd asked him. The other Jess spotted me in the same instant and appeared spooked too. She even put her hand to her mouth in an old-fashioned gesture of shock. I bit my lip. She bit hers. I felt suddenly hot all over and was getting hotter, like you do just before you faint – which I was determined not to do. I took a couple of steps towards her as she took two or three towards me. She had a neat little clutch bag under her arm too, in the same red as her jacket, and she was wearing heels. Her dark eyes were fixed on mine.

'Jessica?' she mouthed. I nodded. My mouth was dry and, what with the heat and my headache and the odd, oppressive stillness, I had the strangest illusion that the world was holding its breath waiting for us.

I felt very self-conscious about my scruffy trainers and bare midriff. I'd had a bit of a wardrobe crisis before I came out. My favourite tops were all in the wash and the only thing I could find to wear was an old strappy top in pale pink. It had looked scruffy before I'd spilled tea on it and I hadn't had time to change. All kinds of strange thoughts were going through my head, but I knew I wasn't a twin – my mum would never have kept that from me.

We stood opposite each other – the heels gave her a little bit of extra height, but we were virtually eyeball to eyeball.

'It's a pleasure to meet you,' she said awkwardly. Her voice didn't sound much like mine. She had a funny, false-posh accent. She held out her hand for me to shake it and I did and then the world sort of fell apart, smashed into a million jigsaw fragments. I might have screamed.

TWO

It felt like I had been hit by a lightning bolt — it felt like some electric force went straight through me and somehow didn't kill me. I heard a noise, loud as an explosion — some kind of bomb? It could have been behind me — I don't know — it was somewhere nearby and I was scared for Jonno, but I was more scared for me. Whatever it was, it was too close. The sound rang in my ears. There might have been a roaring sound like in the footage of that tsunami, but there was no water. I saw her scream, though I couldn't hear anything but the roaring. Her mouth opened and her eyes shut tightly like a little kid's so that they were just a line of wrinkles in her face. I shut my eyes because the light was suddenly so bright it burnt. I could still feel it — orange and burning, hotter than the sun against my eyelids. When I opened them, she was gone. So was everything else.

I was still on the steps of Waterloo Station. I was sitting on them. I must have fallen because I didn't remember sitting down. The sky was still a pale, early autumn blue. You just, like, know sometimes that everything has changed. I didn't have to turn round to know that Jonno was gone. I turned round anyway and he *was* gone. So was the other Jessica. I ran up the stairs to check and felt that hot, faint feeling all over again. The glass-domed roof and suspended, blue Eurostar sign had vanished. So had the sculpture of Cuneo and the uninspiring café, in fact everything I had recognised was gone. The plain beige polished floor of the concourse was now a complicated, multi-coloured marble design. There were a number of boys in dark purple uniforms, like bellboys, and the kind of hushed atmosphere you get in an expensive shop or a bank. There was a lot of spotless glass and shining chrome, and some people were drinking tea at a gleaming mahogany table by a huge fountain with sculpted, leaping fish and marble mermaids. A live string quartet in dinner dress played something classical on a raised glass bandstand. If this was Waterloo, it was some part of it I'd never been before. The air was scented with flowers and it was almost deserted. There was a woman in a large hat with a brim curled like the crest of a wave. She saw me and she froze, the delicate teacup she held in her white-gloved hand paused halfway to her apricot-coloured mouth which made a little 'o' shape of surprise. She didn't look happy and she wasn't the only one to have spotted me – two of the boys in uniform were homing in on me. They seemed a bit young to be security guards and I wasn't even doing anything wrong.

'Now, miss, we don't have your sort in 'ere.'

'See you later though, darlin',' the other one said, before he was shushed by his companion.

'Lady Balfour's watching. Just get her out of 'ere!'

'OK – get your hands off me!' I said. Their hands were all over me, pinching my bare skin.

'Wot? You some kind of Yank or somefing?' One of them looked pointedly at my jeans.

'Didn't think we 'ad no Yankee tarts out this way. Out you go, anyway. Lord Balfour likes 'is tarts hand-picked and delivered, know what I mean?' The boy winked at me broadly and made a big show of pushing me down the steps, though he didn't push me at all.

'Fancy givin' me one gratis – for gratitude – later?' he said.

The other one, who looked older and seemed more cautious, gave me a hard stare.

'Get out of 'ere,' he said, 'or I'll call the Old Bill. And cover yourself up or the Constabulary will 'ave you inside for soliciting on the public highway. 'Ave you been at the smoke or somefing?'

I was fighting back tears, which wasn't much help, and I couldn't speak so I just shook my head.

'Go inside and reassure the gaffer that I've got it all tolerably pukka,' the taller, older one said. He must have been more senior or something because, although the other one said 'You got a game going?' in a well nasty tone, he did as he was told and slunk back inside, straightening his coat and wiping his hands as if he'd done something tough.

'Is this your bag?' the boss one asked me and bent down to pick up the other Jessica's red clutch bag. I hadn't noticed that she'd dropped it. As he straightened up, I saw that the brass plaque above his head read '1922 Battle of Hong Kong 1924'. There was nothing about the Great War at all.

I think I might have been crying by then because I was more scared than I'd ever been. I wanted Jonno and I knew he wouldn't have left me alone. I knew I was somewhere he couldn't get me, but where? I knew Waterloo well enough to know that there was no huge fountain, no uniformed attendants, no live music nor marble concourse scented with fresh flowers. The uniformed boy, who, I suddenly realised, must be a porter, sighed as though he thought I was putting it on. 'Come on, put a stopper in it. I weren't born yesterday.' He opened the bag. 'You're Jessica Allendon?' he asked, rifling through it. He pulled out a couple of silver coins. 'I'll take these for my trouble and then I'll put you in an 'ansom. I don't know what you're doing dressed like that over 'ere, your address is respectable enough – for Soho. You're lucky I'm a God-fearing gent. Now do yourself a favour and stay off the smoke.' He slipped the money – I didn't know how much it was – into his jacket pocket.

His jacket was lined with dark blue silk, shot through with a logo 'Deutsche-British National and Imperial Railways'. Whoever they were, they were a lot posher than South West Trains.

'Stay here for the driver,' he said curtly. I probably should have asked him about a train back to Sheen, but I wasn't thinking straight and I did as he told me in a bit of a daze. The porter went inside the station and a moment later a sleek black vehicle, gleaming with chrome in unexpected places, drew up beside me. It didn't look like a cab, in fact it didn't look much like any car I'd seen before. The man driving it wore a grey and lilac uniform, a hat like an airline pilot and black leather driving gloves. I only knew they were driving gloves because my mum once bought a pair for my uncle when she couldn't think of anything else to get him for Christmas. The chauffeur guy looked me up and down, as if I were a speck of dirt on his immaculate uniform, but opened the rear door for me without saying a word.

'Miss Allendon would like to be driven to Thirty-six Soho Square.'

Miss Allendon didn't know what she wanted and at that moment was too disoriented to do anything off her own bat. I was like a sleepwalker. I got into the back of the car while the porter paid the driver with money from the red bag, for which I was grateful. I slunk into the soft, caramel-coloured leather seats as though I was ashamed. I

13

don't know why; I hadn't done anything wrong. There was no seat belt and the car smelled of expensive perfume. There was no glass barrier between me and the driver and no meter either. I had to hope it really was a cab.

The driver kept looking at me in the mirror and I folded my arms over my bare middle and carried on sobbing quietly to myself. I didn't know what had happened, but I knew it was serious; like Dorothy said in my mum's favourite film, I didn't think I was in Kansas any more.

Crying stops being useful after a while. I rooted in the other Jessica's bag and found a hanky – I thought I might. She'd be lucky to find a scrunched-up tissue in my handbag – if I'd had one. My money and keys were still in my jeans along with my phone. My phone! I tried to pull it out of my too-tight back pocket without wriggling around too much – I didn't like the way the driver was looking at me. There was no signal – nothing. It was dead. I slipped it into the clutch bag. There wasn't too much else inside it. The other Jessica was a lot neater than I was. There was a lipstick in a silver-coloured case, a comb, the handkerchief, a small ring of keys, a purse with a few thick paper notes and some coins: they looked like the money my mum had from pre-decimalisation – a sixpence, a threepenny bit and a half-crown. I didn't understand. There hadn't been coins like that around since the seventies. I couldn't have gone back in time, could I? There was also a notebook with my name and the other Jessica's address written in the kind of elegant cursive hand I could never do. She had no phone.

A good portion of the car was glass, though it must have been the kind that looks black from the outside because I hadn't noticed much glass when it had drawn up beside me. The transparent sides gave me a great view of London, just not the London I knew. There was very little traffic, barely a traffic light. We went over what should have been Waterloo Bridge, but I couldn't see the London Eye, the South Bank or Shell Mex, only a series of extraordinary buildings in white Portland stone with immense windows of bright stained glass. The driver said something about there being a bomb in Whitehall so we'd have to go the back way.

I tried to work out where we were from the street signs but that didn't help at all. There was a real market where I thought Covent Garden should have been and we drove through narrow medieval streets past buildings I'd never seen before. Shaftesbury Avenue was a wide street full of trees and Old Compton Street was narrow and dirty and full of men who stared at me through the windscreen of the car in a way I did not like at all. It's not like I know London that well – but I remembered enough to know that nothing was as it should be. No one was dressed right either. All the women I saw wore hats and gloves and all the men too, even in Old Compton Street, and yet they didn't look old-fashioned. They were dressed in no style I recognised. I wasn't that rubbish at history – I did a project on fashion and, as my mum is keen to remind me, I could shop for England. I knew I'd never seen any of that stuff before. We passed a couple of metallic scarlet trams. They were sleekly bullet-shaped and almost silent. I thought I saw some horse-drawn carriages, though the carriages looked more like futuristic cars. I couldn't make sense of it.

It didn't take long to get where we were going. There were no hold-ups at all, though once the driver stopped for a woman who was wearing a long green velvet coat embroidered with silver and bronze leaves and a matching turban; she waved at him like she was royalty. I began to feel faint again and wondered if I could actually make myself use the keys and walk into the other Jessica's house. I'd never had a panic attack before. Em at school says she gets them all the time, though she likes to be the centre of attention so I don't always believe her, but if this wasn't a panic attack I don't know what is. The car pulled into a square with a garden in the centre of it and stopped in front of a large Georgian town house. It wasn't *EastEnders*, I know that much. I made myself blow into an imaginary paper bag because I did that with Em sometimes. The chauffeur opened the door for me and I stepped out.

'You got a card or something, miss?' he said. 'You're a good-looking poppet. Maybe we could do business together again.' He gave me that look men do sometimes and I was glad I wasn't in the car any more. It occurred to me then that maybe I should have stayed at Waterloo, tried to find my way back to Sheen, but it was too late. I didn't answer the driver and he muttered something under his breath and drove away. Should I have asked him to take me back to the station? It probably would have been more sensible. Instead I fished out the key ring from my bag and walked up the steps to the black front door. I guessed that the largest of the keys would work in the front door. My hand was shaking so much I could barely get the key in the lock. Maybe the other Jessica's parents would help me get home. Looking back, even now I'm not sure what else I could have done.

THREE

I knew as soon as the door groaned open that I had made a mistake. I was in a large entrance hall – all silk wallpaper, pictures and gleaming black granite, like something from a magazine. I knew it was black granite because Jonno's mother had wanted some for her new kitchen worktops and it was too expensive. There was a lot more than a kitchen worktop's worth here. There was a strong smell of wax polish and the heavy scent of lilies coming from a huge urn filled with an elaborate flower arrangement on the polished hall table – the kind of display you usually only see in big hotels. There were no shoes by the front door or dropped bags – nothing to show that it was the home of a teenage girl. A huge chandelier hung from the ceiling and dominated the space – it was made of curving crystal leaves and tiny silvery drops like rain. I'd never seen anything like it. On the other wall was a gilt-framed landscape – a real oil painting. I could even see the signature in the corner: 'A. Hitler' – an unfortunate name for an artist, I thought. I was staring at the decor so intently that I didn't hear the man arrive. I was well shocked when he spoke.

His voice was very low and so menacing that I think I actually shivered.

'And just what in the name of all that's holy do you think you're doing, using the front door and dressed like that?' He was quite young – early twenties with long, carefully trimmed sideburns and one of those peculiar beards that is only allowed to grow on the chin and nowhere else. He was right in my face and glaring at me. I know I must have looked guilty – maybe the other Jessica didn't live here?

I couldn't speak. I mean I opened my mouth, but it was like one of those nightmares where you're being chased and you can't cry for help. No words came out of my mouth, which opened and closed silently like I was a guppy. I kind of gawped at him like some stupid person.

'I know you.' He inspected me as if I were a piece of meat he was thinking of buying. 'You're the mistress's secretary. You're a straight-up-and-down bad girl, aren't you? Who would have guessed it? A wolf in sheep's clothing. Mrs Lansdowne, she doesn't approve of poppy poppets, now does she? No, she does not. Does she approve of girls who work on their backs? No, I think you'll find that she does not. I don't expect you'd want her to know that her prim little office girl has a few ungodly vices.' His forefinger skimmed my cheek. 'Very above-board and proper respectable is our Mrs Lansdowne . . .' He left his sentence unfinished and, as I flinched away from him, lightly touched the bare bit of skin above my jeans with a smooth, cool hand. I couldn't pull away. I was shaking and I wanted to be sick again – sick even came into my mouth, but I swallowed it down. It wasn't so much what he did, but the way he did it. He made me feel more exposed than if I'd been standing in the hallway stark naked. He put his face so close to mine I could see the wet pinkness of his mouth and I thought for one scary minute that he was going to kiss me. He might have done too and I don't know what I'd have done about it, but then we both heard footsteps coming our way.

'Get on with you!' he hissed, pushing me away so suddenly I almost lost my balance.

'Get yourself respectable. Get up the backstairs before anyone sees you!' He pulled me back towards him by my hair and looked me straight in the eye. 'You'll owe me for this, poppet, and I make sure people always pay me what they owe.' As I turned away, he muttered, 'Nice arse!' and slapped me, hard enough for it to sting, even through my jeans.

Tears came to my eyes and I'm ashamed to say I just ran away. I didn't stand up for myself at all. I didn't even yell at him. Yeah, I was humiliated, but I was too panicked to think straight and more than anything else I was scared. Like I said, my mum is protective, and I have to be careful about where I go and who I go with.

For the first time I grasped what Mum had meant with all her warnings and understood her worried looks when I'd worn a skirt that was short and a top that was tight. I wished I could run to her. I could barely see through my tears so it was more by luck than anything else that I blundered upon the backstairs before anyone saw me. They were more ordinary than the grand, sweeping main staircase, but I still climbed them feeling like a thief. This wasn't Jessica's home, and even if it was where she worked, going upstairs in this house didn't feel quite right. I felt I was asking for more trouble, but I didn't know how to get out of the house except by the way I'd come in and I wasn't going anywhere near that man again. I don't know what I'd have done if Edie hadn't spotted me – though I didn't know she was called Edie then. She was a girl just about my own age, with thick blonde hair swept into a high bun. She caught me by the arm as I stumbled past her.

'Jessie? What in hell has happened to you?'

'I – I don't know . . .' was all I could manage to get out, and even that was a kind of a choked sob.

'Hush! The master'll hear you.' She glanced round furtively. 'Tell me upstairs!'

She led the way up the steeper, narrow staircase to the attic rooms. She opened the door to one of them and I followed her into a small, plain room, empty but for two cast-iron beds, two chests of drawers and a wooden wardrobe. I didn't get more than the impression of barracks-like neatness, but she opened the wardrobe and pulled out a dark dress like the one she was wearing.

'Here! You'd better change before any of the nobs see you. Where in hell did you get those rags? You look like a Yank tart – cover yourself up!'

I didn't want to lose my own clothes, but I didn't want anyone else mauling me or staring at me either so I turned my back on the girl and changed. The dress fitted so perfectly it dawned on me that it might actually be Jessica's. Edie, her nose wrinkled with distaste, gathered up my clothes from where I'd dumped them on the bare, painted boards of the floor. I'd managed to slide my keys out of my back pocket and I slipped them unnoticed into the other Jessica's bag where I'd put my phone.

'Is this where I live?' I asked. I didn't think trying to explain what had happened was going to help – call it instinct, call it cowardice, but I felt that it would be a mistake to try to explain what had happened to me. I couldn't very well start screaming that my world had disappeared. All I could do was to pretend to be the other Jessica until I'd worked out what was going on.

'What has happened to you? You go out on your half-day looking a proper lady, you come back like a tramp. Someone do something to you, Jessie? You've not turned to the smoke?'

'I don't know what you mean.'

'Oh, come off it, Jessie, don't come on so primaninny. There's more poppy dens in Soho than fruitsellers in Covent Garden. Why didn't you say if you wanted a pipe? My brother could have got you some pukka stuff without you going to some low-class bawdy hole. He takes cash. And he's reliable.'

I still had no idea what she was talking about, but I didn't want to be called primaninny again – whatever that meant, it was obviously bad. I changed the subject. 'Where can I wash my face?'

'Khazis and bathrooms haven't moved,' she sighed. 'Come on! I'll show you the way since you're still in Xanadu.' She led the way to a small old-fashioned bathroom along the hall and I washed my face with water so cold it took my breath away.

'All better?' she asked sharply and I just nodded and followed her, like Mary's little lamb, back to the bedroom.

'I've got work to do. All the stinking fires need blacking and someone we know has fixed it so I get all the skivvy work – again. I can't stay here gassing with you. Rest up here until you're more yourself. I'll ask Cook for a tray of scraps and I'll bring it up when I can.' She looked at me. I must have looked well pathetic – staring at her like a zombie. Her face softened. 'Did anyone see you like this?'

'At the door someone –'

'You came in the front way?'

I nodded, numbly aware that had been my first mistake.

'James saw you? Oh Jesus, Mary and Joseph! What did he say?'

I cleared my dry throat and croaked, 'He said I'd owe him.' I didn't know what that meant exactly, but it was clear enough from Edie's expression that *she* did.

Her mouth tightened and she looked worried. 'Jessica! Whatever possessed you? You'll have to find a way to buy some time. I can't talk about it now, but I'll think while I'm getting on with my drudge-work downstairs. Don't they teach you brainy types anything in secretarial school?' Her look told me she thought I was an idiot; *I* no longer knew what I was. 'Stay here. Sleep it off,' she said with an exasperated sigh. 'I'll tell them in the kitchen you've got a headache. I don't know what you've got yourself into, but I don't want any of it landing at my door. And for God's sake don't leave the bedroom!' I waited until I was sure she'd gone and then pulled out my phone. It was still dead. Maybe the electrical storm or whatever had brought me to this place had damaged it. To be honest, I hadn't expected it to work, but it was still the last straw and I ended up crying again. I cried until I had no tears left and then blew my nose and began to pull myself together. I know I sound like a wimp but I was frightened and more alone than I'd ever been. When I stopped crying, I wondered if I might be able to find my way back to the station and try to get home from there. I didn't like the thought of meeting with the porters again but perhaps I wouldn't have had so much trouble if I'd not been wearing jeans. People obviously didn't wear them in this place unless they were 'Yank tarts'. My mother called Americans 'Yanks' so I assumed that's what they meant.

There was a long mirror in the door of the wardrobe. My face was pink and swollen from crying, but I combed my hair so that I looked neat and respectable and un-tart-like and tried to open the chest of drawers in order to find something to tie it up with. Both chests of drawers were locked but there was a small key on Jessica's keyring and it fitted the chest of drawers nearest the wardrobe perfectly.

I opened the drawers a little hesitantly, not knowing what I would find. I felt awkward because it wasn't my stuff and Mum was seriously moral about things like that. If I was supposed to be Jessica, I thought it would be strange if I didn't use her things. There was underwear – pretty silk stuff, much nicer than my M&S thongs – lace hankies, a small washbag and some cosmetics – not much, not compared with the heap of bottles and tubes I had at home – cake mascara, a cake of kohl, lipstick, some cream and hairgrips, the kind that look like bent metal. There was also a small bundle of letters, a diary and most heart-stoppingly a picture of my mum and me sitting with my dad at what looked like Richmond Riverside. I looked about fourteen in the picture, my hair hanging loose to my shoulders, beaming like my face might split, but of course it wasn't me or my mum and dad. My mum had never worn her hair in the strange, curly bob of the woman in that picture nor had my dad ever worn a hat. I was so shocked I couldn't even cry out. I wasn't just like Jessica – I *was* Jessica, with the same parents and everything. I made myself do that imaginary blowing into a bag thing again or I might have had a proper panic attack. I was not in London. I was in another place, another version of the world, a world where another Jessica worked in this house and in which Dad was still alive. My own dad. The dad who'd never worn a hat, had never sat with a fourteen-year-old Jessica by Richmond Riverside. The dad who'd died when I was ten.

# FOUR

I spent a long time looking at that picture, wondering what it would have been like if my father had been with us at least until I was fourteen. Mum had tried so hard to make sure I didn't miss out, taking me swimming and to football matches she would never have gone to had he been alive. After a bit we'd quietly dropped the football matches and taken up tennis instead, but I missed him and sometimes I panicked that I couldn't remember his face. Seeing my father's face as it might have been had he lived a bit longer made the loss of him raw and painful again. I didn't want those feelings back, so eventually I put the picture away, but my heart felt like a heavy stone in my chest.

I worked it out then. The photo clinched it, though everything else that had happened to me had led me to the same conclusion. There had been an electrical storm or strange bomb and the other Jessica and I had swapped places. I was in some parallel world where my father hadn't died in a plane crash, where somehow I'd become a secretary in another London. It might surprise you that I took so long to work it out, but although I watched

Doctor Who and some old episodes of *Star Trek*, I wasn't into science fiction and I never thought any of it might be true. Jonno was always going on about things like parallel worlds. Now though, I wished I'd listened to him instead of taking the piss, but I was certain that he had never told me anything about getting from one possible world to another in his – what did he call it? Multiverse?

I was about to open the other Jessica's diary when there was a knock at the door and Edie walked in with a tray.

'He's going to have you all right,' she said as she pushed the door open with her back and I was so lost in my own thoughts that I didn't know what she was going on about for a minute, then it clicked – James. 'He told me to tell you he had his eye on you. I don't know what's got into you, Jessie. You don't want to come a cropper with him, you really don't.'

She sat down beside me on the bed, lifted the silver metal covering off the largest plate on the tray and picked a small piece of meat from it.

'You were in luck. All the nobs are out tonight and Cook had made a good old Raj curry, thinking the master was having his cronies in. The Ecski is on the blink again – damn Deutsche technik, they should have bought Nip, but they're too patriotic – so Cook couldn't freeze the extra and so here we are – a feast fit for our betters if not the King himself!'

I didn't get much of Edie's conversation. I was so out of it I didn't even have the wit to ask which king, but the curry smelled great. I didn't know how late it was: I don't wear a watch – I use my mobile – but my stomach told me it was too long since I'd last eaten. We shared it in the end and I think it was the best curry I've ever tasted. Edie had managed to bring some cake up too, something homemade and spicy, as well as a pot of tea.

'Thanks,' I said when we'd finished and were sitting in friendly silence, amazing since she had been a total stranger to me a few hours before.

'So what are you going to do about James?' she said, in the gossipy tones of one of my friends from home. I didn't know how to answer. My plan was to get home to my own London and my own mum and Jonno. I thought maybe getting back to Waterloo would be a start, but I couldn't tell Edie that. In fact I couldn't tell Edie anything. I shrugged – it was all I could do.

'You're still not yourself, are you? You must have taken some bad stuff. Mary and Joseph, Jessie, next time you want to go off the rails you come to me, right? I've got the contacts.' She tapped the side of her nose and I nodded without understanding. It was dark outside and, as there were no curtains at the small sash window nor carpets on the floor, it was cold in the room and I shivered.

'We'll talk later. You'd best sleep and get your head facing forwards for tomorrow. There was another hoo-hah while you were out enjoying yourself. The master found that his personal security had been breached. The Lord alone knows what that means, but he's blaming the mistress and she's slamming doors and carrying on. Anyway, the Security will be around tomorrow, you can count on it, and we'll all be interviewed again. If she finds out that you've been wandering the streets dressed like a threepenny whore, you'll be out on your ear, gal.' She deftly stacked the dirty plates and cups on the tray and stood up to leave.

'I'll try not to wake you when I come in. I've got a little assignation with Johnny. I need to make a play for him before the Security arrive. I don't want them knowing who I fancy. Anyway, you'll be glad to know my romantic campaign is going well. He definitely flirted with me today and what with my charm and good looks I reckon it will all be over by Christmas!' She grinned and winked broadly, then left, closing the door behind her.

The room was lit by a single, central naked bulb, which shed a bleak and unforgiving light on the spartan room. I couldn't sleep so I crept to the bathroom, taking the other Jessica's washbag, towel and night things. I didn't want to use her toothbrush, but I didn't much want my teeth to rot either, so I washed it as best I could before I used it and consoled myself with the thought that if she was in some sense another version of me, her germs probably wouldn't do me any harm.

No one saw me and I didn't hang around. There was no heating and no hot water and the cotton sheets of the bed were so cold they felt damp. I got as warm as I could and then opened the other Jessica's diary. I needed to find out what I could about her. Most importantly, I wanted to find out if she'd swapped with me on purpose – if this was all because of something she'd done. I thought back. Had she done anything to cause the explosion that tore the world apart? The lightning had begun before we met, but everything had been more or less normal until she shook my hand. I thought back. I'd made the first contact, hadn't I? She'd fixed the meeting, but I'd made the first contact. Could she have planned this? I did not see how. I'd rather we were both victims of some bizarre cataclysm than that I was here because she'd stolen my life.

The first thing I noticed was the date. It was 8th September 2008 – the same date as at home. The second thing I noticed was that the other Jessica was unbelievably neat. I'd tried writing a diary once, and a blog, but neither lasted longer than a week and I'd doodled over the diary as I couldn't think of anything interesting to say. Jessica's diary was noticeably short of stylised flowers, bloodshot monster eyes and variations on her signature, but she didn't seem to find much of interest to say either. Though there was an entry every day, most were short and uninformative. What did she mean when she said *'Mrs L asked me to watch. I don't know whether I have made a mistake. I don't know if she is of the right pack and I dare not ask'*?

All the other entries seemed as cryptic. Jessica was a girl of few words. She seemed serious too. My diary, when I had bothered to write it, was full of gossip and 'Oh my God! Rich told Em he fancied me!' kind of stuff. Jessica never used an exclamation mark and she didn't talk about boys at all. The only thing I took away from her diary was a kind of sadness and I don't know where I got that from. I wondered too why she lived in this poky little room with Edie rather than at home with her mum and dad, so painfully similar to mine.

Perhaps it was foolish, I don't know – but I felt that I had to continue her diary. She hadn't missed an entry for a year that I could see, and if she ever got back to where she belonged – as she would, as I would – she'd need to know what I'd done.

To be honest I wasn't thinking that clearly – my thoughts kept whirling around. I didn't want the other Jessica messing up my life either, but I reckoned on Jonno helping her. That made my stomach lurch a bit, the thought of her with Jonno: he was my best friend. What if he liked her more than me? I knew that she and I were different – she was neat where I was messy, serious where I was an airhead. Maybe there were other differences? Was she also enjoying my life more than hers?

What would Mum think? She'd know the other Jessica was not me the moment she saw her. I decided not to go there. I blinked back my tears. My brain couldn't cope, so instead I wrote about what had happened to me since I'd arrived at our meeting point at Waterloo Station. I wrote it all down in my best writing, which was a horrible scrawl next to the other Jessica's, but quite good for me. When I'd finished my entry, I hid the diary back where I'd found it, buried beneath her underwear, which probably qualified as lingerie, and then I locked the drawer.

I had not expected to sleep I was so full of fears and my thoughts kept leaping like a demented butterfly from one horrible idea to the next. I think it was exhaustion that did for me in the end – all that crying. I didn't turn off the light because Edie hadn't come to bed, but even that didn't prevent me from falling so deeply asleep that I didn't hear her when she did get in. I don't think I dreamt. My imagination was as exhausted as the rest of me. How could there be such a thing as a parallel world, and by what mysterious process had I ended up in one?

FIVE

The sun woke me up, shining through the window right into my face. Edie was already up, brushing out her hair and pinning it up in a complicated hairstyle. I watched her silently for a moment while I got over the shock of still being there, of still being where I did not belong.

'Well, are you fixed right now?' she asked as I stirred.

'I'm better,' I said carefully. I wouldn't be fixed right until I was out of that place. I wasn't used to sharing a room and I wanted to go to the bathroom at the end of the corridor, but was worried about meeting other people there.

'Get in the khazi queue for me, there's a love . . .' Edie said. I was about to leave the room in Jessie's high-cut flannel nightdress, which covered me as thoroughly as a burka, when Edie shouted, 'Put your dressing-gown on, hussy, or you'll have all the men in the house in here.' She wasn't kidding either. 'What's got into you?'

She glanced at me and then at the back of the door, on which hung two grey-brown garments. I'd assumed they were coats, they were so heavy looking, but apparently they were dressing-gowns of the kind a very old-fashioned great-grandfather might wear. What was wrong with this world where if you showed an inch of flesh all the men thought you were some kind of prostitute? It was a weird attitude if you ask me, but I didn't think it wise to say so. Instead, I smiled apologetically.

'Sorry, I'm losing the plot,' I said as breezily as I could by way of explanation, but Edie only gave me an uncomprehending stare.

I won't bore you with the many small humiliations of that morning, queueing for the loo and the bathroom with about ten other strangers who weren't supposed to be strangers, dressing in Jessie's smart but awkward clothes, which included stockings – a nightmare to put on – and low-heeled lace-up shoes. I couldn't do my hair in anything close to Edie's style so she did it for me, tutting and shaking her head, yanking my hair so hard and pulling it so tight that she made my eyes water.

We ate breakfast all together in the kitchen, like something out of that film *Gosford Park*. Everyone was very formal. Cook was a large Indian woman, dressed all in white, and she seemed to be in charge. Everyone called her Mrs Gowda and even Edie called me Miss Allendon in front of everyone else. There was a lot of banter – like in a family, but everyone was much more polite – and James said grace before we started. There was no breakfast cereal, but porridge, which I've always thought makes a good concrete substitute.

I coped with all that quite well. I sat bolt upright like I was Queen Victoria and remembered to eat with my mouth closed. James was there, looking at me as if I was something he'd scraped off his shoe. I could have dealt with that but sitting nearest Cook was a face almost more familiar than my own – Jonno. I wanted to run to him and throw my arms round him – I can imagine what Edie would have said about that. He wasn't my Jonno, of course, and I kind of knew that straightaway. His head wasn't shaved for a start. His hair was parted at the side in a neat line which showed his scalp. He was wearing one of those Indian-style suits with a high collar in a soft grey – it made his eyes look very blue. I caught him looking at Edie while she was joking over something with Cook. I wondered if her 'assignation' had worked out as she'd wanted. My stomach did something strange at the thought. Jonno's double didn't look at me at all. I wanted to cry – again.

James banged the table with a fork for silence and then made some announcements. It was like listening to the headmaster at assembly, only no one mucked about.

'Today Mr Lansdowne has warned us to expect a number of members of the Security Services, who may want to interview certain among us . . .' he paused and gave me a brief but spiteful look, 'following the breach of his office security systems. He asked me to remind you that it would go badly for anyone who was not open and honest in their dealings with them. Biological testing might be necessary.'

There was a kind of anxious silence after that and after finishing up their cups of strong tea one by one they made their excuses and got up to go about their business. The large dial clock on the wall said six o'clock: no wonder I felt knackered – I never got up before seven thirty at home. I don't know if I looked as much like a spare part as I felt, but when everyone went off to do whatever they did Jonno's double came to talk to me and I felt a moment of hope.

'Miss Allendon, Miss Grace told me you were feeling a little under the weather. Shall I accompany you to the office?' I worked out that Miss Grace was Edie straight away and I was grateful to her once more for helping me out. All I'd managed to understand from Jessica's diary was that she worked for Mrs Lansdowne as her private secretary and that she liaised a lot with a Mr Roberts, who was Mr Lansdowne's secretary. I hadn't been able to work out what either of the Lansdownes did exactly that required a secretary apiece but I got the feeling that they were demanding employers. I wasn't wrong there. Jonno's surname was Roberts and putting two and two together cheered me up. Perhaps this Jonathan Roberts was the same kind of friend to Jessica that Jonno was to me – that would make a difference. It was clear enough that I needed an ally, someone with local knowledge, to help me get home. Unfortunately hope didn't outlive our first meeting.

Jonno's double took my elbow and gently steered me through the kitchen and up the stairs to the first floor. Once more I was struck by the extreme cleanliness of everything – the rich shine of polished parquet, the clear sparkle of the chandeliers. He guided me towards double doors of dark mahogany, the handles of which were shaped like stylised panthers and gleamed with the distinctive light that told me they were made of real silver. Mum would have loved them.

Mr Jonathan Roberts opened the doors and guided me so forcefully into the large and opulent reception room that he more or less pushed me. I noticed the high ceiling and a huge fireplace before he closed the door firmly behind him, planted himself in front of me and began hissing at me. 'Listen, Miss Allendon, if you go down you are not bringing me down with you. I need this job. Have you understood me?'

I fought back yet more tears. I couldn't believe how pathetically emotional I'd become, but to get such hostility from Jonno, even though my brain told me it wasn't Jonno – I couldn't deal with that. I didn't know what to say to him. He looked at me very hard. 'Miss Allendon, are you crying?'

'No. I'm fine, thank you. I'll try not to cause any more trouble.' This was not me! What had happened to make me apologise when he was the one having a go at me? The problem was I was trying to speak as I thought the other Jessica might and I had her down as a polite old-fashioned girl: more than that, it's hard to be self-confident when you're dressed as a servant and treated like one. I felt so lost. Jonathan was looking at me and I took my chance to ask for help.

'I wonder if you could help me. I . . . I mean, I can't remember what I was working on.' I put my hand to my temple quite dramatically. 'I've been having these head-aches, you see.' I saw Jonathan take in my grubby, bitten nails, still partially decorated with the remnants of 'pink blush', and I saw what little sympathy I might have gained disappear down the toilet. His face hardened.

'Cook will have some varnish stripper in the dispen-sary cupboard. You'd better get your nails in some kind of respectable shape before Mrs Lansdowne starts work. She'll be here by eleven.' He sounded disgusted. So OK my hands were a mess – it was hardly a capital crime. I don't know why I got embarrassed – it wasn't anything to be ashamed of – and yet I don't think I'd ever blushed quite so hotly before. If he'd been my Jonno, I'd have hit him.

I wouldn't have thought I was the kind of girl to meekly do as I'm told, but in Jessica's world I felt as if I had no choice. I accepted Cook's disapproving stares, removed the last reminders of my own twenty-first century, and did not try to run away. I wanted to, but I was too afraid of what I'd find beyond the front door. I am not proud that I was so pathetic, but it was hardly a normal situation.

When I managed to find my way back to the elegant reception room, I could see that Jonno's double was sorting out papers in the room just beyond. I was rubbish at filing. I didn't understand how to do it, even though Mum had shown me when I went in to help in her office for work experience. The office manager at Mum's place told me that, for an office clerk, I made a very good lumberjack – I think it was supposed to be a joke.

'Mr Roberts?' He stood up almost guiltily. 'I don't know what has happened but I really can't remember what I should do. I don't want to get either of us in trouble, but if you could just show me where everything is and explain to me what I'm supposed to do, I will try and conduct myself properly.' I was proud of that sentence. I think I might have nicked it from some book we'd had to read in English, but it sounded right and Mr Roberts looked a little less frosty. Somewhere between the kitchen and the reception room I had made a decision: I had to carry on pretending to be Jessica until I could find out more about what had happened to us. Until I knew better, I'd assume we were both victims and so do my best not to get her fired. If I was lucky and she was enough like me, she might do the same for me.

There were three adjoining offices – one decorated in chrome and walnut was Mr Lansdowne's and I wasn't allowed in there; one which was full of curved lacquered cabinets in peacock colours was Mrs Lansdowne's and Mr Roberts wasn't allowed in there; the third, which was decorated less dramatically with a mismatch of desks and metal filing cabinets, was our office and both of us could go in there although neither of the Lansdownes did. It sounded almost as complicated as netball the way Mr Roberts explained it. He spoke slowly with exaggerated patience, as if I was brain-damaged or drunk or something. Anyway, he tried to help me and that was something. When I was a little kid, I had one nightmare I've never forgotten: everyone I knew looked like themselves but they weren't themselves, like they'd been swapped by aliens or something. Being with Mr Roberts was like being in that nightmare. I kept thinking he was going to turn round and crack some kind of Jonno joke and then it would all be OK, but he didn't and the nightmare carried on.

SIX

Mrs Lansdowne was a striking blonde. I'm not very good at guessing ages, but she was probably what Mum might call 'well-preserved early thirties'. She wore her hair in a short glossy bob and had an air of expensive, honed fitness about her. She was wearing a narrow cream skirt and a white shirt appliquéd with geometric shapes in pale greens and blues. It looked good. She didn't pay me a great deal of attention after her first, cursory ' 'Tag, Miss Allendon,' which I guessed was a version of 'hi'. I was kind of grateful to be ignored. I got on with filing according to the system Jonno's double had outlined and at about eleven thirty Mrs Lansdowne rang for coffee and Jonno's double and I went down to the kitchen for elevenses.

Edie was in the kitchen, apparently looking for something, when we got there. 'What kind of mood is she in today then, Johnny?' she said flirtatiously when Cook was out of earshot.

'Johnny' shrugged and poured us all some coffee from a large pottery coffee jug on the table. We all had cups and saucers and I gathered from Edie's joking that this was a daily ritual, that Mrs Lansdowne insisted that the secretaries had a coffee break each morning and a tea break each afternoon and that more often than not Edie managed to find herself in the kitchen at around that time. Cook didn't seem to mind. To me it seemed normal to have a tea break but apparently domestic servants rarely got them: domestic service was beginning to look a little bit like slavery to me.

I didn't say much – it seemed safer and I reckoned the other Jessica was the same because neither of Edie nor Jonathan acted as if I was being unusually quiet. Anyway, I doubt if Edie would have noticed if I'd grown a second head she was so busy accidentally brushing Johnny's sleeve and laughing. He was a bit like my Jonno after all, because he didn't respond in any obvious way and I wondered if he might be embarrassed. I didn't think she was getting very far with him, but what did I know? I can't say I was happy sitting there listening to Edie's chatter, but I felt I was coping OK, that I was only slightly desperate.

It all went pear-shaped after that. James swaggered into the kitchen as we were leaving. Apparently two Security men had just arrived and would be interviewing us about the security breach. I got that feeling of panic I was beginning to recognise – rapid heartbeat, sweating hands, dry mouth and a weird kind of squirting feeling in my guts. I was as worried about James as about the yet unknown threat of the Security men.

I tried to sidle closer to Johnny, but Edie had his full attention. James put his hand round my wrist and pulled me. I looked at Johnny for help but he didn't seem to notice me. James's grip was painful and maybe I should have cried out, but I didn't, and though I tried to pull my wrist away, I didn't fight him – not properly. He led me into one of the small rooms off the kitchen – a kind of larder full of cake tins and pickle jars. It was windowless, cool and almost dark. He pushed me against one of the stone shelves and pinned me there with his superior strength.

'So, how are you going to stop me telling Mrs Lansdowne about your habit, then?' I didn't need to see him clearly to know that he was leering at me as he spoke. I wondered what would happen if I screamed. 'A good-looking poppet like you knows what's what. You don't need me to tell you that Mrs Lansdowne is very picky about the kind of "young lady" she lets loose on her letters. Shall we say I'll see you tomorrow, in the backyard after supper? If you don't come to me, I'll find you.'

I couldn't speak – the pressure of fingers on my wrist was hurting. He smelled powerfully of some lemony aftershave and peppermint. I tried to get him to release my wrist and struggled a bit. If I hadn't been so inhibited by trying to fit in and be ladylike, I would have kneed him where it hurt. I'd done self-defence classes and yet I was acting like I didn't have a clue. I pulled myself together and struggled a little, but I'd let him get me cornered and all that happened was that I knocked over a large jar of pickles. There was an explosion of broken glass and vinegar splashed everywhere. James said something that sounded like cursing in a foreign language and I heard Johnny call out sharply, 'Miss Allendon, we must be getting back!' James didn't so much release me as push me out of the larder so that I almost lost my footing. As I struggled to regain my balance, he sauntered out of the larder and I felt his hand patting my backside proprietorially. Cook saw him and gave me a hard look and I think I must have gone red again. James made some remark to Cook over his shoulder and left.

My heart was still beating to some crazy techno rhythm and I had to blink back yet more tears of frustration, but by the time I'd got back to Johnny I was more or less in control of myself. He said nothing about my flushed face or the all-pervading smell of pickle until Edie had gone back to work. As we climbed the stairs together, he wrinkled his nose in a fastidious way, like I stank of something a lot fouler than vinegar. 'Straighten your hair,' he said in a voice icy with disapproval.

'I . . .' I began to try to explain, but his response was quick and quelling.

'I'm not interested in whatever game you're playing with James, but you bring your troubles down on me and you'll know it.'

We walked back into the office suite in silence. Mrs Lansdowne wanted to see me immediately. She rattled off a series of instructions about what files she wanted to see and then leaned towards me so close that I could see the dusting of powder on her face and the slight bleed lines of her pale coral lipstick. Her scent was something subtly flowery.

'You know my husband has brought in the Security Services to find out about the breach. If you had anything to do with it, you will be dismissed, and if you tell them anything about the errands you have run for me, you will be dismissed. Is that clear enough?' she said in an undertone. I nodded. She looked disappointed by my response and pursed her lips. 'Miss Allendon, there were over a hundred applicants for this post. Most of them were from mature women of much greater experience than yourself. I earnestly hope that you are not going to turn out to have been a mistake on my part. I do not like making mistakes. And please try not to turn up in my office smelling as if you work in a pickle factory.' She had a hard face, I decided, and she was not going to age well. I lowered my eyes like I was in some Jane Austen novel and mumbled something about hoping to please.

The door of Mr Lansdowne's office banged and she was suddenly crisp and businesslike. 'I have spooled some letters I want you to transcribe immediately. I want them to go out first post after lunch.' She gave me a small white disc-shaped object about the size of a bagel but thinner, which was labelled with the date and a series of initials. I took it from her reluctantly because it was quite clear that I wasn't going to be able to bluff this one.

The good thing about having things to do – especially impossible things to do – was that I did not dwell too much on what had happened with James in the larder. Every time I did chance to think about it I found myself getting all hot and panicky which, sadly, only made the stale vinegar smell stronger.

Johnny was working at his desk when I went back to our office. He was wearing a black plastic helmet, like a smaller version of a crash helmet, and was typing at a keyboard. I looked around 'my' desk and found a mahogany box with a keyboard in one of the drawers. There was also a square box with a rounded perspex top and a slot roughly the size of a bagel. I could work this one out. The keyboard wasn't much like my keyboard at home – though it still had the letters arranged in the familiar qwerty sequence. There was no screen as such, just a small clear tubular display which showed whatever I typed – a line at a time – in bright red letters. The helmet contained headphones and after a few minutes of messing about I had sorted myself out as a touch-typist.

I'd never done it before, although I'd done a typing course at school, but it was OK – when I'd worked out how to pause the disc and erase my mistakes. I didn't want to ask Johnny anything else. The system used cables so I followed the cable to one of the cupboards where there was a huge printer and by lunchtime I'd done one of the letters. I didn't see anything of the much talked about Security men.

When Johnny left to go to the kitchen, after carefully locking away his keyboard and all his work, I stayed to catch up. He came back about an hour later with a cold beef sandwich wrapped in a linen napkin.

'Don't let Mrs Lansdowne see you or you'll be in the soup,' he said. It was nice of him. When I smiled at him, he smiled back and he looked just like Jonno.

SEVEN

After lunch, Johnny told me to post Mrs Lansdowne's letters in the square. The stamps he gave me were much like the stamps at home but with a king's head on them. I made an excuse to go to my room, grabbed Jessica's clutch bag with her money and my phone, and then slipped out into the street. I should have used the servants' door but I still wasn't sure where it was and – as James appeared to be elsewhere – I furtively used the front door. After only one day in Jessica's world this seemed like an act of rebellion.

Soho Square looked leafy and green, much like it did in my own London. It was a mild sunny day for September and so I was surprised that the beautifully maintained square was quiet. There were a few children playing a chasing game, watched by a bored-looking girl in some kind of nurse's uniform, and that was it. All the office workers and shop assistants, visitors and students who would usually sunbathe and eat their lunch there were missing. They were probably slaving away, polishing the brasswork in the other big houses round the square. Instead of the roar of traffic, I could hear birdsong and music coming from the church across the square. There were no more that twenty cars parked on the street all together. Each one was large and gleaming with polished chrome. I didn't recognise any of the marques: Wolsey-Siddeley, Achilles-Benz, Daimler-Jaguar. They were beautifully designed, like sculpture. I thought of Jonno – his father had been mad on cars and Jonno knew every make and model at a glance. I suppose after all these years of playing the 'What car?' game with Jonno, so did I.

I didn't dare dawdle long, but if I'd had any suspicion that my London was anywhere near, it disappeared as I briefly stood to admire the square. It even smelled different.

I thought I knew the way back to Waterloo. Normally I would have taken the tube, but I have a good sense of direction and thought I might manage to find my way on foot. I had to hope that some landmarks would be the same. The memory of my taxi ride didn't reassure me. I would have liked to have smuggled my trainers downstairs with my phone but I had had no way of hiding them and, as I hadn't seen anyone wearing trainers, I thought they might draw unnecessary attention to myself. I posted the letters and found that my hands were trembling. That didn't matter. So I was scared – so what? Somehow I had to get back to the station and find whatever portal had brought me to this other London and get home. I had to do it at once before James got his hands on me. My only regret was that somewhere in this strange version of 2008 my father was still alive and I would not get a chance to meet him.

I didn't give 36 Soho Square a backward glance. I started walking as briskly as possible, hoping that I wouldn't have to wait for another electrical storm for the portal phenomenon, thingamy, whatever to work. I didn't think about what would happen if both of us Jessicas ended up in my London. One step at a time. I don't think I'd taken above four steps before I felt a strong hand on my shoulder and a man's voice in my ear. 'Miss Allendon, I hope you weren't going anywhere. We'd like to interview you now.' It was a tall man in a grey double-breasted suit and pale yellow shirt. It didn't take a genius to work out that he was one of the Security people. For the first time it occurred to me that the breach of security might have had something to do with my namesake and perhaps with the events that had led to my coming here. That was a scary thought. Could I be punished for something the other Jessica had done? Of course I could and would be, if I didn't answer their questions properly. It was like going into an exam for which I'd done no revision, in a subject I'd never studied.

The Security man led me through the front door of the house. James shot me a sly, lecherous glance as he took the man's hat with a kind of mini bow. James showed us into a small reception room on the ground floor which was beautifully decorated in red and gold with some kind of

Indian theme going on. There was a woman in the room waiting for us. She was sitting at a mahogany writing desk, pen poised, ready to take notes. She was introduced as Miss Shadrake, secretary and chaperone – like I needed a chaperone! Did people think that the minute I was alone with a guy I was going to leap on him or something, or that he was going to leap on me? What was wrong with these people?

Miss Shadrake was very blonde, petite and pretty. She gave me a prim little smile of encouragement. I sat on one of the high-backed winged armchairs and the Security man took the other one. I kicked my bag discreetly under the chair. I did not want this man to find my phone: I didn't trust him. I hadn't seen anyone with a mobile phone, so owning one seemed very likely to get me into some sort of trouble. Miss Shadrake watched us closely, smiling pleasantly all the time.

'So, Miss Allendon, you know why we're here?' the man asked.

I shook my head. 'Well,' he leaned forward and spoke to me as if I were a small child with learning difficulties, I was afraid he was going to pat me on the knee, 'someone broke into Mr Lansdowne's office last week and gained access to a communication device not usually available to the general public.'

I felt my stomach sink – surely that had to be the internet? Of course Jessica would not have had access to the net unless there were internet cafés or some such equivalent. I should have thought of that. I kept my face as blank as if I were being questioned by the head teacher at school. I can do unreadable well – or so I'm told.

'I don't know anything about a device,' I said timidly, making my voice as little-girlish as possible and my eyes wide. 'Could you tell me what it looks like? I'm sure I'd have noticed if there was one in the office.'

The man laughed delightedly as if I had said something particularly cute. Miss Shadrake's eyes narrowed. She, at least, was not taken in. The grey-suited man asked me a few more questions about how I liked my job and my employer, and as he turned to lead me out of the room, I fished around under the chair, grabbed my bag and tucked it under my arm – a manoeuvre which did not escape Miss Shadrake's notice. I tried not to show my relief that I had not been asked anything more difficult and returned to my office under the watchful eye of Miss Shadrake, who escorted me back to the first-floor office on the pretext of stretching her legs.

I may have been mistaken, but I thought something passed between her and Johnny, a small sign of recognition perhaps. It wasn't important – what was important was that I could not leave as I'd planned, not without causing a scene, and instinct told me that was to be avoided.

I had been given a very useful clue, however – somewhere in Mr Lansdowne's office there was a computer with internet access. All I had to do was find and use the computer, contact my double and get the hell out of her world. How hard could that be?

I got back to the pile of work that had been left for me. At home I would have found something else to do, anything else, but this world was getting to me. I sighed and got on with it and was working so intensively that I almost failed to notice the opportunity when it arose. Johnny had been called out to get something urgently for Mr Lansdowne. Mrs Lansdowne had retired for her afternoon nap and I was alone in the office when I heard a kind of electronic bell. It took me a moment to notice it, as I was typing with such concentration that I could only hear Mrs Lansdowne's voice on the tape. My ears had begun to get sore from the pressure of the hat and I took it off for a moment and then I heard the bell more distinctly.

I am nosy and it wasn't a sound I'd heard before, so I got up and peered into Mr Lansdowne's office. A small part of his desk was raised to show just the upper part of a computer screen. I checked to be sure that there was no one around and hurried into the room. There was a piece of paper preventing the screen from sinking into the desk and disappearing from sight. I just knew that this was what I'd been looking for, that this screen was part of a computer which could give me internet access. I didn't have time to do anything with this new knowledge as I heard footsteps and scuttled back to my desk. The man who had inter-viewed me wandered into the office and gave me an appraising look. 'Don't you look the proper little secretary bird?' he said, smiling at me like I was some kind of cream cake. He patted his knee and beckoned me to come and sit on it. What the hell did he think I was?

'Come on, Miss Allendon, we're alone for the moment – what's to stop us engaging in a little bit of spooning?'

The scathing response that was on the tip of my tongue fortunately did not need to go any further as I was saved by the timely reappearance of Johnny.

'Can I help you at all, sir?' he asked the Security man and then looked pointedly at the wall clock. 'Miss Allendon and I are finished for the day now, so perhaps any further questions might wait until tomorrow? I'm sure Mr Lansdowne would not expect you to upset the normal office routine without good reason.'

His manner was polite enough but there was an edge to it that made my interviewer look suddenly ill at ease. 'Well, then,' the grey suit said, 'I'll be continuing my investigations in the morning.'

Johnny waited until the Security man had left the room before speaking to me. 'Are you unwell, Miss Allendon? You look very pale. I hope your interrogation was not too uncomfortable?'

I shrugged and mumbled something, but then I knew. I knew that Johnny thought that Jessica had done it, had breached Mr Lansdowne's security. What I didn't know was what he was going to do about it.

EIGHT

I abandoned all thoughts of going back to Waterloo that evening. It was getting dark and I wasn't sure that it would be safe for me to wander around the London streets on my own. Since I'd arrived, I'd barely had an hour free of the fear of some kind of sexual harassment. I thought it was bad at home but I was beginning to realise I'd lived a very sheltered life. I wanted to try to email the other Jessica but it seemed clear that I was not going to get much opportunity to use the computer while the Security men and Jonathan Roberts were watching my every move. I was exhausted with the work which I wasn't used to, and the terrible strain of trying to be somebody else. I would have slunk upstairs to bed, but I could smell pastry and the delicious aroma of cooked meat and I realised how hungry I was.

The staff ate early, which was just as well because I could barely stay awake. We all sat in the same places as at breakfast. Cook placed two huge meat pies on the table, a vat of potatoes and a similar sized vat of cauliflower. Everyone was extraordinarily polite and there was lots of 'Please pass this and that', but there were a lot of undercurrents in the conversation that I couldn't understand – it was a bit like joining a soap several weeks into the plot. I was too tired to concentrate properly on who said what to whom – I just caught the odd phrase which made me curious.

'Well, Mrs Lansdowne obviously would ask Nancy to do that – I always get the worst of it.'

'Enough of that gossip. We will not discuss grievances over dinner.'

'Been staying well clear of the grey suits, have you, Edie? Girl with your connections . . .'

I worked out the hierarchy – that was easy enough. Everyone deferred to James and Cook, though Johnny kept himself a little apart. A very young girl, who only looked about twelve, was at the bottom of the pecking order. I think she did the washing-up and all the dirty jobs. I'm not sure why she wasn't in school. Johnny and I were treated differently because we were 'office' – there were several jokes about tea breaks, which Johnny ignored. He was not very friendly, this Johnny, he barely spoke throughout the meal.

Everyone but Cook and someone called 'Mr Eccles', who apparently repaired stuff when it broke, was young – well, under thirty anyway. Even through my exhaustion I knew that there was something going on under the politeness – you know how you pick up a conflict kind of 'vibe'. I didn't know what it was and I didn't feel up to working it out, but I knew it was there, under everything like a bad smell.

I tried so hard to keep myself together through all the strangeness. I ate everything put in front of me and only looked up from my plate when I had to. More than anything else I did not want to catch James's eye.

I left the table as soon as I could and I was about to go upstairs and get ready for bed when Cook took me to one side.

'I'll not have any goings-on in my kitchen, Miss Allendon. I'm not running a bawdy house here and you'll kindly not use my larder for assignations the minute my back's turned. The pickles will be docked from your wages.'

I was about to explain that it wasn't my fault but James's when I remembered that Cook and James were both senior servants. If they were anything like senior teachers they would stick together and blaming one of them would only get me in worse trouble. I bit my tongue – there was a lot of tongue-biting in the other Jessica's life. It nearly killed me but I did my demure lowering of the eyes, like those films of Princess Diana when she was young.

As I turned to go she said, 'Are you not watching the visuals tonight, Miss Allendon? I thought you liked *Families of the Empire*?'

I shook my head. I had been aware of everyone moving the table back and settling down to do something, but I hadn't realised that they had a television. It was locked up in a cupboard so I hadn't noticed it. Everyone arranged themselves so they could see the screen. The men took out pipes and cigarette cases and then James turned the television on with great ceremony. It was black and white but had a wide screen like a cinema. I was intrigued but couldn't stay once I had said I was going to bed. The very formal tones of a terribly posh announcer followed me as I stomped upstairs, blinking back tears of exhaustion and frustration. I couldn't stay another day here. I had to find a way of using Mr Lansdowne's computer and making contact with Jessica. Failing that, I had at least got to try to get back to Waterloo and take my chances there.

I filled in the diary – I don't know why – it seemed the right thing to do and I didn't skip anything either, not even the bit about James in the larder and the pickles. I was all too aware that when I got away from that place my double would still have to pick up the pieces. Of course if she had arranged for this to happen, she would deserve anything she got, but I didn't like to think that the other Jessica would do that. I didn't like to think that another version of me would deliberately screw up the life of another person.

I got ready for bed as quickly as I could: the attic bedrooms felt about ten degrees colder than the rest of the house. Edie burst into the room just as I was settling down to try to sleep.

'What happened? It's not like you to miss *Families of the Empire*. You missed a good episode too – Lilian has decided to emigrate to Calcutta and Ginny has got a job in the draper's.' She paused to register my expression. 'Go on! Tell me. I can see you've got a face on you like the Siege of Shanghai.'

I told her about James in the larder and the pickles and Cook's reaction. Edie didn't seem at all surprised.

'James is too young to be butler – no one knows how he's managed it. Reckon Mrs Lansdowne fancies him and is grooming him for something.' She touched the side of her nose and looked knowing. I didn't have a clue what she was talking about.

'You've got to turn up and meet him or he'll have you fired,' Edie said firmly, and I believed her. I didn't think it would be right to get the other Jessica fired.

'Now the thing is, I have it on good authority, that our James's days here are numbered. Doreen, who goes to St Patrick's with me and works for Commander Martin, has a sister in the know and she told me that James is Welsh! His family apparently has links with some of the most dangerous separatist groups: all of them are big noises in the IBI. How he got past the Lansdownes' screening God only knows, but the IBI lot are clever, that's for sure. They must have forged his papers. Apparently the antiterrorist lot are getting the case against James together now and, if it's straight up, he will be in the clink within a couple of weeks.'

As usual with Edie, the part of her comments that I didn't understand almost overwhelmed the part that I did. I was very slow that night. Eventually I said, 'So – what? He'll have to leave me alone?'

'No – he can do you a lot of harm while he's still here, but he won't be around for ever. You'll have to stall him. Tell him you'll "do it" with him but that you don't want to lose your position. Knowing what the mistress is like, you would if anything went wrong – so tell him he'll have to get you some contries, that you won't do anything without the contries.'

'Contries?' I was still trying to take in the first part of what she'd said about sleeping with him to keep my job. The bit about the Welsh and about terrorists went over my head then – I only remembered it later. This place was worse than I'd imagined.

'Jessie – don't you know anything any more? Contraceptive pills. If he's working for the mistress, he'll be able to get them as one of the perks of his job. She has a storeroom full of them. She's big in Women for Reproductive Freedom and keeps them to give to the poor sods with too many kids already, plus all her 'fallen women' she's forever trying to rescue. If you ask me, she does altogether too much falling on her own to be so high and mighty. Anyway, that's as may be, and the contries are worth a bob or two on the market – if you don't want me to sell them on, I might have a use for them myself if all my groundwork with Johnny-boy pays off. Anyway, you get James to get you those, and by the time they put you in the clear – a fortnight at least – he'll have got the sack. You don't have to deliver on your side of the deal and I've got something out of it too! Brainy enough to be an office girl I am, don't you think?' She winked at me and I smiled back hesitantly.

I must have looked blank because she patted my hand like I was demented. 'By all that's holy! You know you can only get them if you're a married woman over thirty with the vote or if you're a married woman with a chitty from your husband saying he has given you his permission. Now you're not married, you're not over thirty and you haven't the vote so the only way is the black market – we should look on your problem as an opportunity. Trust your Auntie Edie – James will go for it, I know he will. He doesn't want the hassle of a backstreet gin-and-bucket affair. He's ambitious and it wouldn't look good for him. The Welsh dissidents are nonconformists, but they can kill you with disapproval when they've a mind to.'

I thought I'd understood: Edie wanted me to put off James by promising I'd sleep with him after he'd somehow got me contraceptives. I didn't like her suggestion at all.

'Can't I just say no?' I asked and Edie laughed a hard little laugh.

'He'll have you one way or another. Better willing than forced – trust me. He's butler here. He'll deny wrongdoing and he'll be believed. Welcome to the real world, Jessie. Your best bet is to stall and with any luck he'll be fired before you've any need to use the contries. Come back from Xanadu yet?'

I felt sick. It wasn't right and yet I didn't for a moment not believe her. Cook had blamed me for the pickle jar, but she must have seen James following me out of the larder. The way I ran out of there like a scalded cat, she must have guessed I hadn't been there with him because I wanted to be. This was a horrible place. There were no equal opportunities here. I wanted to go home. It came over me – a wave of nausea more like seasickness than homesickness. This place disgusted me. I hid my face in the pillow – I didn't want Edie to see me cry.

NINE

Waking up that second day knowing I was no closer to getting home was one of the worst moments of my life. I didn't want to get out of bed – the thought of being the other Jessica all day was too much for me. I buried myself under the bedclothes hoping that if I just wished for it hard enough, I would be in my own bed, my mum yelling at me that my toast was getting cold. But it wasn't my mum yelling at me, only Edie who had threatened to get the butler, James, to get me out of bed. That worked.

I managed to get my hair into something like the bun Edie had done for me the day before, and I didn't struggle so much with the fastenings on the clothes, but although those practical things were easier, I felt terrible. 'Despair' is a big word, but I don't think it is too big to describe how I felt, I so didn't want to be in that situation. I had never been so lonely.

It was as I was straightening my bed that it struck me – I could be stuck in this unfair, sexist, awful place for my whole life. I think I actually cried out, because Edie gave me a hard look.

'Are you all right? You're that pale you look consumptive. Put a bit of rouge on, and rub it in so you don't look like a tart.' She gave me a small glass jar of pink blusher and I did as she said. I looked in the mirror in the wardrobe and was frightened by how little like myself I looked. The hairstyle made me look older, it accentuated my cheekbones and my eyes, which are too big anyway and make me look like a bushbaby even on a good day. Edie was right. I was pale and haunted-looking. What else could I expect? I put on some of Jessica's dark red lipstick, then blotted most of it off with her hanky so I looked a little less bloodless, and followed Edie downstairs. This morning, Cook was listening to the radio.

'Oh,' said Edie, 'It's *Good Morning with Mr Thrubb*!' I gathered that she was talking about a radio programme. The music was not like anything I'd heard before – it was rhythmic, syncopated and sort of jazzy but with an Indian feel. Some guy was singing about loving the veldt, which really confused me, but Cook was happy and the smell of bacon and eggs mingled with the stale smoke of the previous night.

I couldn't eat the breakfast. I usually only have cereal or toast, and my stomach was not awake enough to manage a cooked breakfast before seven o'clock. Edie and Cook both watched me carefully and I managed to drink a couple of cups of weak tea and nibbled at a piece of buttered toast. James sat opposite me, which was enough to kill what little appetite I had. I tried not to watch, but the sight of him eating a fried egg almost turned my stomach. It wasn't that he was a disgusting eater or anything, I just found him and everything he did made me frightened. I had never been frightened of a man before.

'You've got a half-day tomorrow, haven't you?' James said to Johnny, fussily wiping the yellow yolk from his upper lip.

'No, I'm taking the whole day, Mr Leonard. I've cleared it with the master. I'm owed some time in lieu.' Johnny managed to be polite without sounding deferential and James gave him a calculating look.

'You're going Sheen way, aren't you? Maybe you could drop off a parcel for me on the way.' Johnny nodded, colouring slightly, and once more I had the feeling of things going on below the surface that I didn't 'get'. What I did get though was that Johnny was going back to Sheen. I felt suddenly hopeful. If I could contact the other Jessica and arrange another meeting, I might be able to go with Johnny to the station or to a meeting point in Sheen that she could get to easily: more than that I might get the chance to see my dad again one more time before I left.

People talk about your heart skipping a beat, but I swear mine did when I thought I'd come up with a plan. I followed Johnny eagerly to the office after that, trying to think of a way of asking him to take me to Sheen that wouldn't seem mad to him.

I busied myself in our shared office for a few moments then said, as casually as I could, 'What way do you go when you're going to Sheen?'

'There's a good tram service, but I usually take the tube and then the train from Waterloo, but you know that.' He gave me that searching look that Jonno does when he thinks I'm bullshitting him and I didn't know what to say. Fortunately Mrs Lansdowne swept into her office at that moment and called for me, like you might call for a dog. I gritted my teeth and forced a smile. She lit a cigarette and placed it in one of those long cigarette holders you see in films. I was surprised. She hadn't struck me as a smoker. Her long pointed nails were painted an elegant eau de Nil.

'Miss Allendon, I have some errands I'd like you to do for me this morning. I'd like you to take this envelope and deliver it by hand. I don't trust the mail when it comes to items of great importance. I especially don't trust it when we have the Security here. Come what may, my charity work must go on. There are too many people who depend on my largesse. Now get your coat and hat. I have written the address so you shouldn't have any trouble. Keep your wits – you know what Soho is like. Should I ask Mr Leonard to escort you?'

I shook my head more violently than was strictly necessary, earning me a curious look from the mistress, who was today wearing something between a kaftan and a dress, with a turban of turquoise silk and a floor-length embroidered

67

waistcoat. A pale aquamarine the size of a quail's egg caught the light as she took a long drag on her cigarette. She viewed me, cat-like, through half-closed eyes. 'You'd better take the car then – have Francis drive you to the end of the street at least. Be as discreet as possible.' I thanked her, though I didn't know what for, and resisted an urge to curtsy. Mrs Lansdowne was so imperious and regal I had to remind myself that I was Jessica Allendon and, as my mother was fond of saying, as good as anyone.

I hurried up the backstairs to get my coat and ran past Edie and Cook discussing something in lowered voices. They started as I went past and Edie even looked embarrassed. I supposed that meant they were talking about me. I said the first thing to come into my head to hide my discomfort.

'Oh, Edie, I have to go out and I don't know where I left my hat and . . .'

'That's all right – borrow mine and my coat too if you like,' she said, a little too quickly, and she and Cook exchanged looks.

'Thanks,' I said, quite pleased with myself for remembering that the other Jessica had worn her jacket and hat to meet me at Waterloo and from the look of her wardrobe did not own another one. Edie had a rather nice cornflower blue fitted full-length coat with a swinging skirt. It was a little bit big and perhaps a bit warm for autumn, but covered me from my neck to my sensible shoes. I found a black hat and gloves too, though I didn't know if it was the kind of hat to go with the coat. I know it seems stupid to care about such things but I had already come seriously a cropper, as Edie would say, by wearing the wrong thing and I did not want to do it again. Edie had gone by the time I got downstairs and Cook just looked me up and down and said, 'Very ooh lah lah!' As I didn't know what that meant, I had to hope that was a good thing.

Johnny didn't say anything to me when I went to pick up the letters.

'Mrs Lansdowne said for Francis to take me and I . . .' I began. I was going to ask him where I would find Francis, even though I was sure that the other Jessica would have known.

'He has just gone to take Mr Lansdowne to the City. Where do you need to go?'

I showed him the address on the letter. He gave me an appraising look.

'You know that area, do you?'

'I'm not sure,' I said, uncertain whether Jessica would be expected to know the geography of Soho or not: every small thing was so difficult when I didn't know how anything worked.

He took a pocket watch out of his waistcoat and said, 'I can spare half an hour. Mr Lansdowne won't be back for a while. I'd like to get away from this lot.' He gave a brief glance in the direction of one of the Security men who was sitting in Mr Lansdowne's office working intently at something I couldn't see.

Was he on the internet? Annoyingly, I couldn't get any closer because Johnny was still talking to me and blocking the route to his boss's office. 'I'll escort you,' he said decisively. 'You ought not go down there on your own. I'll get my coat.'

I have always been too nosy for my own good, but I had to see what was in Mrs Lansdowne's letter that could not be trusted to the mail. The gum on the envelope had not been stuck down properly and I managed to open it with the minimum of damage. Obviously I hid my activity from the Security man. The envelope contained money, a great deal of money, in used hundred-pound notes. I sealed it up carefully when I heard footsteps. They belonged to Johnny. He was wearing a long dark coat with an implausibly large collar, a broad-brimmed hat and leather gloves. He ought to have looked ridiculous, but the surprising flamboyance of it suited him. Jonno would have died rather than wear anything so dramatic. Relieved that I didn't have to go out alone, I followed him out of the house the back way – the servants' entrance through the scullery led into a narrow alleyway and to a couple of garages.

'I'm not licensed to drive that class of vehicle,' Johnny said, looking longingly at the shining silver and green vehicle parked in one of the garages, 'or I suppose I might

70

have borrowed it. Still, I'm sure a walk would be good – clear the cobwebs.' He talked like somebody's grand-father, then he offered me his arm and I took it. With my black gloves and hat, I felt like a character in a play. It felt good to hold on to him even though he wasn't my Jonno. His arm felt strong and I badly needed something to hang on to, especially as I nearly tripped over a blind beggar sitting just outside the alley. He had a sign written on a tatty bit of card in a scrawling uncertain hand: 'Veteran of the Kenya campaign. A wife and two children to keep.'

'You won't get anything here! Clear off!' Johnny said harshly, and put out his foot as if to kick the man. I pulled him away, shocked that he could kick out at a beggar.

'I bet he's no vet, either,' Johnny said, but then out of the corner of my eye I felt sure I saw him drop something into the beggar's upturned hat before leading me firmly and rapidly away.

'Why did you try to kick him?' I asked in horror, unable to stop myself.

Johnny looked surprised. 'If Mr Lansdowne knows there's a beggar by his door, he'll have the King's Constabulary's Vagrant Control round. You know them – shoot first, ask questions later and admit to nothing.' His tone was bitter. Surely he didn't mean what I thought he meant? I was lost for words.

We turned out of the alley back towards the square

across a wide road, which to my surprise had horse dung strewn across it.

'The damned new London road tax has really impacted on tradesmen – even the butcher is thinking of going back to horse-drawn. It makes for a mucky street,' Johnny said. As if in response to his remark, a bright red car shot into view and took the corner at such great speed that Johnny had to push me out of the way. 'Of course the ones who can afford the tax, the insurance and the fuel think they've paid for the bloody road so they needn't take any care for the rest of us,' he said. 'Are you all right?'

My heart was beating wildly and my hat had ended up over my eyes. I straightened it carefully with one hand, still clutching Johnny's arm with an increasingly desperate grip. Two days in a strange place and I'd turned into Tara Bridgstock, a girl in my class who spent most of her life entwined like a kind of ivy round her boyfriend. Johnny got us both on the pavement just before a second low-slung racing car took the corner of the square on two wheels and squealed after the first.

'Nobs!' Johnny said with acid in his tone.

There were a couple of women in nurse's uniform and elaborate starched wimple things on their heads outside the women's hospital. Johnny raised his hat and said, 'Ladies,' and they both giggled like schoolgirls, which they could have been as they looked about my age. We walked past St Barnabas into Greek Street, which was full of cafés and bookshops. I felt Johnny tense, though I couldn't see anything to tense about: he didn't know I was carrying a few thousand pounds of Mrs Lansdowne's cash in that slim cream envelope. As for me, I would have been nervous carrying that anywhere.

It was *so* not my London – overhead I could see several huge balloons with vast baskets underneath. I only recognised them as airships as my history teacher had included some pictures of them in last year's end-of-term history challenge. They glided silently high above the city. I could just make out the name in scarlet letters on the silver and gold metallic background of the balloon: 'Ariana 11 Goodyear-Zeppelin'.

Away from the relative quiet of the square, the streets were busy. Most of the traffic was horse-drawn and the few car drivers trying to progress along the clogged street were tooting their horns and gesticulating wildly at the hold-up; no one took any notice. The stench of horse manure and petrol was as unfamiliar as the sight of the pavement crammed with pedestrians all wearing hats and gloves like in an old film. We passed an electrical shop which sold a combination of pianos and electronic devices. A small crowd had gathered outside the window where a colour television showing some kind of romance was prominently displayed. Music blared out from the partially open doors. The music wasn't what I was used to, but its pounding rhythm and electronic origins were definitely twenty-first century. The horse manure was not the only unusual smell either. Something pungent and sweet lingered on the air and, when I peered down narrow side streets, I saw groups of men in flat caps leaning against walls and women in exotic gowns with fashion-model poses smoking pipes. Was this 'the smoke' that everyone was going on about? The smell caught at the back of my throat. I felt a moment of panic when one of the women clocked me watching, and I looked hastily away as if I'd seen them do something illicit. I told myself I had no reason to be scared. I mean, I know Soho's reputation, even in my own London, but it was bright daylight and the streets were busy.

We turned into Old Compton Street and off that into a narrow alley where the atmosphere immediately changed. There were many more men just sitting around smoking and laughing loudly. One of them tipped his hat at Johnny, who shook his head slightly and the man turned away. I didn't like the way they looked at me. I checked the address on the envelope: this was the place. The buildings were dilapidated and I had trouble working out the numbers. Rubbish was stacked up on either side of the street and spilled into the road. I'm sure I saw a rat skitter away as we approached. The stench was putrid and there was that other smell, cloying and sweet. I gagged slightly and Johnny looked disapproving, as though that reaction let him down.

'It's just past the smoking parlour up there on the left,' he said, indicating a derelict-looking building with graffiti scrawled over the walls. I couldn't read what any of it said as it all seemed to be in a foreign language. I checked the letter. It was addressed to a Ms Finlock of the Women's League for Universal Enfranchisement. One of the buildings had a small handwritten notice pinned to the door declaring it the 'WLUE' so I supposed I had the right place. It looked very shabby. No wonder it needed a donation. Beside the notice there was also a small brass letterbox hidden beneath an iron cage. 'What's the cage for?' I said curiously.

'To stop bombs of course,' Johnny laughed. 'Not that it's much good against letter bombs or some of the newer types of contraptions. Let's hope no one mistakes us for the kind of person who might plant one of those.'

I slid the letter through carefully. His words made me nervous. 'Should I ring the bell or something?'

'I wouldn't do that, no,' said Johnny, his face suddenly hard and wary. A second later we were both being manhandled against the wall. This time I'm glad to say I remembered some of the self-defence stuff I had been taught. As I was grabbed from behind, I threw my head back wildly, making contact with my assailant's nose. At the same time I kicked him as hard as I could with Jessica's high heel, catching him just behind the knee. He let me go and I started to run, but the men who had been leaning casually against the wall now formed a menacing line, blocking my way out of the alley.

TEN

'Johnny!' I shrieked. I turned and Johnny was punching someone enthusiastically in the face, with sharp, deliberate strokes as if he knew what he was doing, and as if he quite enjoyed it. Johnny's victim's companion was bleeding from the nose. I think I must have head-butted him in exactly the right place; something bright and metallic shone in his hand.

'Johnny! Knife!' I shrieked. Johnny needed no more information. He let go of the man he had been punching, who fell groaning into a heap on the floor, and turned to face the man with the nosebleed. Neither he nor his opponent spoke and then Johnny kicked the other man hard in the groin. As he doubled up in agony, Johnny grabbed my hand and pulled me towards the line of men who stood between us and the street. I suppose we could have gone the other way – I'm pretty sure the street was not a dead end – but I didn't think of that and Johnny seemed to be quite happy to take on anyone.

'You going to try to stop me?' he said to one of the men facing us in the street, a short skinny guy with a long knife-scar down his face.

'You're outnumbered – is your little tart going to fight for you too?'

Johnny said something in a foreign language. It didn't sound all that polite and then he ran at the scar-faced man, dragging me behind him. Scar-face got out of the way, though whether it was because Johnny was twice his size or because he never intended to stop us in the first place I couldn't say. We ran gloved hand in gloved hand all the way up Old Compton Street until we got back to the relative civilisation of Greek Street. I had to stop then. I can run. I used to be in the cross-country team, but I haven't run for a long time. I was scared and panting and I had a stitch in my side. Johnny looked surprisingly calm.

'Your hat is lopsided,' he said. I straightened it, aware that I was probably red in the face and that passers-by were giving me curious looks.

'What was that all about?' I asked, trying to sound as if that kind of thing happened all the time and was no big deal. I pinned up a stray strand of hair and hoped that he didn't see that my hand was shaking.

'Don't play little prissy innocent with me, Miss Allendon. I know you got into Mr Lansdowne's office. I know you're an undercover and you know damn well what that was about.' I opened my mouth and then closed it again. What was an 'undercover'? Maybe the other Jessica did know what it was all about, but I didn't and now was probably not the time to tell him that. He wasn't Jonno: Jonno couldn't fight his way out of a hamburger wrapper. Johnny's face was hard and closed, where I could read Jonno like a PC screen. I glanced at Johnny, who was unclenching his fist and cracking his fingers as though beating the crap out of someone was something he did every day. Perhaps it was.

'We should get back,' I said. 'Thank you for helping me.'

'They wouldn't have hurt you though, would they – not if you're on their side?'

The look he gave me was one of cool indifference and I wondered how much he had fought for pleasure and how much to help me out. I didn't have any answer to give him so I shrugged. I didn't know who the sides were, let alone which side was Jessica's. Were Johnny and Jessica on different sides? Was that why they weren't friends?

We walked the short distance back to the house in silence. He did not offer me his arm and I did not try to take it. I wanted to ask him to take me to Sheen, but dense as I can be about other people's feelings sometimes, I knew that it was not a good time to broach the subject. When I went to return the borrowed coat, the forlorn, set face in the wardrobe mirror looked even less like mine.

Johnny and I worked in near silence for the rest of the day. I typed letters and watched: I watched Mrs Lansdowne, I watched Johnny and when Mr Lansdowne arrived later that day I watched him too, as best I could, through the chink of his almost-closed door. I didn't know what I was watching for exactly, other than an opportunity to try to contact Jessica on the machine in Mr Lansdowne's office: none came.

Mr Lansdowne was as plain as his wife was lovely. A short squat man with a huge leonine head set on an equally disproportionate pair of shoulders: his upper and lower body might almost have belonged to different people. He was dressed in a dark brown tunic that reached virtually to the floor and was decorated from top to bottom with horizontal black frogging, like some imitation military uniform. He had a cascade of grey hair which reached to his shoulders. To be quite honest he looked weird and not a little frightening. He barely glanced at me, for which I was grateful. He and Mrs Lansdowne made a big show of greeting each other with lots of 'darling' this and that, but his eyes were cold like a hawk's, while hers were sharper than any bird's. They did not touch each other but there was something powerful between them, an electric kind of connection – there was no doubt about that. I don't know anything about marriage but theirs seemed weird.

Mr Lansdowne smoked a pipe, so between her cigarettes and his pipe the room quickly became very smoky and I had to struggle not to splutter. What with the fug, Johnny's hostility and the strained relations between the

Lansdownes, the atmosphere was well nasty and I was glad when suppertime came, or rather I would have been had it not been for the fact that I was supposed to meet James and I was no nearer escaping either him or this nightmarishly violent world.

After dinner as everyone moved the table back ready for the nightly 'visual', Edie signalled to me to meet her on the stairs. 'Get yourself smartened up!' she said. 'You look a right bluestocking. Change into something pretty and act like you're interested in him. You look like a pot of cold porridge at the moment!' I didn't tell her to go to hell. She was an ally of sorts, though if she'd asked me I would have told her that she was unlikely to get too far with Johnny. I didn't think she was his type. I wanted to rebel, to wear my jeans and tell James where to stuff his job, but I couldn't and I wouldn't even if I'd found the courage: something about that house and my role in it knocked the fight right out of me.

I changed into a less sombre dress – Jessica didn't have many, but she had something quite pretty in an unusual shade of olive green. It wasn't a colour I would have ever chosen, but it looked OK. I redid my hair so that it was a little looser and reapplied Jessica's crimson lipstick, all the time wondering what I thought I was doing. Jessica's clothes were sort of neat and fitted. If I'm honest, they were more flattering than my own clothes – I don't think I owned a dress.

I found a small bottle of scent with some German name and dabbed a bit behind each ear, hating myself for playing along. It smelled musky and exotic, not what I had expected at all.

I wondered if I could get away with not meeting James. Short of running away into the hostile night of an unfamiliar city where they shot vagrants, I could think of no way out. Speculating about that got me downstairs and past Edie and Cook, who exchanged a knowing glance. Did everybody know my business?

James was waiting for me in the back alley. He was wearing some kind of jumper in place of his usual suit. He was smoking a pipe and leaning against the back wall of the house like someone in an old-fashioned knitwear advert. Another time I might have laughed – he looked so ridiculous, but there was nothing funny about James or my predicament. Would he try something on here, now, and if he did would anyone come to help me? I felt sick and my stomach squirmed like I'd swallowed worms. I so did not want to do this.

'Jessica?' he said.

'I'm here.' I found myself folding my arms defensively round me and wishing I'd worn something warmer – like Edie's blue coat – that was more suitable armour for this encounter than the clingy green dress. He made a clumsy sort of grab for me and the next minute had me in his arms and was slobbering all over me like some kind of overenthusiastic Labrador.

'Wait, wait a minute, James, let's just slow down . . .' I began, trying to shove him away with something that didn't look quite so obviously like revulsion. I don't want to remember exactly what I said – it's too embarrassing – I think I've wiped it from my mind. I think I did all right. It was almost dark, so he couldn't see my expression too clearly, and anyway I looked down modestly while I spoke. I managed to control my voice so that I sounded about a billion times more enthusiastic than I felt. Perhaps he expected it because he didn't sound too surprised when I explained about the pills. I don't know what his expression was because I couldn't look. I think it is probably the most uncomfortable conversation I've ever had.

He calmed down a bit then, so that he seemed a little less like an octopus touching me wherever he could. I tried to chat with him normally, as I would do with my friends at home, but he seemed to find that too much to deal with. He didn't want to *talk* to me. Anyway, I survived without having to head-butt him or try out my other self-defence moves. It was as if he was more confident that he would get what he wanted, so he didn't have to pressure me quite so much.

'I'd better go in,' I said as soon as I decently could. 'I'm tired and I have a lot of work to do for Mrs Lansdowne tomorrow.' I was cold too, but I didn't want to mention that in case he grabbed me again in a misguided attempt to warm me up. He let me go with just one more wet kiss. I ran upstairs to scrub my face until it was pink and to clean my teeth to get rid of the taste of him. I hadn't done anything other than endure an unwanted kiss – but I felt demeaned somehow, like I'd just sold myself.

Johnny saw me come in and as James followed a few moments later he must have cottoned on to what was going on. He wasn't my Jonno, but I still didn't want him thinking badly of me. It upset me to imagine what he must think. If I was lucky, it would soon be Jessica's problem again, not mine, but somehow thinking that didn't help. I put the barest details in the diary and then cried myself to sleep again. I didn't hear Edie come in, which was as well, because I did not want to give her a blow by blow account of what had gone on. I wanted to pretend it had never happened.

ELEVEN

I avoided an intimate chat with Edie simply by getting up before her and getting downstairs before anyone else. The little girl, Ruby, was cleaning boots in the scullery. I offered to help her but she told me to 'eff off'. It was the first time I'd heard that particular word in Jessica's world. Roberta probably thought I was after something. I walked outside for some air. There was no one around, no one to stop me if I took off and made my own way to Waterloo. Would there be an entrance to my world there? An equivalent to the Narnian wardrobe or did I have to wait for another electrical storm? Every moment I stayed in Jessica's shoes I felt like I was being changed, turned into someone who got more fearful each passing day. For a moment I found that I couldn't believe in my own situation – it was too far-fetched – a kid's story. I watched as some sort of motorised milk cart, which was also pulled by a horse, dropped off a large metal milk churn at the house opposite. 'Hello darlin',' the driver shouted. 'Fancy a nice bit of cream in your jug?' I don't know what he meant by that but he winked at me broadly and I retreated back inside. Cook was up and getting the breakfast organised. This time I didn't offer to help, but she asked me to anyway. I was glad when she put the radio on: I couldn't think of how to fill the silence. I realised too late that I'd probably missed the one opportunity to get away I was likely to get that day.

When Edie came downstairs, she gave me a quizzical look and I gave her the thumbs up sign. She grinned at me and didn't appear to think I'd been avoiding her, or if she did, she wasn't holding it against me.

At the table James kept trying to catch my eye and I nearly went bog-eyed trying not to look at him. We were all startled when the music from the radio was suddenly interrupted by a news flash. There had been a bomb attack at a government building – the Ministry for Foreign Affairs, the Commonwealth and the Colonies. There was extensive damage to the fabric of the building, but no one had been injured. Police suspected the IBI. King James III had urged the people to remain calm and to put their faith in the hands of His Majesty's Constabulary, the regular police and, of course, the Security Services. His Majesty's government would not be bullied or blackmailed by anti-colonialist terrorist factions. They were the enemies of the state and would die as enemies of the state.

Johnny groaned. 'Well that's my day off cancelled, then.' I was puzzled by his reaction until the newsreader continued in his clipped posh tones: 'The Minister for

National Security and Public Order, Mr Lansdowne, expressed his grave concern and promised that the investigation into the apparent security breach will be dealt with as a priority. Armed officers will be stationed throughout Westminster and public access to the centre of London will be tightly controlled . . .'

I didn't take too much notice as details were given of the street and tube station closures. I didn't remember there being a Minister for National Security and Public Order at home. Mum always said I didn't pay enough attention to current affairs – but I didn't think Britain had any colonies. And I knew that there was no James III. Who the hell was he?

Everyone was strangely silent after the announcement. Johnny looked grim and I don't think it was just because of his missing his day off. From my point of view, I thought it was possibly good news, assuming he could take his day off soon – it would give me more time to make contact with the other Jessica and maybe ask Johnny if he would take me with him to Waterloo.

'Damn and my Aunt Alice,' Cook said. 'We'll have the Constabulary and the Security round here under our feet now. Sniffing into my jam jars and checking my receipts. The Security are one thing but the Constabulary are all jackboots and efficiency – put the fear of God into a Godless heathen, they would.'

'It may not be that bad,' James said deliberately. 'Just

make sure that everything is above board, twinkle clean and pukka.' He looked at me and I felt immediately guilty, even though I didn't think I'd done anything wrong. Cook looked at me too and I had to try not to notice. I didn't know what they thought I'd done that wasn't 'twinkle clean and pukka'. James caught me on the stairs as I was on the way to the office. He grabbed me and kissed me enthusiastically; I tried not to struggle.

'I've been thinking,' he said. 'I agree about the contries. I've made my enquiries. I can see that you can't afford to put a foot wrong or it's the municipal workhouse for you and no girl of mine is going to end her days doing hard labour there. Just remember, Jessica, I'm a person of influence here, so don't think you can go playing fast and loose with me.'

It was a threat, of course it was, but I was more stunned by the revelation that if she lost her job Jessica would end up in a workhouse. Surely in my world we'd got rid of those years ago? I thought back desperately. I'd done modern history. 1930 – the date arrived in my head. In my world workhouses had been abandoned in 1930. I felt a kind of vertigo and had to grab the wall for support. Everything I learnt about this world made it more hellish than the one I'd left. A sudden wave of homesickness overwhelmed me. Tears pricked my eyes again. I'd sworn I was going to stop being so emotional, but I was out of control.

'Oh, my sweet!' James said. 'There, there, I didn't mean to wobble your lip. Don't worry your pretty head. I'll look after you.' He spoke in the voice old ladies use to talk to babies – eugh! If I hadn't hated him already, I would have started then. I hate people talking to me like I'm something cute and helpless, like I can't look after myself. A smart-arse reply was in my mouth but I swallowed it down. There was no point in antagonising him.

'Have to go. I'll be late!' I said through clenched teeth.

He waved a small box wrapped in brown paper in front of my nose. 'You can have them for a kiss.' He kissed me again, an assault I accepted without resistance, then I broke free and ran up the stairs.

'Catch!' he said and threw the packet after me. I didn't catch it and when I bent down to pick it up, he pinched me. 'See you later, Jessie darling,' he said. If he thought the grimace I gave him was a smile, he wanted his eyes testing.

I put the box in my pocket. It wasn't much of a pocket – designed for a ladylike lace hanky and not much else – but I didn't think I had time to run to the top of the house and lock it in my drawer. I was late. Johnny had already gone and I didn't want to endure another of his disapproving looks.

The office was in uproar when I arrived. Mr and Mrs Lansdowne were in there and 'exchanging words'.

'I will not have His Majesty's Constabulary in my house, disturbing my staff and creating a climate of suspicion. The Security I will accept – they are at least nominally under your control, but the Constabulary! They have an agenda all of their own which may suit neither of us.' Mrs Lansdowne's voice was coldly angry. I hadn't quite appreciated how steely she was beneath her polished, glamorous exterior.

'We do not have any choice, my dear. There has been a serious breach of security this time – the King has got himself involved, and you know that means the Constabulary. I might personally be a target for terrorists and we will need to security check the staff – again.'

He touched her then, lightly on the arm, and leaned towards her, so that he all but whispered in her ear: 'This is not one either of us can win, but I advise you to be very careful. Remember the King has very little interest in the weak of this world and regards philanthropy only as a tool of sedition.' He spoke in such an urgent voice that Mrs Lansdowne was silenced. She fixed him with her pale eyes, and nodded slowly. I felt I was intruding and looked away, but not before I saw them exchange a very intimate, intense look. She loved him, I realised; whatever else was going on between them, she loved him.

Mrs Lansdowne then turned her back on him and walked into her own office in a flurry of silk robe, tossing her blonde hair. The door slammed so that the paintings on the wall trembled on their hooks. I wasn't sure that a tantrum was the most effective way of dealing with what was surely some kind of a warning, and I looked at Johnny for some hint as to what I should do. Mr Lansdowne sighed. 'Inform the officers that we are expecting them. I have to go to the Ministry. Hold the fort here, Jonathan, and see that Miss Allendon takes care of my wife.'

He left then, leaving me staring at Johnny.

'What did he mean, take care of his wife?'

Johnny waited a second as if to be sure Mr Lansdowne had truly gone and that we were alone and then he whispered: 'Mr Lansdowne is worried about some of Mrs Lansdowne's activities. Normally, he pretends not to know about them and you know the lengths she goes to to keep her activities secret from him. Politically they don't agree and that's a very big deal, as you can imagine. Everyone expects him to rein her in and have her behave as a dutiful wife, but he never has. They play this big game of always being at loggerheads but, well, you can see – the truth between them is more complicated and Mrs Lansdowne is not quite the radical she seems. She does her good works, but when it comes down to it I'm not sure of her commitment – she's a toff after all. Mind you, the Constabulary are evil bastards. Mr Lansdowne wants you to help her get rid of anything incriminating.' I must have gone pale, because Johnny's expression suddenly turned sympathetic. 'Yes, that does put you in danger, Miss Allendon, but Mr Lansdowne won't worry about that.'

I waited a decent interval and then knocked on the door and was told to enter. Mrs Lansdowne was in what appeared to be her dressing-gown. She wore no make-up and she looked older; the cold morning light showed the cobweb of fine lines round her eyes. She had ordered the lighting of the fire in her office and was feeding it with papers. She looked scared.

'I must dress,' she said. 'I must be ready to greet His Majesty's Constabulary with elegance and charm.' She sounded bitter. 'I have some more letters you need to deliver for me. You have to go straight away and it would be better if you did not involve any of the others. I trust you will not tell the Security men about these errands, when they arrive. Remember that life without my patronage and with the antagonism of the Lansdownes would be a harder, colder place.'

That was a threat all right. I did not like the sound of it. She clearly expected me to keep her secrets – perhaps that was part of being a secretary. Of course the fact that I didn't even know what her secrets were made keeping them easy. She passed me a couple of brown envelopes, hastily addressed in a scrawled version of her beautiful hand, but she dropped one on the floor and as I went to pick it up the small packet of pills slipped out of my shallow pocket and landed at her silk-slippered feet.

'What is that?' she asked sharply, her long fingers scooping the small packet from the thick pile of the carpet before I could reach it.

'This looks very familiar,' she said grimly, and opened the packet as though it were hers, as if a secretary had no right to privacy at all. Her manicured nails ripped through the brown wrapper and tugged at the white cardboard box – thirty or more small pills scattered everywhere. She held one between her thumb and forefinger.

'Contraceptives,' she said. 'Contraceptives destined for Women for Reproductive Freedom. What is the meaning of this?'

I stared back at her, my mouth half-open like an idiot. My mind went blank: I'd no idea what to say.

TWELVE

'Miss Allendon, I am not having a good day. I do not expect to find a trusted employee with illegal drugs in her pocket. Where did you get them from?'

I took a deep breath. What would happen if I landed James in trouble? Would he take it out on me before I could get away? I was afraid of him; I was not used to being pushed around.

'I'm not sure I can say, Mrs Lansdowne,' I began.

'Don't get pert with me, young lady. I took you on Mr Roberts's recommendation. He said your family was known to him and that you were an intelligent and well-mannered girl. I did not expect to find you engaging in immorality in my house.'

I accepted this, conscious of the heat in my cheeks. 'Mr Roberts,' she'd said. Mr Roberts had recommended me – that was Johnny – were we on the same side after all?

'I'm sorry, ma'am,' I said. I didn't know why I used the 'ma'am' like a police constable on the TV, but it kind of fell out of my mouth.

'Pick up the pills! I don't have time for this. You have to deliver my notes now. The Constabulary will be here any second. They would have been here earlier but for some issue of jurisdiction Mr Lansdowne has concocted. I'll discuss this with you later.' She swept out of the room and I found that I was shaking. I didn't seem to be doing very well at being Jessica . . . It was looking less and less likely that when we swapped back to our own lives she'd still have a job at the Lansdownes'. Whatever else I did, I had to try to keep her from the workhouse.

I picked up all the pills and put them back in the packet and then ran to lock them in the drawer, which is probably what I should have done in the first place. While I was there I grabbed Edie's coat, hat and gloves, hoping that it would be OK to borrow them again. My hands were still shaking with nerves and haste, and it took me ages to do up the buttons. I forced myself to calm down and carefully pinned Edie's black hat on my head. It had a little half-veil I had not noticed before and I pulled that down so that my eyes were largely hidden. When I arrived back in our office, Johnny was waiting for me.

'Mrs Lansdowne isn't happy,' he said flatly.

'I know,' I said, trying to keep my voice equally non-committal.

'She told me to give you this as you are going into a difficult area.' Jonno slipped me a small tan leather handbag about the size of an exercise book, with a long strap – like a satchel. I took it from him and put it over my left shoulder, crossing it over my chest so that it hung at my right hip. I always did that with bags at home as it made them harder to snatch. I had no idea why I would need a handbag except perhaps to keep the letters safe, but I accepted it just as I was having to accept so much else. Johnny looked momentarily amused, a half-smile on his lips. 'Aren't you going to look inside?' he said.

I looked inside and felt faint. Inside there was a gun.

'Are you sure Mrs Lansdowne wanted me to have this?' I asked, swallowing hard. 'Why didn't she give it to me herself?' I was suspicious because, as I was rapidly learning, nothing in this place was straightforward and I didn't know who to trust. I especially didn't know whether to trust Johnny. Why would Mrs Lansdowne give him something to pass on to me? I'd thought he was her husband's man, not hers.

Johnny smiled his devastating smile, so much like Jonno's but somehow more powerful for being rarer. 'She had to change. She was in a hurry and neglected to give it to you.'

I put my hand in the bag and pulled out the gun – it had a pearl handle and was highly decorated. It was beautiful, if you like that sort of thing.

'Don't get it out here, you idiot girl!' he said under his breath. 'It looks fancy but it's a straightforward, standard issue revolver. Nothing you're not used to. If you have to use it, get in touch and I'll sort it out.'

I was too startled to answer him. When did I get into a spy movie? I couldn't believe that he wouldn't be able to see my heart pounding underneath the blue coat. I didn't want a gun. A more practical problem struck me, as things do, even in unreal situations: how did I get in touch with him? There was an old-style phone in the office – one with a dial and a big heavy receiver made of the kind of stuff my mum called bakelite. The other Jessica would have known the office number. I did not.

I nodded at him as if I understood what he was talking about, and tried to look purposeful as I went back into Mrs Lansdowne's office to collect her letters. I could feel his eyes on my back, so I was careful to stand tall and straight like the other Jessica and not betray my feelings.

Inside the privacy of the office, I let out a long shaky sigh and slumped in Mrs Lansdowne's red leather chair. It was safe enough – it would surely take her a while to transform frustration and fury into elegance and charm; the Security men were in Mr Lansdowne's office and the feared Constabulary had not yet arrived. I took out the gun cautiously, as if it were a wild creature that might bite me, and examined it more closely. What kind of world was this where it was OK to have a revolver but not contraceptive pills?

My hands were sweating as I put the gun away and my fingers were so clumsy I was frightened I was going to set it off by accident. Did it have a safety catch or something?

I tried to remember everything I'd ever heard about revolvers: it didn't amount to much. I checked the addresses on the envelopes, which were both tightly sealed. The first one bore the same address as her previous letter: the street where Johnny and I'd had to run for our lives. Oh. My. God. Did I have to go back there – was there not some way out of it? The second letter had an address I didn't know on it. Surely there must be an equivalent of an A to Z somewhere? I took a series of long, calming breaths – like I was breathing into the imaginary paper bag again. I could not afford a panic attack, however well justified. I went back to my office. There it was on the bookshelf by my desk next to *A New English Grammar* and *Who's Who (Imperial Edition)*. I grabbed *An Alphabetical Guide to London and its Environs*. It was just small enough to fit in the bag, alongside the revolver and the letters. That done, I had an overwhelming urge to run to the loo and then to run to Waterloo. I had a chance – no one would miss me for a while. I had a gun and so I could defend myself if attacked again. I didn't know how to use it and I didn't know if I would use it, but still, I had a chance. There were two things that held me back. The first was straightforward: I was afraid. I was afraid that I wouldn't be able to get back to my London unless Jessica also came back to hers, that I'd get to Waterloo and have to turn round and come back without having run my errands.

Then I'd be sent to the workhouse and I very much doubted they had internet access. The second thing was sort of crazier and had to do with Mrs Lansdowne. She was not a nice person in the usual sense, but from her letters and the money she'd had me deliver she did genuinely seem dedicated to helping all kinds of causes – causes that, from what I'd seen, needed supporting. Women for Reproductive Freedom, the Women's League for Universal Enfranchisement – they all seemed to be trying to right the terrible injustices that were going on in this hellish London. I made my decision. I would deliver Mrs Lansdowne's letters first and then try to find Waterloo: both decisions scared the pants off me.

THIRTEEN

I slipped out of the house the back way just as there was the sound of running feet and a bit of a commotion at the front door. I guessed that would be the Constabulary arriving. I had only just got away in time.

It was early and the air was still damp and cool, the streets were not busy and there was that strange waiting feeling in the air you get sometimes before the day has properly started. A man with a flat hat and fingerless gloves was cleaning the pavement with a broom. He was whistling and chewing tobacco at the same time. Every now and again he spat out the tobacco and swept it up. A woman in a huge hat was walking a pair of rangy Dalmatians, and a couple of magnificent cars cruised slowly round the square; I wondered if they too belonged to the Security Services, as all the other cars I'd seen had used the square like a racetrack. I was glad the veil hid most of my face. I thought it would be good to be anonymous.

I walked confidently – that was the first thing they taught us at self-defence: don't look like a victim. I had no trouble remembering the way, though I did wish I had Johnny's arm to hold on to, even though I wasn't sure where his loyalties lay. I never thought much about Jonno's sheer size – I'd known him too long – but Johnny's muscular bulk, his physical presence, was intimidating and at that moment I felt that being intimidating was a good idea. I was very scared by the time I turned up the alleyway off Old Compton Street – so scared that my knees felt rubbery and my legs boneless. I felt spineless. I also wished I'd got trainers on instead of Jessica's heels; I felt much more confident in trainers. Jessica's shoes forced me to take small mincing steps and I needed to stride.

When I turned the corner, the first thing I noticed was how quiet it was, the second was how clean. All the bins and overflowing rubbish were gone and the street had been swept and sluiced down with disinfectant. Yet still the sweet, pungent smell I'd noticed before lingered on the air, not quite erased by the acrid stench of bleach. At first I was relieved to see that the men who had been idling in the alley were missing, but then I saw the other ones who weren't idling but stood like on-duty guardsmen at intervals down the street, watching. They wore smart grey suits and trilbies – the kind of hats gangsters wear in movies. These changes made the street, if anything, even more menacing and I gripped the strap of my bag tightly so that no one could see my hands tremble. I felt it would have been overkill to hold the gun, although

I wanted to. I could not honestly imagine pointing it at anyone, let alone attempting to fire it.

A tall lean man with his hat tipped at an angle ambled towards me. He was smoking and acting relaxed. All the others watched him as he approached me. My mouth went dry and I'm sure I was trembling noticeably. I could see the netting of my veil quiver like a leaf in the wind, only there was no wind. The man raised his hat. 'Miss,' he said by way of greeting and I nodded at him graciously, like I was an important lady or something.

'Can I ask your business in this street, miss, please?'

I was tongue-tied for a second but somehow, channelling Lady Bracknell, I managed an imperious 'What business is it of yours?' I was quite pleased with that in the circumstances. The man reached into his inside pocket and I froze with fear, losing what little confidence I'd managed to cobble together – what if he had a gun too? I don't think I breathed until he pulled out a flat, leather wallet with some kind of document inside it, which he handed to me. The paper was very fancy, decorated with squiggles in different coloured inks like a five-pound note. I skim-read it quickly, though nerves made it difficult for me to focus. The document said he was an Officer of His Majesty's Forces for the Prevention of Terrorism and Public Disorder. I noticed that the florid signature at the bottom of the document belonged to T.E. Lansdowne. Should I say that I worked for him?

It was a split-second decision. Some reluctance to identify myself in any way prevented me. My brain was whirring like a tyre stuck in the mud, but unfortunately it wasn't producing much in the way of useful thoughts. I said nothing.

'So,' the officer said, with a slight edge to his tone, 'would you mind telling me what your business is in this street and could I please see in your bag, miss?'

'Oh, shit,' was my first thought, and I didn't have a second because my mind went from fairly blank to completely blank in the blink of an eye. I began to open the flap of the bag with trembling fingers and was about to take it from my shoulder when there was a roaring sound like thunder and then an almighty bang. The ground shook as if there was an earthquake and the air was suddenly thick with grey dust and falling debris. This time I was in no doubt that a bomb had exploded. Something clipped my face, I covered my head with my arms and then was immobilised by a fit of violent coughing. My eyes streamed and my ears were ringing. The officer dived to the floor. I didn't. I know what I did next was stupid, but, as I've explained, I seemed to have given up thinking. I was determined to deliver Mrs Lansdowne's letter, so against all logic, common sense and instinct, I ran towards the smoke and confusion. Bits of wood and plaster dust were falling all around. The building I wanted was still intact, as was the letter box. I thrust the envelope into the letter box under cover of the smoke. The explosion had taken out much of the building opposite. There were men lying on the floor and broken glass everywhere. I felt it crunch like ice under my feet. I didn't see any blood, but I didn't look. I don't think the men were dead or anything – I think they had dived to the floor when the bomb went off. I think I should perhaps have stopped to check if anyone needed help, but I can honestly say that never entered my mind at the time.

I ran towards the other end of the alley. It was lucky that it was not a dead end. I had no idea where it led. In the strange silence after the bomb, all I could hear was the panicky clip-clop staccato rhythm of heels against the road and a choked sort of sobbing. It took me a good minute to realise that both sounds were coming from me. I found it hard to breathe – the cloud of dust seemed to cover a good area, but eventually I emerged into a broad road full of shoppers, smart women beautifully dressed and a steady stream of cars. People were looking around in bewilderment for the source of the sound of the explosion, a few were walking briskly away. I was stricken by a sudden attack of coughing and as I put my hand to my mouth I saw that Edie's coat was covered in a thick layer of white dust. So I was really going to be able to pass unnoticed in a crowd.

I looked up to see a girl of about my own age standing

across the road looking anxiously out into the street. She saw me and stared straight at me. She was dressed in a long black dress with a white apron over it and even from across the road I could see that she was amazingly beautiful: she looked Indian and her long dark hair hung in one huge thick plait to her waist. She had seemed to be looking out for something and when her dark eyes settled on me it looked like she'd found it. She smiled and put her fingers to her lips and then beckoned me towards her. I was mesmerised by her appearance, which sounds stupid, but she was virtually the first non-white person I'd noticed in Jessica's London and she looked like a Bollywood film star. I don't know why I moved towards her. Perhaps because the good guys in films are always beautiful, perhaps because I was lost and shocked and very suggestible, I don't know, but I crossed the street in a daze causing a car to toot me. I stumbled up the pavement, getting in the way of some woman who uttered an outraged, 'Well, really!'

The girl was standing at the entrance of a tea shop. The sign above the door proclaimed 'The Raj' in red and gold letters, and, because she invited me in, I stepped inside.

'Bore da,' she said. That was what Jessica had said in her email, which was very weird.

'Bore da,' I mumbled and I stared at her in a kind of glazed fascination. Her huge eyes were almond-shaped and she had the longest eyelashes I'd ever seen. 'Take off your coat and hat,' she whispered quickly.

'Why?' I said too loudly.

'Shh! Keep your voice down. We've got customers and we don't want to be heard. Take off your things – they're dusty and people will think you were involved in the bomb. The Constabulary, the Security and the ordinary police will be pouring through this street any minute,' she said impatiently.

I looked at her wide-eyed and once more I was gobsmacked into silence.

'It was an IBI bomb – yes?' she said and I shrugged. I was pretty sure it was a bomb but that was about the limit of my knowledge.

'You can wash in the cloakroom downstairs. Do it quickly while I brush down your coat.'

I held on to my bag and wondered about sides again. I didn't know who the IBI were or if they were Jessica's side or her enemy, but I was not in a position to turn down much needed help. She pointed to the Ladies, and I more or less fell inside. There was a mirror above a blue and white porcelain basin. I was a mess. My face and hair were both pale with dust. There was blood on my cheek too – something had grazed my skin. My eyes were like two dark pits. I looked more than a bit mad. I cleaned up as best I could. The cut was a small one and it stopped bleeding almost at once. As I rested my head against the wall for a moment, someone knocked sharply. I opened the door. The girl was waiting for me with my coat and hat. She gave them to me without a word. I put them on equally silently.

'A cup of tea is good for shock,' she said and led me to a round table by the window covered in a white linen tablecloth, brought me a silver pot of tea, poured it into a china cup and helped me to three lumps of sugar with silver sugar tongs from a pretty bowl etched with roses. I don't take sugar in tea, but I was glad of it. I drank it down, though it was actually much too hot.

'I have no money,' I mumbled eventually. She shook her head. 'It's a gift of the house – from the grateful to the brave. Come now, it would be good if you left the back way. Pretend you are going to the cloakroom again.'

Through the window I could see that her prediction was correct. The road had filled with uniformed police officers who were checking shops and questioning passers-by.

I finished my tea calmly and walked after her. I felt like I was in a dream.

The girl led me through a narrow kitchen, where the radio was blaring out Indian music. I squeezed past a couple of men who very deliberately did not look my way. I think they may also have been Indian – they were certainly speaking to each other in a foreign language. The back door opened on to a dirty back alley. Grey dishcloths and red and white tea towels hung on a makeshift line.

'Thank you,' I said to the girl. It wasn't exactly a speech, but it was heartfelt.

'Lighten my darkness,' she said with her dazzling smile and unexpectedly kissed my hand. 'Turn left and left again and you should be able to get lost in the crowd.'

Before I could say anything else, she had turned and gone back inside. I did as she told me and soon found myself carried away in a crowd. She was right; I was completely lost.

FOURTEEN

I walked for a while without knowing where I was going. I crossed roads and changed direction in a daze. I think I was still in shock and I kept running over the events in my mind. Why did Mrs Lansdowne give me the gun – didn't she guess I would be stopped? I thought back to the morning's radio news. There had been talk about security measures in London and surely in giving me a gun she was putting me at risk, unless of course it *was* normal in this place to carry a gun. I kept on going over the same ground again and again. Maybe I should have identified myself in the alleyway. Maybe I should have said I worked for the Lansdownes, rather than running off as I had. It was difficult to know what was the sensible thing to do, when the rules in this place seemed so different. I walked on, hoping to recognise some land-mark. My feet were blistered where the hard back of Jessica's leather shoe rubbed against my heel. I was beginning to feel very wobbly when I finally saw some-where I thought I recognised: St James's Park. I cheered up a little. The sun had come out and although I had no idea what time it was, the light suggested it was still quite early in the morning. Every bone in my body ached with the tension of being questioned by the officer, the explosion and my meeting with the Indian girl. I found a park bench and cautiously took out my map, taking care not to touch the gun. I still had the second letter to deliver. As I checked the route, I noticed more of the grey-suited men in trilbies. I could see at least four of them wandering around giving every appearance of enjoying the park, but they were all the same lean, athletic-looking types, and they were getting nearer. Any moment now I was going to find myself being questioned again. My hand shook as I put away the map and I got up as casually as I could. I felt weak, still footsore and unaccountably weary. I spotted one of the men talking into something. I couldn't see what it was and I didn't want to stare, but it was certainly possible that it could be some radio transmitter or even a mobile phone. The more I thought about it, the more concerned I got. What if the officer who'd stopped me in the alleyway had circulated my description? Edie's blue coat suddenly seemed too bright and too distinctive. I started to walk purposefully towards The Mall, but the way was blocked by mounted officers in splendid regimental red uniforms and those helmets which have horsetails hanging from them. I changed direction and spotted more and more grey-suited men standing around, apparently just watching. They were like stars – the more you looked, the more you saw. I was sweating even though it was not hot. What if the officer had thought I'd had something to do with the bomb? I had to get away.

I wandered over to a tree and pretended to be watching a red squirrel run across the grass. I checked that none of the grey-suited men were looking my way and then I stepped behind the tree and took off my coat. I folded it so that only the pretty burgundy lining could be seen and put it over my arm. I took off my hat, and unpinned my hair with clumsy, gloved fingers. I tucked the veil on the hat away and then pinned it higher on my head in the hope that it would look different. I waited until I saw a couple of young women in nurse's uniform with prams and then I walked across the grass to join them. I managed to get between them and cooed a bit at the babies, which I think they thought was rather odd, but I stayed with them until the grey-suited man who may have had a phone was out of sight. I felt more myself with my hair once more round my shoulders. I was Jess, not Jessie, and I lengthened my stride to something approaching my normal walk. Jessica's shoes still pinched though and the blister on my right foot was really bad. I said goodbye to the young women, who were apparently nannies, and made for Green Park. It was a little cool not to be wearing a coat, but I hoped I'd get away with it. I held my breath as I passed one of the grey-suited men, but he just wolf-whistled. At home I would have said something stroppy – here I just smiled, grateful not to be stopped.

Once I'd reminded myself of the geography of that part of London, I managed to make my way back towards Mayfair and delivered the letter without too much trouble. I kept to the main roads, kept my head down and did not linger even for a moment to look in shops or admire the views.

The roads were full of trams, buses, cars, cyclists and horses, so the smell was quite strong in places and men with carts risked their lives to clear up the mess at regular intervals. There were uniformed policemen everywhere and an air of unease in the streets. I saw members of what I guessed were His Majesty's Constabulary too, and my heart almost stopped. This is going to sound very ridiculous, but they looked like SS officers in old war films. I don't think the uniform was exactly the same, but the look and the attitude was, and everybody gave them a very wide berth. In fact everyone was doing that very London thing of not noticing whenever a policeman stopped a passer-by to ask questions.

I did my best to get to Waterloo. I even got quite close to the station, close enough to see it anyway. It was swarming with members of the Constabulary on horseback, and Security men. Perhaps I should have tried to get past them, but my nerve failed. I walked back the way

I'd come on bleeding feet, always staying among prosperous-looking shoppers.

I got back to Soho Square just in time for lunch. There was a grey-suited man watching the back door. He asked my name before he would let me in. That set my pulse racing again. When I got through the door, I ran upstairs to my room to redo my hair and clean myself up a bit, hang up Edie's blue coat and take off my shoes for a minute – I had massive blisters on each foot. I did not know what to do with the bag and gun. Should I give them back to Johnny or to Mrs Lansdowne? In the end I just took out the map and locked both the bag and gun in my drawer.

Everyone was very subdued at lunch, not least because there were five new faces at the table, four dressed in grey suits, which I now recognised as the civilian uniform of anti-terrorism officers, and one in the dark, beautifully cut uniform of the Constabulary. They watched us and each other with suspicion etched on their faces. I hoped I didn't look guilty. I was afraid I would be arrested for involvement in the bombing.

I was exhausted too, having walked for miles round London. I felt too sick and nervous to do more than pick at my food and I was aware of both Johnny and James watching me. It was a relief when the meal was over. I got up when Johnny did, so that I would give James no opportunity to corner me as I limped up the servants' stairs.

'No trouble then?' Johnny asked in an undertone as we walked together towards the office.

'No,' I said, 'it was fine.'

'According to the news, a bomb went off opposite the WLUE building,' he said with an intense stare. I must have looked blank because he added, 'Didn't you go back there to post the letter?'

'Er, yes, I meant it was fine, apart from the bomb,' I said. Aware that sounded unconvincing, I chewed my nail nervously, then realised that it wasn't a Jessica thing to do and stopped, embarrassed.

'You didn't think a bomb going off worthy of note? What exactly do you count as trouble?'

I shrugged and he stopped questioning me as we got within earshot of one of the grey-suited men.

If I'd thought the worst of the day was over, I was wrong: all that afternoon Mrs Lansdowne was hard work. She was annoyed that I'd taken so long to return from my errand and berated me for being lazy and untidy. She criticised my hair, the dustiness of my shoes, the state of my fingernails and then she started on my morals.

I didn't need a lecture on why sleeping around was a bad idea and I could have done without her graphic accounts of backstreet abortions. She went on about her work at the women's hospital offering assistance to those without husbands, supporting their babies and rescuing fallen women. Then she started on the pills. I thought that since she was so opposed to 'the iniquities of the backstreet abortionists' she would have approved of contraception but she didn't or at least not for unmarried women. Apparently the pills were the property of a charity of which she was chairwoman, which was established to distribute contraceptives among the poor in the overcrowded slums of the East End, and unmarried girls of my class had no business taking them. She was very disturbed that they had been taken from her stores and she wanted to know how I'd come by them. I won't bore you with the details of the conversation. Mrs Lansdowne used very long words and difficult sentences – I found understanding her a strain. I felt tears prickle at the back of my eyes so I looked at the floor. I felt even worse because the door to my office was open and Johnny was in there typing. I could hear him so he was certain to be able to hear Mrs Lansdowne. I hadn't wanted him to know about the pills. So I just stood there taking it from Mrs Lansdowne, not answering back, not pulling faces – my mum would have been stunned.

'Miss Allendon, if you do not tell me I'm afraid I'm going to have to let you go. I cannot have a thief in my employ.' I have thought about this a lot since. I'm not a snitch but it was a straight choice: I told the truth about a man who was threatening me and who, I was fairly sure, would not hesitate to hurt me, given half a chance; or I lost Jessica her job and condemned her to the workhouse.

I made my decision. My lips were dry and I heard Johnny stop clattering away on the keys; I knew he was listening. I spoke as quietly as I could in the hope I wouldn't be overheard and I told her. I told her I'd been given the pills by James.

She was very angry and I wasn't sure if she wasn't going to sack me anyway. She went white and her eyes seemed like hard blue glass set in marble. She dismissed me from the room, though not, thankfully, from her service, and slammed the door. I was not entirely sure why.

There was a grey-suited man sitting in our office at Johnny's desk. It wasn't Johnny at all! A moment later, Johnny came into the room, a sheaf of papers in his hand and I knew by the look on his face that he'd heard too. I blushed down to the roots of my hair. Johnny didn't say anything either then or later when we went to the kitchen for tea break. I mean, it wasn't that he didn't talk, I think he said something about the weather and the fact that one of the officers would need to see my identity card at some stage, to verify my details, but he didn't say anything personal about the pills or James or the bomb or anything and I wondered why. Jessica and he had worked together a while – he must have known her before, at least slightly, to get her the job. They were the same age and everything so I couldn't work out why he didn't talk to her.

There was a Constabulary officer in the kitchen watching Cook and you could have cut the air with one of her carving knives. She was muttering to herself in Punjabi and was most startled when the officer spoke back to her in the same language. Johnny tensed visibly when that happened, but again he said nothing. Edie, unusually, did not appear at all.

'Do you know any Punjabi?' I asked Johnny on the way back to the office, because you don't just talk about the weather to people my age – not in my world.

'How did you know it was Punjabi?' he countered.

Now, I know a few words because Amrita in my class at school had taught me and I recognised a couple of the things Cook mumbled, but I did not know how the other Jessica would have known that. 'Oh, Cook taught me a few words,' I said casually, though, even as I said it, I thought it was a bit far-fetched. Cook didn't seem to like Jessica much. He glanced at me sideways.

'I know bits and pieces of most things – you pick the odd word up here and there in my line of work,' he said. I think he expected me to say something else. It felt as though he were dropping me a hint about something, but it seemed reasonable enough to me, so I didn't say anything else.

Mr Lansdowne didn't return until my working day was over, but I heard Mrs Lansdowne lambasting him loudly on the phone. I didn't know whether to listen or not. She tended to behave as though I was more or less invisible unless she needed me for something. Yet she kept some of her papers and things hidden, locked away. I couldn't work it, or her, out.

I was knackered by the end of the day – completely drained. I couldn't face playing the avoidance game with James. I was worrying about that when suddenly he was called into Mrs Lansdowne's office. Johnny glanced in my direction, then made a huge play of checking his fob watch.

'Time to call it a day, I think,' he said loudly and pointedly so that our resident grey suit heard, glanced at the wall clock and gave what passed for a smile. I tidied my desk so that it would meet even Jessica's exacting standards and followed Johnny gratefully down the backstairs. As I closed the office door, I could hear Mrs Lansdowne's shrill tones and I realised what was happening: James was in trouble. Johnny had been kind enough to get me away.

'It might be a good night to retire early,' he said. 'I'm going to the gym myself. Sometimes it is expedient to get out of the way.'

If he mentioned the gym to draw attention to his physique, he needn't have – I'd already noticed.

The television was already on when we got downstairs and the table wasn't even laid.

There was mention of the bomb opposite the WLUE

building, in some office alleged to have links with the Foreign Office. That bomb was being blamed on the IBI, who were also being blamed for the bomb at the government offices.

The IBI stood for the International Brotherhood for Independence, and that group was also allied with the WLUE, Women for Reproductive Freedom, as well as a number of smaller groups – the Welsh and English Miners Association and the Union of Railway and General Transport Workers are the only ones I can remember now but there was quite a list. There was an on-screen diagram showing the links between the various organisations. The IBI was the umbrella group who had been running a long-term bombing campaign to get the British government to grant universal suffrage to all adults over eighteen and to grant independence to all countries wishing to secede from the Empire. I am not stupid. I'm expected to get quite a few A*s in my GCSEs, but even so it took me a while to work out that I had been delivering letters from Mrs Lansdowne to what almost amounted to a terrorist organisation. It didn't fit with what I knew of her, and who could not support organisations intent on giving women the vote and the right to control their own fertility? Worse than that, there was coverage of the explosion from this world's equiva-lent of CCTV footage. The area had apparently been under surveillance. The images were grainy and of poor quality, but if you peered really hard and knew what you were looking for, you could see a figure in a long coat and hat disappearing out of shot. Had they also got footage of the fight that Johnny and I had got into in that same alley? Whatever appetite I'd had disappeared at that moment. I hoped Edie hadn't recognised her coat.

FIFTEEN

I skipped dinner and just lay down on the bed upstairs, grateful to take Jessica's shoes off and think. Mrs Lansdowne supported organisations linked with terrorism, while her husband was in charge of national security? How could that be? And yet Johnny had suggested that Mr Lansdowne knew about his wife's activities? Did he sympathise with those causes too, or didn't he take his wife seriously? And what about Johnny? Was he against workers' rights and all that other stuff they'd talked about on the news? That didn't fit what I knew about Jonno, who was obsessed with justice, nor did it exactly fit what I'd seen of Johnny, but I didn't know, did I? I could see now how the household staff might choose to support one or other of their patrons, be employed by and maybe even spy for one or other of them. What I couldn't see is how the two of them – Mr and Mrs Lansdowne – managed to be together when such huge issues divided them. It made no sense. I didn't know anything. I didn't want to know anything either – they were all the problems of another world. I could see they were important. Jessica's world was a horrible, unjust mess but none of it had anything to do with me. All I wanted was to go home.

I thought about what I'd be doing at home. On week nights Mum insisted we had a meal together when she got back from work at about six o'clock and we'd sit and talk about what we'd been doing. I know my friends didn't do that very often, but there was just the two of us so I knew quite a lot about Mum's work and she knew more than most about my life though, obviously, I only gave her the edited version. Sometimes Jonno would eat with us too – he could always make Mum laugh. As I thought about it, I knew that there was no way Jessica would be able to fool my mum that she was me – not if she spent any time with her at all. Would Jonno have found a way to keep it secret from her? Maybe, if he'd found a way to get Jessica away for a few days in the hope that we'd find a way to get back into our right worlds. Yes, I decided. Jonno loved my mum – he would try to protect here from what had gone on for as long as he could. He was clever was Jonno, and he could always get round my mum. That made me feel slightly better. I didn't want to think of Jessica taking my place at the table – it hurt me. By the time Edie came up, I had exhausted myself with yet more tears.

'What's up with you?' she said breezily. I sort of shrugged and got off the bed unsteadily to go and wash. I felt giddy and light-headed from too much crying and not enough food. I staggered slightly and had to hold on to the door to get my balance. I caught sight of my face in the small mirror in the bathroom. My eyes were two dark raisins in my swollen and puffy face. My nose was twice its normal size and my skin was pale and mottled everywhere it wasn't red and blotchy. I never could cry attractively. I washed my face in the icy water. When I got back to my room – clean, if nothing else – I felt better.

'Are you still on the smoke?' Edie said, eyeing me critically. 'You're losing weight by the day, you're not eating, you're barely talking – you haven't cracked your face or a joke in days!'

I had to adjust my mental picture of Jessica then – as I'd not thought of her as a girl who cracked jokes. She'd seemed from her diary, her clothes and her desk, a neat, quiet person who, in my head at least, was rather sad. I think I must have looked a bit startled and it took me a second or two to think of something to say.

'I, erm, I haven't been feeling well, but I'm not on the smoke.'

'You were gone long enough today and you borrowed my coat, which smells of all kinds of things. It didn't get that way just posting letters. You might think I'm just a housemaid, Miss Uppity Secretary, but I'm not thick and I've got eyes in my head. You're acting like you've been kicking the gong around, like you're a pipie. I'm worried about you.'

I still didn't know what she meant about being a pipie, though having seen those women in the alleyways off Soho I was getting the general idea. For some reason I did not want to come clean about the bomb to Edie. I couldn't tell you why exactly – I just had a feeling that dropping letters off at the WLUE was not something I ought to tell the world about, and I had a suspicion that what Edie knew, the world would know sooner rather than later, so I just said something about being caught up in the security cordon and having to go the long way round. By her look she didn't believe me and I didn't want to lose Jessica someone who, for all I knew, might have been her only friend, so I tried to make things better – friendlier – between us.

'I'm sorry if I've been a bit funny, Edie, but you know all that business with James . . .'

'Well you know on that score – I've been talking to Cook and she reckons that you might have led him on. She thinks you're a bit of a flirt with your red lipstick and little bit of lace.' I knew she was talking about Jessica's underwear and fancy garters which, now I came to think of it, didn't entirely fit with the picture I'd been building of her.

'Oh,' I said, grateful for a means of changing the subject. 'By the way, have these! I shouldn't need them now.' And I tossed her the pills.

'You did it! He gave them to you!' I smiled as she tucked them away somewhere about her person. She came over and hugged me like we were real friends.

I wondered if Jessica *had* flirted with James: she smiled, she cracked jokes, she broke into Mr Lansdowne's office to use a computer, she was the kind of person Johnny would give a gun to. I didn't really know her at all.

Edie thanked me profusely and said she owed me. Contraceptives were worth more than gold to her, she said, and after that she left the subject of my smoking alone.

I fell asleep eventually, but I slept badly, haunted by dreams of bombs going off in my face and killing my mother, and of Johnny shooting me and fighting Jonno, beating him up until his face bled. I woke some time before dawn barely any less tired than when I went to bed, hot and sweaty from the aftermath of my terror, with a banging headache and eyes so puffy from all my tears that they felt stretched and strange like they belonged to somebody else. I tried to get back to sleep, but I was frightened of what I might dream about next.

In the end I got up and got dressed, rapidly and carelessly, without bothering to pin up my hair, and crept downstairs. I had no idea what time it was, but I had decided, sometime in my troubled sleep, that I had to try harder to contact Jessica. I had to find the computer that Jessica had used; I had to email her.

Edie was lying flat on her back and snoring. She did not stir as I opened the door and crept barefoot along the pitch black landing and down the servants' stairs. There was a large window illuminating the hallway that opened on the offices. The curtains were open and the distant street lights of London filled the hall with shadows. There were fewer street lights in Jessica's time than in my own and they glowed more dimly and with orange-coloured light. It was a menacing kind of light. It only occurred to me then, as I tried the locked door of the office, that the house might have CCTV cameras for all I knew, or an alarm system. Maybe I ought to have found that out before wandering the house in the middle of the night. I let my hand fall from the elaborate door handle and turned to go back upstairs. It had been a stupid idea.

You can imagine how I felt when I saw the handle of the door turn slowly. I literally stifled a scream by clapping my hands across my mouth. I backed away like some pathetic soon-to-be-axed victim in a horror film and then ran up the stairs. I peered through the bars of the banister into the hallway to see what emerged. It was the tall and unmistakable figure of Johnny, dressed in dark clothes. He locked the door with unhurried efficiency, and then I fled, terrified that he would see me.

What was he doing there in the middle of the night? Finishing off his work? What would he do to me if he thought I'd been spying on him? He was not my friend.

It was hard to remember that, especially in those rare moments when he gave me Jonno's smile. But Johnny was not Jonno – he was dangerous and I did not want to cross him. I moved as hastily and quietly as I could back to my bed and tried to quiet my noisy, panting breathing. I did not hear Johnny pass my door and I lay awake, shivering under the covers, listening for his footsteps. It was a long time before I fell back to sleep.

SIXTEEN

Breakfast was a largely silent affair. The grey-suited men and the intimidating Constabulary officers were there again, even though it was soon after six in the morning. The latter tried to engage us in conversation but no one was willing to chat. There was no sign of James. Edie looked pleased with herself and exchanged a satisfied look with Cook. Johnny did not look at me at all and the rest of the staff seemed as uncomfortable as I did. I looked shit. There was nothing I could do to make my eyes look normal. Even with all the products I had at home, serious crying was hard to disguise. Jessica's meagre selection of creams and cosmetics was not even up to the attempt.

Johnny waited until we were out of earshot of everybody and said in a low and faintly menacing voice: 'What were you doing on the stairs last night?' He'd seen me then. I tried to keep my tone guilt-free and natural.

'I couldn't sleep.'

'Not a good enough reason, Jessica,' he said, his breath warm on my neck as he whispered in my ear. I got goose pimples. 'Whose side are you on?' he mouthed at me as one of the Security men came into view. I dropped my eyes. Johnny scared me, but not like James had scared me; Johnny got to my guts and twisted them.

Mrs Lansdowne did not appear to notice that I looked any different from usual. She arrived just before ten, wearing a simple dress of raspberry-coloured silk and a paisley shawl; her nails were stained to match. I half expected her to ask about the gun, but she seemed to have forgotten about that. Instead she said brusquely, 'Miss Allendon, I must have those pills. Where did you put them after you picked them up off the floor?'

'I don't . . .' I began and before I had time to splutter anything further Johnny walked in with such immaculate timing that I wondered if he'd been listening at the door.

'Mrs Lansdowne, Mr Lansdowne has employed a new butler to replace Mr Leonard. He wondered if you wished to meet him before he begins his duties later today.'

She grudgingly agreed and waved at Johnny to send the man in. He was a very handsome, very dark-skinned African named Mr Kwanele Green. I found out later he was what they called a 'regimental by-blow', fathered by a British soldier on a local woman and raised largely through regimental charity; Mr Lansdowne had long been his patron and Green's loyalty to him was, in return, indisputable. Edie had suggested that James was Mrs Lansdowne's man – whatever that might mean.

If Mrs Lansdowne had sacked him because of me, she would be angry. Perhaps Edie and Cook favoured Mr Lansdowne's side and would be happy that James's replacement shared their views? If Edie was for Mr Lansdowne then would she be friends with Jessica, assuming that Jessica was on Mrs Lansdowne's side? But Johnny, who was obviously trusted by Mr Lansdowne, had helped get Jessica her job – did that mean she was actually on Mr Lansdowne's side pretending to be on Mrs Lansdowne's, or that Johnny was on Mrs Lansdowne's pretending to be on Mr Lansdowne's? And why had he been in Mr Lansdowne's office in the middle of the night?

It made my head hurt and by coffee time I had still come to no conclusion other than that I hoped Jessica knew what was going on.

'When are you having your day off, Mr Roberts?' Cook asked. 'I'll make sure I don't serve your favourites that day.'

'Tomorrow. I think things are calming down at the Ministry and Mr Lansdowne won't need me.'

I thought about that. I needed to do three things urgently: I needed to contact the other Jessica, though I still did not know how, I needed to ask Mrs Lansdowne for a day off, even though she was probably furious with me for the part I played in James's downfall, and I needed to persuade Johnny to let me go with him to Waterloo.

Not much to do then. I decided to leave asking Johnny until last – until after I'd got the day off sorted and somehow contacted Jessica – so I was surprised when the first thing I said to him was: 'Can I go with you tomorrow?' It just kind of came out without me intending it – a real 'Did I say that out loud?' moment. But I did say it out loud and couldn't unsay it. Not surprisingly, Johnny looked very taken aback.

'Have you got the day off?' he said logically enough.

'I haven't asked yet. I – I wanted to go back to Sheen, but the way things are with Mrs Lansdowne . . .'

'Oh,' he said stiffly, 'I had forgotten the date. Would you like me to ask Mrs Lansdowne on your behalf?' I hesitated; did that mean he was really working for Mrs Lansdowne, that he had some influence over her?

'I suppose so, if you wouldn't mind. I don't think I'm her favourite person at the moment.'

'You're not important enough for her to hold a grudge against you for very long,' Johnny said. 'She will be angry about something else this afternoon. I'll ask her then.'

'Thank you,' I said. My face was burning again with something like embarrassment and I found it difficult to meet Johnny's eye. Johnny was obviously the kind of boy who liked to be asked for help. At teatime he told me he'd sorted it out and we would leave together directly after breakfast. Mrs Lansdowne had mellowed by the afternoon as Johnny had predicted. She had noticed that

I didn't seem to have a coat of my own and offered me one of hers from several seasons ago. She said Angie, her personal maid, would drop some things off in my room later. I was grateful because I didn't want to borrow Edie's coat again, but at the same time I didn't like the feeling of owing Mrs Lansdowne something – it made me uncomfortable. I didn't know what she was playing at. Her moods were unpredictable and it also made it more difficult to snoop around looking for evidence of the computer. Instead I worked particularly conscientiously, typing letters and filing. Most of them related to her charity work, which was extensive and involved everything from 'fallen women' to supporting schools in the colonies and much in between. She was one of those women, I decided, who wanted to do what was right even against their own nature. I don't think she was kind by instinct – she didn't strike me as being that way – but kind on principle and it made her seem rather hard.

I supposed that being kind on principle was better than not being kind at all and I tried a bit harder not to dislike her. She was certainly more admirable than her husband, whose job seemed to be to defend the status quo.

I had the day off, I had Johnny's guidance to get to Waterloo; all I now needed to do was to make contact with Jessica.

I hovered as near to Mr Lansdowne's office as I could

get for most of that afternoon. There was a filing cabinet quite close by and I kept checking files in an unnecessary way, trying to look busy and to ignore the resident grey suit, who was ogling me the whole time. My persistence was rewarded, just once, with a glimpse of Johnny typing into something that looked suspiciously like Google, only the logo was different and it was spelled 'Googol'.

I have good eyesight and by squinting and screwing up my face I could just see the luminous blue-lit screen. Unfortunately Johnny, who seemed to have a sixth sense as far as I was concerned, saw me dawdling by the open door and pressed something on the desk so that the screen retracted. His body blocked his hands from my view so I couldn't see the location of the hidden keyboard or the controls for lowering and raising the screen. In fact for all my hanging around wasting time, all I'd done was confirm what I'd already known – that Mr Lansdowne had internet access.

'Can I help you, Miss Allendon?' Johnny said stiffly. 'You seem to have been busy in that corner for rather a long time.' I thanked him with as much dignity as I could manage, assuring him that I'd now found what I'd been looking for and retreated, shamefaced, back to my desk.

I wished I knew whether I could trust Johnny. He obviously had internet access and could have contacted Jessica for me, but what if he were somehow against Jessica? I knew he'd got her the job but I still could not work out their relationship. I didn't know which way was up by this stage. I just didn't have enough information, and I kept arranging and rearranging what little I had in a variety of interesting and contradictory patterns. It was doing my head in.

I decided that the only thing to do was to return in the night, again, and to try to access the net then. I know it was a desperate sort of a plan with a small chance of success but I had to try. I was not going to be stuck in this alternate London hell for want of a bit of bog-standard courage. My big worry was that the Security Service, or worse the Constabulary, might post guards overnight.

I watched Johnny like a hawk, noting which keys he used for which doors and where he kept them. I also looked around for any signs of an alarm system or the dreaded CCTV cameras. I watched the Security men – I watched so hard and with such focus that by late afternoon my headache was so dreadful that once more I made my excuses early and retired to bed before supper. I noticed Cook and Edie exchanging complicit looks.

I had forgotten about Mrs Lansdowne's clothes. My headache lifted slightly as I looked at them. They were gorgeous in a way no clothes I'd ever owned were gorgeous. The fabrics were amazing and they looked to me like they'd been hand-sewn. There was a wide pair of long culottes in a dark blue heavy linen with a short fitted jacket that was a shade lighter: it had appliquéd flowers of the darker colour in silk and linen all over one sleeve and down one half of the jacket front. I've always loved asymmetric shapes. This was quality. There was also a kind of a trench coat that reached almost to the floor in a dark dusky pink with tiny navy stitches on the belt, collar and cuffs, and a navy hat – shaped a little like a bowler. They smelled of expensive perfume and wood. Call me shallow, but when I discovered that they fitted me perfectly, I did feel a little cheered, though my situation had not really improved at all.

I almost failed to notice a small pair of low-heeled ankle boots which were more or less my size. They would certainly give me blisters, but in different places from my current crop, which I thought was a result.

SEVENTEEN

I pretended to be asleep when Edie came noisily to bed. She smoked for ages with the window open in a way that might have been inconsiderate, if she'd known I was awake. I watched the bright red dot of her cigarette glow in the darkness, like a malevolent eye. I could not begin to imagine what she thought about staring out of that open window. I dozed until she finally closed the window and crept into her own bed. I waited for her even breathing to tell me that she was asleep. I waited until the loo's noisy flush had rumbled its last and then I waited even longer. All the servants who lived in slept on this same attic landing and I knew that Johnny had the room next door. It was impossible not to know where everybody slept when everyone trooped to and from the shared bathroom. His was a tiny eaves room so small that he didn't even have to share – a source of some jealousy. I wasn't sure if I would have the nerve to steal into his room and take his keys, but I didn't actually have any other options. I had to get away from this nightmare place. I had to get home. I put on the thick, dark dressing-gown and once more crept barefoot out of my shared room. I think all floorboards creak and the ones on the landing were pretty bad. Every creak sounded as loud as a shotgun and I hoped that everyone slept soundly. They all worked so hard I'd be surprised if they didn't. I tried the door of Johnny's room; it was unlocked. You know when people say their heart was in their mouth? I don't think I'd ever understood what they meant until that moment. My heart was not in its usual place and I couldn't breathe or swallow, so it might well have been in my mouth were it not biologically impossible. I slowly eased Johnny's door open. It squeaked as I opened it – in fact it sounded like one of those doors in a horror film it was so noisy. Still, I could hardly turn back then. I only opened it a small way, just enough to allow me to slide my hips inside. I held my breath and then I felt a hand over my mouth and something cold and metallic pressed against my head. As I should have guessed, Johnny was a light sleeper.

'Now, Miss Allendon,' he said quietly, 'suppose you tell me what is going on.'

I couldn't speak at first – the heart in my mouth thing, I suppose – and when my voice finally emerged from my constricted throat it came out as a pathetic squeak.

'Put the gun down, please,' I said.

'Sit on the bed,' Johnny said and I obeyed him, wondering what the hell I'd let myself in for.

Johnny had a bedside light, which he turned on so that I blinked at the sudden brightness. He wasn't wearing a shirt and I could see the dark hair of his chest and the smooth curve of muscles under the skin. His hair was all ruffled and disordered from sleep. I swallowed hard. He leaned towards me so close I could smell the sweetness of his sweat. I wasn't at all sure what he was going to do and then he sniffed my hair.

'You don't smell of opium. Is Edie right? Are you on the smoke?'

I shook my head. I didn't seem to be able to stop trembling and I felt that I had made a terrible mistake.

'Then, if you are in your right mind, what are you doing creeping into my room?'

I made myself look at him; he seemed genuinely confused and in spite of the gun in his hand, looked strangely vulnerable.

'I don't understand you, Jessie. I don't know what game you're playing or what side you're on any more. You have been so strange.'

He touched my cheek in an unexpectedly intimate gesture and I tensed – was there something going on between him and the other Jessica? That hadn't occurred to me.

'Look, I know it's been difficult, and I know Mrs Lansdowne can be hard work, but you can't let yourself go like this. If you lose this job, I can't protect you, and if

I find you've been recruited by the other side, I *won't* protect you. Now, why did you come in here?'

His response was so confusing. I couldn't make sense of it. Were he and Jessica friends, lovers, enemies or some mixture of all of them?

'I wanted to borrow your keys.'

'And you couldn't ask?'

'I didn't want to compromise you,' I said in a flash of sudden inspiration.

'Why did you want my keys?'

I decided to tell a little bit of the truth, mainly because I could not think of a suitable cover story – I'm a rubbish liar. 'I needed to use the internet.'

'The internet?' Shit. It wasn't called the internet here. 'I needed to find someone, secretly.'

'You wanted to use the Root? Again?'

'Yes.' Surely 'the Root' had to be the internet, didn't it?

'Jessica, who are you working for that you need that? It's for academics, politicians and the military. Who can you know in any of those places? You must realise you are putting more than yourself at risk – dabbling in all this. If you know what you are doing, you are braver than I can imagine, and if you don't know then stop for God's sake.'

Johnny had put the gun down and was looking at me with some bemusement.

'Can we talk about this tomorrow?' I said, feeling as pathetic as I sounded. Now the immediate danger had passed I felt exhausted. Maybe I should have told him then. I wanted to. Every day that I stayed in that place, the truth seemed more unreal and more distant to me. Jessica's life was a sticky spider's web of fear and obligation and I was getting more and more entangled in it. It would have helped to have told someone and as Johnny had internet access he could have helped me.

I got to my feet with difficulty – my blisters were still sore.

'I don't want to hurt anyone or cause trouble,' I said as I limped towards the door.

'You're hurting yourself, Jessica, coming to me like this. You should be more careful of your reputation.' I shrugged a bit dismissively. My reputation was the last thing on my mind. Then I remembered it was Jessica's reputation, which I probably should be guarding.

Johnny got to the door before me, barring it with his body. He seemed so big suddenly, an unpredictable giant of a man. What had I been thinking of?

'I mean it, Jessica,' he said with a strange kind of intensity. 'You can't enter people's bedrooms in the middle of the night without getting people talking.' He moved towards me and for an instant I thought he was going to kiss me, but he didn't – he just opened the door and I slunk out. I could not meet his eyes. My heart was beating so fast it was almost painful. I should have realised Johnny was not Jonno.

EIGHTEEN

I was almost late for breakfast. I overslept and then, discovering that there was hot water for once in the servants' bathroom, washed my hair and had a bath. It was bliss to have a few moments to myself to get really clean without other people knocking on the door demanding their turn. There was probably a rule about using hot water on a weekday or something, some petty restriction which I'd infringed, but I hate having dirty hair – I wash it every day at home – and I reckoned I would never get away from Jessica's place if I tried to keep to the rules.

I got dressed in my borrowed finery, with a certain amount of hope. I think in some very childish corner of my brain I thought that just going back to Waterloo might be enough to whirl me back into my own world. It would take a miracle, but then what exactly had brought me here? Is there a word for a miracle that you don't want? I must have had more than a trace of hope because I quickly made sure the diary was up to date, just in case. If I didn't manage to get home, at least I would see my dad again. That made me feel strange – sad and optimistic together, excited and fearful; he might not be the same here.

I had a bit of a problem filling in a diary entry for the previous night. I just said that I'd gone to Johnny's room to find the keys, but hadn't managed to get them. I didn't know what else to put. To write 'nothing happened' might be misunderstood – the other Jessica might think I wanted something to happen, which obviously I didn't, and yet if I didn't write anything she might worry about her reputation. In the end I left the entry unfinished. I suddenly realised I was in danger of missing breakfast, which would not have been good because, after skipping supper the night before, I discovered that I was ravenously hungry.

Edie gave me a very pointed look when I slipped into my place just before breakfast was served. Everyone was sitting there including the new butler, Mr Green, a couple of grey suits and the inevitable Constabulary officer.

'Jesus and Mary, look at you!' Edie said, with something that was not far off a sneer. I wondered what I'd done wrong. Did she object to me having Mrs Lansdowne's cast-offs?

'Don't you like it?' I said anxiously.

'I think you look charming, Miss Allendon,' Mr Green said in his beautiful rich baritone and I smiled, and I think Mr Green smiled and so did Johnny, and then I saw Edie's face and the room grew a little colder.

'You off somewhere nice, Jessica?' Cook said in barbed tones as she ladled out bowls of thick porridge.

'I'm going back to Sheen,' I said quietly.

'Are you going with Mr Roberts?' Edie said, in surprise. 'You never said.' She flashed Johnny an accusing look.

'It was a last-minute thing,' he said evenly. 'Miss Allendon mentioned it yesterday and I thought it would be a good thing if I could accompany her.' He took out his watch and said, 'We'd better go.' When I went up to get my new hand-me-down coat and hat, Edie followed me up the stairs.

'So, minx, you show yourself in your true colours!' she said angrily as we reached the upstairs landing. 'You really are nothing but a tart. First James, now Johnny!' Her face was blotched red with fury and then she lurched forward and slapped me so hard on my face that she took my breath away. I didn't hit her back – I was too shocked.

'What was that for?' I said a second or so later when I'd regained the power of speech.

'What kind of fool do you take me for? Do you think I don't know you've been sneaking around meeting Johnny in the middle of the night? Have you no shame?'

'It isn't what you think,' I said feebly. How could I explain without telling her what had happened? Edie did not strike me as the kind of girl used to believing impossible things.

'So when you go to a man's room in the middle of the night it's to play tiddlywinks, is it?' she spat.

'Please, Edie, I'm not after Johnny.'

'You could have fooled me. You don't think I've seen the way you look at him? Miss Butter Wouldn't Melt – all big eyes and long looks. They say the quiet ones are the worst and since you've gone quiet you've certainly got worse. What have I ever done to you?'

I found myself blushing – how had I been looking at Johnny? Of course blushing was just about the worst thing I could have done.

'Well may you blush, Miss Allendon. I tell you, I'm not having it.' Edie stormed back down the stairs. I walked to our room in a bit of a daze and sat down on the bed, wondering if it would have been possible for me to screw things up any worse.

Fortunately I didn't have time to dwell on Edie. I had to get my coat, Jessica's bag, what money I could find in her drawer, my phone and house keys – just in case. Then I had to fix the hat, which sort of perched to one side of my head. As I scrabbled in the drawer for money and hair pins, I wondered about the bag with the gun. Should I take it with me? Jessica's red bag didn't work with Mrs Lansdowne's clothes, and was really a bit too small – it didn't shut properly with the phone and keys inside it. After a moment's hesitation I put both my things and the other Jessica's in the gun bag, and relocked the drawer.

When I got back down to the kitchen, Edie had gone and only Cook remained to flash me disapproving looks. She muttered to herself, in English so I would understand, something about young girls today getting ideas above themselves and dressing like nobs when they were only servants. I tried to look like I hadn't heard her. I wondered if Mrs Lansdowne's clothes looked ridiculous – how would I know? But the grey suit who was still studiously finishing his tea gave me an approving look and winked at me. I didn't know whether I was supposed to respond, but winked back anyway because he seemed to be taking my side against Cook. I think that was probably a mistake. Johnny gave me a speculative look. He was dressed in what I supposed must have been casual clothes – a buttoned-up jacket in peacock blue, dark trousers with turn-ups and a pink cravat. I tried to imagine Jonno in that particular combination and almost cracked up. His mother had once bought him a pink sweater because they were fashionable and he'd been too embarrassed to wear it and had given it to me. This Johnny had no such reservations. He put on the same large-collared coat and hat he had worn before, on our last ill-fated outing together, after checking the time on his fob watch against the kitchen clock. His eyes widened when he saw the brown bag I was wearing satchel-like over my chest.

'Expecting trouble?' he asked softly.

' "Be prepared!" – that's my motto,' I said. How I wish that I had been.

Cook gave the grey suit some tea and while he was engaged in drinking it I saw her surreptitiously slip Johnny an envelope.

'James left this for you,' she whispered.

I didn't want her to know that I'd seen her so I turned away and shouted over my shoulder, 'See you later,' as cheerfully as I could, all the time hoping against hope that I wouldn't.

NINETEEN

'Now,' Johnny began as we left the house on Soho Square behind, 'are we going to talk about last night?'

I sighed. Unpleasant things were happening in my stomach. Every time I ran through it in my head I squirmed. Edie's response that I could only have gone to Johnny's room for one thing made me wonder if he had made the same assumption. 'Do you mind if we don't talk about it?' I said. 'I mean – I'm sorry if I startled you. I shouldn't have come to your room. I see that now and I'm sorry if I've made things difficult with Edie.'

'With Edie?' Johnny said in an incredulous voice. 'Why should it have made things difficult with Edie?' I decided to quit before I messed things up any further.

'Oh, she was angry with me this morning, that's all.'

'You think there's something going on between me and Edie?'

'No. Yes. I believe she thinks so . . . I don't know,' I said, confused.

'I would have thought it was obvious that one of the first rules of the game is not fouling your own nest,' Johnny said cryptically, but I thought I got what he meant. That certainly suggested that there was nothing going on with Jessica either. I was relieved, sort of. He gave me his arm and I felt a little better about taking it now I knew it was funny old-fashioned manners and nothing more.

'I thought we could walk, if you don't mind,' he said. 'It's only about half an hour to Waterloo and the trams are packed at this time of day. We can go the nice way and maybe even stop for a coffee or something?'

I smiled, relieved and pleased that he sounded cheerful and unthreatening – it was almost like being with Jonno. The sun had come out and apart from the fact that I was in a parallel London with no friends, family, no means of getting home and a gun hanging at my hip, all was right with the world.

The streets were crowded, but Johnny had a certain air about him, not to mention a certain size, that led people to get out of his way. Men doffed their caps at me, which I found odd, but quite fun in a way.

We wandered through Covent Garden, which was indeed a real market, though by the time we got there the main business of the day was over and it was more or less closing. It was full of noise and bustle, the smell of fruit, flowers, pipe smoke, diesel and horses, and underneath it all, incompletely disguised, the pungency of rotten vegetables. Men yelled out prices still, even while they were packing away and the area was full of horses and carts, as well as vans and open-sided trucks. There were no arty little shops or street performers, just muck and business – it was exciting. I bought flowers as a gift for Jessica's parents, or rather Johnny bargained with the stallholders and I struggled to work out the money, which was the most irrational ever invented, but I still managed to get a huge bunch of pale pink roses for a few shillings. My mum loves roses and I know Dad used to bring her flowers sometimes, so I try to buy them for her when I can afford it.

There were a number of Security men around but I ignored them. I was with Johnny and that made me less afraid.

I was in a strange mood that day – both excited and apprehensive – and yet I did relish that time with Johnny in that other London – the different smells, the fantastic way people dressed, the foreign-looking street signs, the unfamiliar shop names. It was exhilarating – like being abroad in a new place.

We stopped and had 'kaffee and kuchen' because I'd started to limp again. I saw a couple of grey-suited men following us but I think we lost them when we went into the café. The waitresses spoke German to one another and to my surprise Johnny appeared to speak it fluently. I only did German for a year at school, but couldn't really get on with the grammar. Of course, I did not know what the other Jessica spoke – did Johnny expect me to be fluent too? That uncertainty left me momentarily tongue-tied. Johnny had obviously asked the waitress to keep my flowers in water for a time. The waitress was blonde and very pretty, with her hair in an elaborate plaited bun; she could not do enough for Johnny. I found that irritating, as she barely managed to serve me my coffee and plonked my cake down as if she were feeding a dog.

'So,' Johnny said, after we'd both finished off a generous portion of apfelkuchen, 'are you going to tell me who you wished to contact through the Root?' He was looking at me intensely – the charming smile he had given the waitress had been replaced by a harder and less pleasant look. I hesitated.

'Johnny, do you mind if I don't? I'm really tired and I don't want us to argue . . .'

It was a line that might have worked with Jonno, but Johnny seemed unimpressed.

'I don't understand what is going on, Jessica. You've changed and if it's not the smoke, which would at least be understandable, I don't know what it is.' He took a cigarette from a silver case, put it in his mouth and lit it. I hadn't realised he smoked – he didn't apologise or ask if I minded, but when I looked round I realised that most of the men were smoking and the café was lost in a kind of warm fug of smoke and steam. It was a clean-looking place with scrubbed wooden tables and bunches of spring flowers, but the walls were stained a dirty nicotine yellow. I coughed, but even then Johnny did not take the hint.

'So, you've been recruited?' he continued. 'The big question is who by.' His eyes were cold and my guts began to twist with growing fear. 'You have obviously done some self-defence and gun practice too, I suppose? You took the gun readily enough.'

'I took the gun because you said Mrs Lansdowne wanted me to have it.'

'Well, you must have known that was a ruse, as Mrs Lansdowne supports unilateral disarmament among her many causes – she's not going to give you or anyone else a gun if she can help it. She's more likely to give you a dove-for-peace armband.' His tone was mocking, which was unexpected.

'Why did you give me the gun? You must have known there were Security people everywhere.' I must have sounded loudly outraged, as he touched his lips to indicate that I should lower my voice. I'm afraid the gesture incensed me and made me inclined to talk even louder.

'I gave it to you as a test. I didn't think you'd take it. That you took it showed me that you'd changed and gave me a clue that you were working undercover for someone – all I need to know now is who.' He flicked ash into the remnants of the cake; it looked ugly – ash among the apples – and made me feel sick.

Fan-bloody-tastic. I'd taken the gun because I assumed that it was what was expected in Jessica's world, only it wasn't, and by trying to do what Jessica would have done I'd exposed myself as being as un-Jessica-like as it was possible to be. I didn't say anything, but slowly and deliberately finished the dregs of my coffee. I was not going to be cowed by a Jonno lookalike. Johnny's agreement to accompany me to Sheen was beginning to look less like an act of kindness than an opportunity to interrogate me as to what was really going on. I sure as hell wasn't going to tell him now. I finished my coffee and carefully placed the cup precisely back on the saucer.

'You may believe whatever you want, but I'm not working for anyone. I only took the gun because you gave it to me. I thought it was for my protection – I trusted you.'

I said it with as much dignity as I could muster and was pleased that my voice did not even wobble slightly when I said I trusted him. I had. I couldn't help it.

Johhny raised an elegantly curved eyebrow and took a long drag of his cigarette.

'Well, forgive me if I struggle to believe that,' he said, blowing smoke into my face. 'I'll believe a lot of you, Jessica Allendon, but I don't believe you're stupid.' I think my jaw actually dropped. I did not know what he meant and I didn't think I could ask. Why would my double not trust him? What was their relationship?

'Shall we get the bill and go!' he said with a smile that did not reach anywhere near his eyes. The blonde-plait girl was there in an instant brandishing my flowers in an effort to be as helpful as possible. My legs had gone. My knees seemed to have lost the strength to support me. Somehow I got to my feet and limped out after Johnny. The whole situation was getting worse by the minute. I prayed that somehow Waterloo would provide me a route home. I thought I'd been afraid of James, but my fear of him was as nothing compared to the way I felt taking Johnny's arm once more.

TWENTY

The silver tram looked strangely futuristic, but was like an ordinary bus inside. The people on board were no friendlier than in my own London. I kept my hand over the flap of my handbag in an almost reflex action, squared my shoulders and tried to stand my ground. As a fresh wave of people boarded and the uniformed conductor yelled at us to 'Move down the bus please', I was pushed up against Johnny so that my head was pressed into his chest. I held myself stiffly; this Johnny seemed to be Jessica's enemy and our physical proximity highlighted the real distance between us. It was an uncomfortable journey. Why wouldn't Jessica trust him? We got out at the side entrance of Waterloo Station nowhere near the place where I'd met Jessica. There was no sense of an impending storm; the sky was almost cloudless.

'Can't we go in at the main entrance?' I asked as Johnny guided me through the throng, his hand steering my elbow with more force than was really necessary.

'What? The toffs' entrance? No fear,' he said.

'But I need to go there,' I said, panicking, and tried to turn against the press of people, but Johnny had my arm and I couldn't get away from him. I found myself being carried along by the crowd on to the concourse – not the silent place of glass and marble, nor the mall-like version of my own world, but a place of grimy, smoky walls and a green stained-glass canopy through which even the sunlight seemed sickly. We bought third-class tickets from a small ticket booth. There were no automatic machines, just rows of wooden booths and station staff in their braided uniforms and military hats. We were to go on the 'hop-along' as Johnny called it. There was a screen on each platform which divided the marble first-class section from the plain concrete of the rest. A red-jacketed soldier stood on duty at the barrier, a mounted Constabulary officer was on guard. It was impossible to get from where I was to the first-class area. I spotted several men in grey suits and wondered if the Security Services always watched the railway stations. I had the distinct impression that they were following us. I didn't say anything to Johnny.

Johnny helped me on to the train, as if I couldn't manage on my own, which would have annoyed me but for the fact that the combination of blisters and high-heeled ankle boots did make it difficult for me to get on board: that really irritated me. The train was busy with dogs and bicycles, as well as people. It was friendlier than the equivalent local train at home. I overheard two women chatting loudly about their children above a general buzz of conversation. No one talks on trains in my London unless they're drunk, mad or on their mobile.

Our carriage had maroon plastic seats embossed with the Deutsche-British National and Imperial Railways logo. There was navy lino on the floor and the carriage was thick with smoke. We got a seat after Vauxhall when two of the bicycles and several people left the carriage. Unfortunately, there was no tension in the air except between Johnny and myself, no sense of an imminent thunderstorm. What hope I had of a sudden magical translation back to my own world disappeared. I felt deflated, tearful even. The train remained resolutely different. Johnny remained Johnny, sitting slightly stiffly by my side – his hands in leather gloves, his clothes smelling of wool and wood and tobacco. Nothing was familiar except the smell of dirty train. Still, I would get to see my dad again – only he wouldn't really be my dad. What was I doing?

The stations bore the same names, but the signs were blue and used different, more elaborate lettering and each station we passed had well-tended flowerbeds and uniformed porters on duty. At Clapham there were goods trains everywhere, something I never saw at home except on Thomas the Tank Engine videos, which Jonno had loved when we were at nursery together.

We left the train at North Sheen and walked into

green and leafy countryside along a narrow lane. I didn't know where to go and so followed Johnny. 'Would you like me to escort you?' he said. I smiled at him because I was grateful. I'd checked through Jessica's things but I couldn't find any reference to her home address.

I ought to have recognised the road – I'd walked along it enough times – but there was a large, rather beautiful white house I'd never seen before. Where there should have been a superstore there were fields and hedgerows and birdsong. I felt very disorientated. We were passed by a few cars, a couple of vans and several men on bicycles wearing bicycle clips and flat hats; there was no lycra in sight and no traffic lights where the Sheen Road crossed Manor Road. In place of the large petrol station at that crossroads there was a greengrocer's selling local produce, and manure. There was just one, lone petrol pump. I think I had believed, however crazily, that somehow beyond the city I would find life as normal; I had hoped that perhaps home was still home. It wasn't.

A man in a grey suit got off the train when we did, followed us for a while and lurked around at the green-grocer's. Johnny gave no sign of having noticed and we walked on in silence. I had declined to take his arm. Our earlier companionship had evaporated. I had a knot in my stomach. Was this a good idea? Jessica's parents would know I was an impostor at once. How could I have thought this a good idea? My father was dead – he was unique. No one who looked like him, no twin, divided by who knew what experiences, was going to be any kind of substitute. I think I slowed down. I suddenly didn't want to see him or some fake almost-mother.

We walked onwards towards a large stone sign that marked the entrance to the graveyard. There was a big tub of flowers on each side of the gate – I think they were geraniums or busy Lizzies, they were a cheerful orange-red anyway. I was startled when Johnny walked past them and on through the graveyard. Was this some kind of short cut? I hung back a little but Johnny strode forward.

I had only been round the graveyard once in my own London, but the green angel I remembered from that visit still spread her wings as if to shelter what had been lost. It was strange to see her – a rare point of continuity between my London and this one. I shivered. I had never liked that angel – it had always given me the creeps.

Johnny led me until he came to a small plot with a modest stone headstone. He stopped there and removed his hat as a sign of respect. What was he doing? As I caught up with him, I saw the headstone and what was inscribed on it and let out a cry of shock.

Here lies Roger Allendon
13th March 1960 – 13th September 2007
and his beloved wife
Elizabeth Allendon
17th June 1964 – 13th September 2007
Rest in Peace
'What God has joined together may no man put asunder'

The dying remnants of Jessica's last offering lay in a stone vase – a bouquet of pink roses. I didn't know what to say. I would never see my dad again, never see his smile; Jessica was an orphan.

I think I stared at that headstone for quite a long time before I remembered the flowers in my hand. I was holding them so tightly my fingers were bleeding. I ignored that and cleared the dead flowers away, refilled the vase with water from the standpipe nearby and then arranged my own roses in the shallow vase. The stems were too long. I tried to force them in the vase anyway, but Johnny gently took them from me and cut them to size with a penknife he produced from his pocket. I managed all that quite well, but as I replaced the vase in front of the headstone I found myself on my knees and sobbing. My own father was not so long dead that his name on the headstone did not make me weep, and the thought of not seeing my mother again made me cry like a lost child. Johnny didn't say anything but he laid his hand on my shoulder in what I guessed was some kind of gesture of solidarity. Perhaps I should have flinched away, but I was glad of the warmth and the heavy weight of his hand on my shoulder; it made me feel a little bit less alone.

When I had no tears left, I pulled myself together and wiped the dust and gravel from my clothes. There was a wooden bench not far away and I sat down there to wipe my face and regain something like composure.

'Tell me again what happened,' I said – it was the only thing I could think of to say which might give me the information I needed. They had died on the same day – had they been in some kind of crash? I suddenly understood why Jessica worked in that awful house for Mrs Lansdowne, why, if she lost her job, she had not other options but the workhouse. She was alone. The words of her email suddenly came back to me: 'I'm a lone wolf seeking a pack.' Whatever she meant by it – it was literally true. She had no one.

I felt a terrible empathy for her.

Johnny took off his gloves – the day was getting warmer. He had Jonno's large powerful-looking hands and he fiddled with his signet ring as he spoke, the first sign of nervousness I had seen in him. His voice was quiet and he went through what had happened as though it were a story he'd rehearsed many times in his mind.

'Your father and mine served together in the King's African Rifles, as you probably remember. I don't think they saw each other all that often when they went back to civilian life. My father preferred to forget the war – what with losing his leg and everything – he said it didn't do to dwell on what was done. He was angry though – that his pension was so poor and that there wasn't any decent work for him here. He worked abroad for a bit in the colonies, sending money home, but my mum hated it so much he came back. Anyway, when I decided to apply for the job at the Lansdownes' and needed a reference, your father gave it gladly – he was a generous man. I only met him a couple of times, but I liked the way he talked. He would talk about the Mau Mau and some of the other conflicts, as my father wouldn't. I really rated your father; he was a good man. A year later, when I'd begun training for my other job, they needed a safe address, somewhere they could send . . . material – so I would get it. By then my dad had died and my mother was . . . fragile. I didn't want her to know what I was doing – she'd have tried to stop me because she would have been afraid for me. I didn't want her to worry about my . . . less legal activities, and so I asked your father if I could use his address. I didn't go into it too much but I assumed he understood what I was up to. He knew what was what, and from our talks I knew where he stood – that he sympathised with the cause. Then, when I was barely out of training, my cover was blown. There was some enormous mess-up and sensitive, uncoded data fell into the wrong hands. The address was part of that data and your house was firebombed by the very regiment your dad had served. There was a huge stink afterwards when the men found out who he was. Or at least that's what I heard, but by then it was too late.' His voice had fallen so that it was so quiet I had to lean towards him in order to hear him. 'Both of your parents perished in the fire. They should have got away but your mum was ill at the time and your father tried to carry her out. The coroner thought he had a heart attack trying to save her. I am so sorry. It was my fault.'

He buried his head in his hands. I tried to take it in. Was Johnny some kind of spy or criminal, maybe even a terrorist? What were these less legal activities? Jessica knew? If she blamed him for her parents' death that certainly might explain why they were not friends, why his relationship with her was so hard to guess. I tentatively put out my hand and then let it come to rest on his shoulder.

I didn't think it was his fault but the fault of whoever had bombed the house – the regiment or whoever had ordered the regiment to act.

'Johnny,' I said at length, 'I don't think you can be blamed for something someone else did. You did not know they would be at such risk, did you?' He shook his head. 'Then I don't think you are to blame.' I patted his shoulder. 'I don't blame you,' I said, softly. 'You could not have known what would happen.'

I was not Jessica and perhaps it was not my place to forgive him in her stead, but I thought it was the right thing to do.

He lifted his head and I removed my hand from his shoulder. 'No, I did not know what would happen, but they are still dead,' he said heavily, and with that I could not argue.

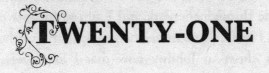

TWENTY-ONE

We sat for a while in the sunshine. There were many questions I wanted to ask him, but for the moment my head was too full of memories – and worries. I was thinking through what he'd told me. My own father had died of a heart attack, though my mother was in robust health so far as I knew. Poor Jessica – how must it be for her meeting my mother? Perhaps she would not want to come back here, but stay where there was still someone to look after her, where she was not alone? That scared me. Going to Waterloo had not been enough – there had to be other things I had to do to get home and she must be part of them. I had done nothing but meet her at Waterloo – what had she done? I should have realised that worlds did not just collide by accident, or other people would have done what I had done. Surely our transfer between worlds was not a freak accident, but the result of some act of Jessica's?

I watched a man in a grey suit remove his hat before a grave. How odd that he should also need to pay his respects at the cemetery!

Eventually Johnny suggested walking to Richmond Riverside through the Park and I agreed in spite of the blisters. He didn't mention the grey suit and neither did I. I felt closer to Johnny now that I knew what the problem was between him and Jessica, but that scarcely helped. I was beginning to realise that getting home might be an even bigger problem than I'd thought.

We walked through the cemetery to a stile where Bog Gate would have been in my world. There was no path and no road, but other than that the park looked much the same – though it was a little wilder. Pembroke Lodge was still a private residence and Petersham Farm was a real working farm, and there was no right of way through the water meadow.

I had taken off my shoes to walk barefoot in the park and Johnny had laughed and taken his off too and rolled up his trousers. He looked well stupid actually – we both did – bare feet didn't work with hats and all the bits and pieces that went with being respectable people. We didn't talk about anything much, just admired the deer and laughed at the dogs chasing each other around the park. It was nice – fun – like being a teenager again. We even had a race, which Johnny won easily.

We doubled back to the main entrance to the park, sat down and put our shoes back on and then walked along the Petersham Road. There was no Poppy Factory, but a pottery and some kind of glass and bottling factory with a

German name. The smell of the river was powerful and tainted by something oily and unpleasant, and soon I could see why – the Thames was packed with riverboats and barges as well as pleasure boats. The river was busier than the road and, on the Twickenham side, instead of posh flats overlooking a picturesque view there were warehouses and industrial buildings, the sounds of engines and the fug of fumes. I was completely startled – it was not what I had expected at all.

There was a working wharf too and loads of dirty-looking warehouses down Water Lane, and some rough-looking pubs with not a wine bar in sight. Trains hurtled over the railway bridge every minute.

I was limping badly by the time we got to the wharf and the press of dirty, oil-stained men downing pints and smoking in their lunch break. I held on to Johnny and my bag, fearful as if I'd never seen dirt or working men before. The wharf was full of the smell of grime, of beer and fags, of grease and sweat and varnish, and underneath it all the powerful metallic smell of the water. That smell at least was familiar.

A couple of men – dressed like the others with flat caps pulled low over their faces so that I could not see their eyes – detached themselves from the drinkers. They nodded at me and then spoke rapidly to Johnny in another language; it was not German, though it was hard-sounding. I tried not to stare or to notice when notes changed hands, nor when the parcel James had left for Johnny was passed on. I didn't know if it was money or information or drugs. I was aware that the grey suit was not far behind us, watching. I had no idea what Johnny was into, only that I felt something violent could explode at any moment, that gradually the milling men had noticed strangers in their midst and were turning with hard, hostile faces to stare. We were dressed all wrong, I suppose, like toffs. I clutched the bag with the gun wondering if there was any way I'd ever use it. I was glad when Johnny's business was over and he turned abruptly and led me back through the throng of increasingly agitated men along the riverside towards the reference library. One man spat in my direction and swore, but Johnny didn't appear to notice.

In my Richmond there's a big riverside development that looks old. In this world that development just wasn't there, but the real Victorian buildings, like the library, were. I worked out where I was from the library clock and realised that the war memorial was missing. It was a big monument in my Richmond with several panels of names and stone sculptures of a soldier and sailor.

Mum used to take me past it when I was little and we used to get the bus to Richmond to feed the ducks and I was well proud of myself when I could identify some of the letters when I'd just started learning to read. It was part of my childhood – feeding the ducks and then having ice cream or chocolate by the war memorial while mum sipped a takeaway coffee and talked about brave men dying, like her granddad. You don't ever forget stuff like that.

'Where is the war memorial?' I asked, because I didn't want to ask about what he'd been doing. If this Johnny was a drug dealer, I didn't want to know – not yet. I didn't want Jessica's parents to have died because Johnny was an ordinary criminal.

'For which war?' Johnny laughed.

'Well, the world ones, of course,' I began and then stopped. Johnny was looking at me quizzically.

'You can take your pick, there's plenty of them all over the world, that's for sure – not counting the cold one with the Franco-Nips and the Yanks,' and he rattled off a load of dates and names of battles I'd never heard of. That was it then. I was in a place where the Great War hadn't happened, nor the Second World War either. I couldn't get my head round it. All of the little bit of history I knew had never happened. I opened my mouth to say something, but as I tried to work out the implications of what I'd finally discovered, I found myself getting all hot and the waistband of Mrs Lansdowne's suit suddenly felt too tight and the world started to get fuzzy and dark at the edges and everything went black.

TWENTY-TWO

I came round to find Johnny's face close to mine and his hand loosening the belt of my raincoat and the waistband of my culottes.

'Are you all right?' he asked as soon as my eyes opened. I nodded and struggled to my feet. One of the men from the wharf was by Johnny's side, a pint glass of water in his hand.

'You have a swig of that, missis,' he said. 'I'd offer you some tea but you'd be better off going to one of the tea shops in the High Street.'

I tried to smile and sipped the water gratefully. I couldn't remember the last time I'd fainted – not for a long time anyway. Johnny helped me to my feet and I said thanks to the man, who said it was no trouble and any friend of Brother Roberts was a friend of his.

I was a bit bewildered by that as it made Johnny sound like some kind of monk, but I smiled anyway, as you do, and then let Johnny guide me to the High Street. We found a tea shop opposite a Victorian department store called Goslings. I drank the hot, sweet tea Johnny ordered for me gratefully.

'I'd leave your skirt unbuttoned until you're yourself,' Johnny said. 'You're not . . .' he began. I looked at him, guessing what he might say next.

'I'm not pregnant, if that was what you were going to ask,' I said angrily. 'I was just shocked, that's all.'

Johnny gave me a curious look. 'So, you're not shocked by being attacked in an alley, being given a gun or by having a bomb go off a few yards away, but you faint because Richmond does not have a war memorial?' He was right, it sounded ludicrous.

'Miss Allendon, I am not stupid and nothing you have done since Sunday has fitted with your previous behaviour. Edie is convinced you've become a poppy poppet, Mrs Lansdowne is concerned that she's hired a scatterbrain, and I have no clear theories but some very worrying suspicions.'

I dropped another sugar lump in my already sweet tea and sipped it. I didn't think I could go on with the charade any longer. Without help I would never work out what had happened to make us swap worlds. Who else could I ask for help but Johnny?

I didn't know anyone else. Edie was angry with me and seemed unlikely to know much about parallel worlds – the same went for Cook. Mrs Lansdowne was disappointed in me and seemed as likely to send me to the workhouse as help me, for all that she placed such store by charity work.

Johnny continued to watch me while I drank my tea and then poured a cup for himself. As he busied himself with the milk and the sugar and the little tea strainer, I couldn't help thinking how the hardness in his face made him seem much older than my Jonno and that even if they had been standing side by side in identical clothes, I would have had no trouble telling them apart.

He was aware of me watching him, and when he looked up and met my eyes I found I couldn't look away. I was almost hypnotised by him.

'I know you don't trust me, Jessica, but you have to believe I will help you as far as I can – for your parents' sake if nothing else. I have a duty to you that I take very seriously and you can rely on that – if nothing else.' I did believe that. He looked and sounded utterly sincere, but more than that there was something of Jonno in him. I didn't get the business with the gun or with the men at the wharf – I don't see how I could have done. How could I possibly work out the rights and wrongs of a world I didn't understand which, even if it had a familiar geography, had a different history? Perhaps it boiled down to this – I had to trust Johnny because there was no one else and I had come to the end of my own resources.

Waterloo had held no magic to whisk me home and my borrowed boots were no ruby slippers. A large tear trickled unbidden down my face and dropped with an almost audible plop into my saucer. I scrabbled for a hanky but Johnny had his out in an instant. I took it gratefully and dabbed at my hot face. 'I'm sorry,' I said. 'It would be such a relief to tell someone, but I don't know if I should talk about it here.' The tea shop was crowded and there was a queue for tables developing at the door.

'Come on!' he said, leaving money for the bill on the table. 'I know somewhere we could go.' He guided me out swiftly, tipping his hat at the waitresses, and then hailed a cab – a rather less grand vehicle than the one I'd taken at Waterloo. It didn't have seat belts either. I still felt clammy and strange, as you do sometimes after you've fainted.

I didn't recognise the streets we drove through – Sheen Lane was a narrow road with a Victorian fire station and one very modernist looking block of flats. The rest was all old buildings and hedgerows like the countryside. We got out at a small cottage near the Sheen entrance to Richmond Park.

'Come on – this is my mother's house but she won't be in till later. She does shift work at the brewery.'

I had been in the other Jessica's world too long because I found myself asking: 'What will the neighbours think about me coming here when your mother is out?'

'Don't worry, Mrs Davies is bedridden and Herr Ehlers is at work. Mum moved here after my dad died because it is quiet and out of the way.'

He took out a key and opened the front door. Inside it was cosy and not unlike Jonno's home in that it was crammed full of odds and ends: every surface was full of ornaments and nick-nacks, dried flowers in dusty vases, all put together with an artist's eye so somehow it looked both homely and stylish at the same time. There were bright throws over the shabby furniture and I sat down gladly in the first place that had felt cosy and friendly since I had arrived in the other Jessica's oddly hostile world.

'Would you like some tea?' Johnny asked solicitously, and although I had enough sloshing around inside me to keep me going for days I said yes, to give me some time to think and to put off the hour of telling Johnny everything. I shivered and he lit the coal fire for me. I wanted to curl up in this place that was almost like Jonno's and rest. I felt like one of my mother's dishcloths soaked in hot water and bleached and then wrung out to dry.

I snuggled up on the comfy armchair, sliding off the uncomfortable boots, and in a moment I was asleep.

I woke to a voice I recognised. 'But Johnny, darling, you shouldn't have brought her here on your own – she has her reputation to consider. Sometimes you don't think things through. You're just like your father. Now get me a nice little sherry and have one yourself – a little one won't do you any harm. Ah, there we are, Jessica's waking. Now, Miss Allendon, would you care for a small, dry sherry? It's a wonderful pick-me-up.'

I quickly took my feet off her chair, embarrassed to be found in such a position; my mum hates me putting my feet on the furniture.

'No, no, my dear, it's lovely to see you so comfortable – stay just as you are and Johnny will fetch you a drink.'

I didn't want any sherry – it tastes disgusting and fortunately Johnny just poured me a tiny bit, while giving his mother a generous glass.

'I can't tell you how lovely it is to see you, Miss Allendon. Now tell me, how is your lovely mother? She is such a smart woman and she has always been so kind to me too. I never see her but that she asks after Johnny.' I glanced towards Johnny, who had coloured slightly in his evident discomfort. He looked like he was about to interrupt her, but then she interrupted herself: 'Oh, dear me no, I have got muddled again. Your mother is . . . Oh, no! I'm so dreadfully sorry, sometimes I get a little . . . would you excuse me for a moment?' And Johnny's mother, so like Jonno's mother in my own world, except if anything even thinner and paler and more diffident, ran from the room. I could hear her sobbing as she clattered up the stairs.

'She'll be fine in a minute,' Johnny explained awkwardly. 'She tries to forget the bad things by pretending they didn't happen and it always upsets her when her fantasies collide with reality.' Anna, as I always called Jonno's mother at home, was clearly in worse shape in Jessica's world than in mine, where her new husband and child had given her back her mental health. In spite of her kind words, I sat up properly and put my boots back on, which was torture; it would have been better not to have taken them off.

Johnny was looking at me intently.

'I'm sorry I fell asleep – you should have woken me,' I said. He smiled.

'You looked like Sleeping Beauty – I couldn't spoil it. Anyway, to fall asleep like that, you must have needed the rest. Do you feel better now?' I nodded, but if I was honest I didn't know how I felt. Anna Roberts was very much the same in this world – even to her taste in nick-nacks. In my world she had got addicted to pills for a while, in this one perhaps it was sherry. In this world she didn't have my mother to talk to – I hoped she had other friends. Johnny left then to find her, and reported that she was 'indisposed'. She apologised for being so confused and hoped I would forgive her as she was having trouble with her nerves.

'It's fine,' I said. 'I know what Anna's like – she never means any harm.'

'What did you call her?' Johnny said, almost angrily as if I'd spoken disrespectfully of his mother.

'I called her by her first name because I know someone exactly like her somewhere else who has a son like you, called Jonno, and who is my closest friend.'

'What are you talking about?' Johnny said, as if I were some kind of gibbering maniac, which was perhaps true enough. I took a deep breath and began.

'Johnny, do you believe that there are other worlds?'

TWENTY-THREE

Yes, it seemed that Johnny did. More than that he seemed to understand what had happened to me with remarkable ease – almost as if it was not a complete surprise to him. It took me a long time to explain – about home and googling for Jessica Allendon and somehow finding myself in another place. All through my story I watched Johnny, trying to gauge his response, but I couldn't decide what he thought. He didn't even say anything when I told him about Jonno. When I had finished, I almost didn't believe myself – it sounded ridiculous when said out loud.

Johnny didn't speak for a long time. The light had begun to fade outside – I suppose it must have been about eight o'clock. We sat together by the soft glow of the coal fire. I watched the shadows flicker across his face. Although it was a very serious moment my stomach rumbled – which was not helpful.

He looked up when he heard the growl and I tried to pretend it wasn't happening.

'I'll make us something to eat,' he said. I followed him into the small kitchen and helped him. Mrs Roberts did not keep large stores but he found lots of vegetables that needed to be eaten up and some old cheese my mother would have called 'mousetrap'. I don't cook that much at home – too lazy – but I know my way round a kitchen, so I chopped vegetables and grated cheese and quite soon the silence was broken between us.

'Me and Jonno used to make cakes with Anna sometimes when she was feeling up to it,' I said. 'My Anna can make something nice out of anything.'

'My mother is a brilliant cook too,' Johnny said wryly, 'when she remembers to buy groceries.' He paused, and asked, 'Your Jonno – how did he cope when his mother was . . . ill?'

'My mum used to go round a lot to check Jonno and Anna were all right and then when things got really bad she went to hospital for a bit and Jonno lived with us.'

'How did you afford the hospital bills?'

'The hospital is free on the NHS.'

'The NHS?'

'The National Health Service – everyone can go to hospital if they need it.'

'You pay for everything here. There are some workers' cooperative hospitals, a few church and charity ones and the workhouse ones, but they're charnel houses by another name. The brewery where Mother works doesn't have access to anywhere that would take asylum patients.'

'But your mum doesn't need an asylum. She's just fragile after what happened to your dad. She can get well, Johnny.' I spoke with all the conviction I could manage. Johnny shrugged.

'Your Anna had more help than I can give my mother. She has been like this for a long time. And now I'm afraid she's going to turn to drink. She's good at hiding it and she's still working but . . .'

'Do you believe me then?' I asked, unable to stop myself. He paused in the act of frying together a mixture of herbs and vegetables in butter.

'Yes,' he said.

Johnny took supper up to his mother on a tray and I found the things needed to lay the table in the small dining room. The main light didn't work, but the table lamp with an orange shade did and it shed a golden glow over the table. After we'd eaten I found myself becoming increasingly nervous. Whatever I'd expected, it wasn't Johnny's calm acceptance of what I'd said.

'Should we not be getting back?' I asked to fill a particularly long pause.

'I don't like to leave Mother like this – she was hysterical,' Johnny said doubtfully. 'There is an early train that would get us back in time for work tomorrow and I will telephone Soho Square to let them know not to expect us back. I think your reputation might take another dent, though. There are some other people I need to contact too.'

'About what I've told you?'

He nodded and I felt my guts twist. I wanted to ask him who he was going to contact, but no words came out.

I so didn't want to go back to Soho Square – I couldn't face Edie's accusations, though I couldn't help thinking that they would be even worse if I were to stay away all night with Johnny. On the other hand I needed to contact the other Jessica and it wasn't going to happen from Johnny's house.

'Will you consent to stay here with me tonight? You may trust me.'

My mouth was dry. I didn't think he'd hurt me, but what of these people he was going to contact?

I said at last, 'I'll stay, but I don't know what the other Jessica would say.'

'That probably,' said Johnny. 'I'm going to have to go out and phone from the pub down the road. I can't take you with me there. It's pretty rough and ladies of the respectable kind aren't very welcome. You will be all right here.' It wasn't a question.

I didn't like it when he left. The branches of a tree outside kept banging on the window and, though Anna had stopped sobbing, her silence was no less sinister. In my world Anna had taken an overdose at least once that I knew of and she could be by turns hysterical and catatonic. When I went to wash up, the light in the kitchen was bright enough to make the darkness outside the window impenetrable. I was scared. I'd never dealt with Anna on a bad day, though my mother had. I could at least hear her walking around upstairs – that was probably a reassuring sign. I cleaned the kitchen up and then, unable to stand not knowing what was going on upstairs, I climbed the narrow staircase.

The window of the box room at the top of the stairs was open and the net curtains were billowing like ghosts in the breeze. The spare room door banged and I jumped and sort of stopped. The cottage had three bedrooms – the box room, the spare room, and the main bedroom. There was no bathroom. I think the loo was outside. The main bedroom was to the right of the stairs and Anna had a dressing mirror draped with beads and scarves and stuff that sat on top of a chest of drawers. The mirror was angled so that I could see Anna sitting up in bed, her dark hair wild about her head, and next to her a man in what might have been a grey suit pointing a gun at her head – his gloved hand was pressed against her mouth. Anna's eyes were wide with terror.

I crept down the stairs, grateful for the banging of the spare room door which masked all other sounds, and ran to the sitting room and my handbag and the revolver. I couldn't run after Johnny – I didn't know where he'd gone – but I couldn't let Anna be hurt.

I grabbed the revolver and crept back up the stairs. I hadn't really thought this through, but when I got to the open door on the landing I shouted, 'Drop your weapon!' like they do on TV. I made my voice loud and authoritative and then in my panic I squeezed the trigger and the dressing mirror shattered into a thousand pieces. Seven years' bad luck, I thought, for no good reason. Anna screamed and I ran into the room to see the man disappearing out of the window. Very helpfully I then burst into tears.

'Oh, don't cry Jessica, love,' Anna cooed. 'You scared the nasty man away.'

I was trembling so badly and was such a useless lump of jelly that I obviously roused Anna's maternal instinct. She got up, put on her dressing-gown, and staggered downstairs to make me some tea. At least that was the same in both worlds – if in doubt, drink some tea. I heard the door bang and I grabbed the gun again, but it was Johnny. I heard his surprise at seeing his mother up again. I couldn't hear exactly what they said but I heard him clambering up the stairs two at a time and bursting into the upstairs room. I heard him running back down them a few seconds later.

'What in hell happened? Mother, are you all right?'
Anna beamed, 'I'm fine. Jessica saved me.'

Johnny hugged his mother and, after he'd established that she really was all right, asked her to make up a spare bed as I would be staying overnight. When she'd gone upstairs, he asked me what had happened.

'I'm really sorry about the mirror,' I said. 'There was a man. He had a gun to your mother's head. I think he was with the Security Services. I ran and got the gun but I got it all wrong and fired at the mirror by mistake and the man ran away. I'll buy another one.' I was gibbering, barely making sense. Johnny said some words I didn't understand.

'You did well,' he said. 'Thank you for saving my mother. I never thought they'd use her to get at me. I was foolish.' His face was very white, though I didn't know if it was with anger or shock. 'The Security have been shadowing us all day. I thought it was routine. James is such a slimy bastard, he set me up.'

James? I couldn't see what he had to do with anything. He was out of the way – he'd been sacked.

'Are you going to call the police?' I asked naively. Johnny laughed without humour.

'Trust me – we don't want the Constabulary involved. The regular police will not interfere with a Security Services' operation. James was one of ours, but the Security found out about his background. He probably traded me for his life.'

'I don't understand,' I said.

He looked at me and sighed. 'No. How could you? Don't worry. My days as Mr Lansdowne's secretary were probably numbered anyway.' He sighed again. 'We're safer staying here tonight. The attack was probably opportunistic. They might have taken my mother as hostage or killed her as a warning, if you hadn't been here to save her. Lucky you had the gun. You gave her attacker a fright. I doubt he'll be back before morning.'

'Should we keep watch?' I asked, as if I were one of the Famous Five.

'I'll sleep on the floor of my mother's room. Don't worry.' He sounded worried and knowing what happened to Jessica's family I couldn't blame him. I was terrified.

I didn't want to ask him about bombs and the like, not in front of Anna, who had reappeared, so instead I let her show me to my room and took what pleasure I could in a cosy bed in a room that wasn't shared with Edie, among people so like the people I loved I could almost pretend for a while that I was home. In spite of everything I slept like one of the dead.

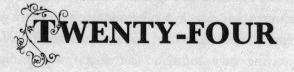

TWENTY-FOUR

It was very early when Johnny knocked on my door – the sun was just rising and when I managed to get out of bed I could see the wild tangle of shrubs and flowers that was Anna's garden: it made me smile. Flowers thrived under Anna's casual husbandry.

I got dressed quickly in yesterday's clothes to find that Anna had somehow washed and dried my underthings – she must have been up half the night. I crept downstairs to the smell of toast and tea. Johnny was already dressed and ready to go. He looked pale with exhaustion and stress.

'Don't worry,' he said, though he was the one looking worried. 'We have dispensation to get in later this morning. I told them it was a family emergency.' I hadn't given Soho Square much thought and I hadn't even thought to worry about being late. I was still worried about 'Almost Anna', as I'd labelled her in my own mind.

'Can't your mother go to your Aunt Fitch?' I blurted out.

'Aunt Fitch and my mother haven't spoken in years. There was a huge row some years ago.'

'They fell out in my world too and then when Anna was better, they met at a funeral and Aunt Fitch was furious that she'd not called on her when she'd been in trouble. She gave Mum an earful too, about blood being thicker than water and how dare she take on a sister's role when Anna had a perfectly good sister of her own.' I had almost forgotten about Aunt Fitch, but I remember my mum feeling bad that she'd never even thought to contact her when Anna had been ill. I could see that Johnny was taking my suggestion seriously.

'Do you have an address for her?' I asked. He nodded.

'It is an idea. I haven't seen her for years, but her husband was killed in Manchuria in '85. He really hated my mother. However, this Fitch may not be the same as your Fitch?'

'She's very manly with a moustache and a booming voice. She runs a kennel in my world,' I said. Johnny gave a strained smile, as though he recognised her from my description.

'She and her husband had a small farm out Ham way; they bred pigs – I don't know if she runs it alone now,' he said.

He got a pad of writing paper from the drawer in the dresser and fished out his fountain pen from his pocket. He found an envelope, which he addressed, apparently from memory, and took a stamp from his wallet and it was done. 'We'll post it on the way, but I think my mother will be angry with me.'

'She'll know you're trying to take care of her,' I said and he nodded. He wrote his mother a note and left it pinned to the larder door; they didn't have a fridge. If the Fitch in this world was anything like the one in mine, I'd feel sorry for anyone who tried to attack Anna in her care.

It was a fair walk to Mortlake station from Anna's house. It was a fine morning but I was nervous and kept expecting grey-suited men to leap out at me from behind every bush, and there were a lot of bushes on the narrow lane. The brown leather bag with the revolver banged against my hip as I walked and I found myself glad of it and frightened by it at the same time.

We walked in silence for a while and then I finally said, 'Johnny, I've been honest with you, don't you think you should be straight with me and tell me what side you are on?'

He shook his head. 'I'm on your side – on a side that might help to get you home. Do you need to know more than that? It can do you no good.'

At his words, I felt the first glimmering of real hope I'd had since I'd arrived. 'Then will you at least tell me what the sides are?' He grinned at that.

'You say Britain has no Empire in your world. Well here it has political and economic control of much of India, Africa and British Canada, not to mention Wales and Scotland. Some people think that's wrong, like they think it's wrong that ordinary people can't get help when they're sick. There's too much power and wealth in the hands of just a few and some people are fighting to change that. Of course it's all much more complicated than that, but I can't tell you everything about the whole history of the world since – when did you say that "Great War" was?'

'Nineteen fourteen,' I said, that being one of the few things I was still sure of.

'Too much has happened since 1914. Let's just say quite a lot of people think that things need to change – some of them have no democratic rights and some of those that have can't find a party that represents them properly, that hasn't sold out to the forces they should be fighting.' Even though I recognised that what he was talking about was simplified, it made sense to me because in my world some of those battles had already been fought. Of course, I knew that even in my own world some people thought that power and influence was still not spread widely enough – I wasn't completely ignorant.

'And is Mrs Lansdowne on that side?' I asked. Johnny laughed.

'Well, Mr Lansdowne is on the side of power and influence, though he was a liberal in his youth. He's not all bad – he has supported limited welfare payments in this country and some devolved government in India, but he is big on the rule of law and refuses to see that, when the law is wrong, sometimes it has to be broken. Mrs Lansdowne is a philanthropist. She is rich as Croesus in her own right and about as privileged as you can get – now anyway. She is the one with the money in the family. Mr Lansdowne is from a good family but he has no independent wealth. Mrs Lansdowne's father was in the army when she was a kid, before he inherited his millions, and she's lived in the colonies so she knows what goes on. She wants to improve the lot of the poor and women and she supports financially a lot of organisations which are allied to the IBI, though she doesn't support independence so much as devolution of some government functions.' He waved a hand impatiently. 'It's complicated. She is an ally of many organisations that have radical wings, but she is careful not to do anything publicly that would undermine her husband's position. They fight about everything, but they stay together. She's Catholic, of course, so that is another factor that sets her apart.'

I tried to take this in. 'And you?' I began. 'Why did the men attack you in the alley? Weren't they with the IBI? Are you on Mr Lansdowne's side or not?'

Johnny paused to light a cigarette. He didn't seem to smoke that much – he seemed to use cigarettes more as a social prop than anything else; all the business of getting out his cigarette case and lighter and faffing about kept him from answering me for a while.

'I'm on my own side, Jessica,' he said at last. 'You really shouldn't get involved.'

I began to feel angry. 'I think I am involved. I could have been shot last night. Could you at least tell me what side Jessica is on?'

He took a long drag on his cigarette and looked at me thoughtfully. 'She did not confide in me, but it was the Security Services who had her father killed. Whose side do you think she was on?'

'Mrs Lansdowne's?'

'I think Mrs Lansdowne wanted Jessica to be her spy in the house – it's a web of intrigue. Mrs Lansdowne is a bit of a tyrant and not someone a girl like Jessica would trust. No, I think Jessica wanted to work for the IBI, but didn't know how to go about it; I'm guessing the message she sent you via the Root was a very foolish attempt to make a connection with IBI people.' He shook his head as if he couldn't quite believe she would take such a step. 'You said she mentioned being a "lone wolf" – that means she wasn't yet part of an IBI cell, but wanted to be. My guess was that she had no idea she was talking to someone like you – from another world. She wouldn't have realised that the Root had been augmented.'

'Augmented? What does that mean? Why didn't she tell you what she wanted to do?'

Johnny ignored my first question though I didn't realise that till later. He just answered my second.

'Jessica didn't know what side I'm on either. I think she suspects I killed her parents. I work for Mr Lansdowne and he is in charge of the Security Services. I liaise a lot with the Security, even on occasions with the infamous Constabulary. I'm just about the last person she would have confided in.'

I suddenly felt quite cold. What if Johnny was with the Security Services, working against the IBI – had I landed Jessica in serious trouble? I think Johnny must have understood my change in expression because he said, 'I owe a duty to the other Jessica – I didn't bomb her house, but if it weren't for me her parents would still be alive and she wouldn't have taken the job at Soho Square. There are easier jobs, but she needed to live in as she was homeless. If she hadn't been working at Soho Square, she would never have considered joining any political organisation – I'm sure of that. I have to find a way to keep her safe and pay my debt.' He looked for a moment like an old man, not a boy at all. He had a lot of responsibilities one way or another. 'As for you – Jess, is it? I will help you because . . . because you helped my mother – just like I will help Jessica because I caused the killing of hers. I'll try to get you home, Jess, but you know I can only do so much . . .'

Hearing him say *my* name, 'Jess', gave me a little shiver

of – I don't know what exactly. It was the first time I felt he had spoken to the real me, not to my shadow-self busily pretending to be the other Jessica. Somehow, it made him seem even less like Jonno. I was suddenly afraid for him – not because he was my Jonno's double but because he was himself, Johnny. I thought that whatever game he was playing seemed quite likely to put him in an early grave. He was only seventeen – a kid – even though he acted older; what was he doing with bombs and guns and all that stuff? I wanted him to stop, to survive to be eighteen, shit, to live to be old.

'Why did you get involved?' I asked. His face darkened.

'I was born involved – everybody is,' he said.

TWENTY-FIVE

We caught the tram into town. Neither of us said much. I had too much to think about and I think Johnny was just worried about his mother. I know my London is violent and everything, but I was either in the wrong place at the wrong time or Jessica's London was a hell of a lot worse. I was beginning to wonder if Johnny were not some kind of double agent – I know it sounds a bit James Bond, but from the way he'd talked it did seem as if his sympathies were with the IBI, even if he seemed to be working for Mr Lansdowne. Of course he could, I supposed, as easily be making out he was in with Mrs Lansdowne and actually be on the side of the Security Services. I glanced at his face in profile, deep in thought. Jonno was easy to read, if you knew him – Johnny's face was hard and closed. I supposed double agents couldn't give much away. They were also as likely to be killed by either side. I didn't want to think about that.

I had certainly given up hoping for any miracle that would get me home the second time I approached Waterloo – and I was not disappointed. There was no lightning flash, no heavy feeling in the air – just the coolness of the early autumn and a certain heaviness in my heart as I remembered Edie.

'I'm going to be in trouble with Edie,' I said, startling myself by expressing the thought out loud. I had to stop doing that. Johnny looked up at me.

'She'll get over it,' he said.

'Does that mean she did think you were going to go out with her?' I asked and realised that somehow in the day and night away something had changed between us – some awkwardness had gone. He was no longer quite the stranger he had been. He knew my secret and, in knowing about his mother and his guilt over Jessica's parents' death, I knew at least some of his.

'She didn't want to go out, didn't Edie – she wanted to stay in,' he smiled. 'She's a good enough sort, but not one to cross, I wouldn't think.'

I didn't point out that if she thought I'd stolen her potential boyfriend, crossing her was exactly what I'd done, because it was clear that his mind was elsewhere. I found his gloved hand with mine and squeezed it. He looked shocked and affronted for a moment and then smiled. 'One of your forward, other-world habits, I suppose,' he said. I grinned back at him, trying to cheer him up. I didn't want him to turn back into Mr Roberts on me.

'It was my forward other-world way of saying that I think Anna will be all right. That Fitch will come.' He let my hand go and nodded his head curtly.

'Yes, well, Miss Allendon, we can but hope for the best.'

I don't know what made him suddenly formal – our arrival at Waterloo or the by now not unfamiliar sight of men in grey suits and trilbies trying to look inconspicuous on the platform. I felt his response as a kind of a rebuff.

We caught the tram to Soho Square and arrived only a little later than usual. All the staff were about their business, which was a relief, as it meant I didn't have to face Edie.

I went upstairs to hang up my coat and change into my work uniform of dark fitted dress and neat uncomfortable shoes. Cook ignored me as I cut through the kitchen to the backstairs, though I gave a cheery 'Tag' like I'd heard people do on the street. I didn't think anything of her lack of response because you didn't have to be around her for too long to realise Cook was a bit moody – 'volatile' my mum called it.

I ran up the stairs and then paused at the door to my shared room; there was somebody in there. I didn't go for my revolver, though I thought of it, which just shows you the kind of state I was in. I gently pushed open the door so that I could see inside without being seen and was surprised to see Edie packing.

'Edie? What's going on?' I asked.

'Like you don't know,' she spat. 'I've been a friend to

you, Jessica Allendon, even though with your stuck-up ways you never deserved one – and how do you repay me?'

'I don't know what you mean,' I said and sat down heavily on the bed – my legs had gone wobbly again. The other Jessica's life seemed to be one drama after another.

'Well, who told Mrs L about the pills if not you? First you disappear off with Johnny, then you make sure you've got no rivals by making sure I get the sack. I should have seen through your Miss Sweet-as-Pie look straight off.'

'Edie, I didn't tell Mrs L anything – she asked but I never said, honest . . .'

'You think I'd believe a word you say? If you told me it was raining, I'd go and check outside.'

'But it's the truth! I wouldn't tell her.'

'No! You expect me to believe that? You got James sacked and now me. You better watch your back, my little poppy poppet. With no mum and dad behind you, you shouldn't go making enemies.'

It felt like a threat – it was a threat. I felt the blood drain away from my face.

'But, Edie – I didn't tell her.' The words came out in a kind of a wail, making me sound desperate: I suppose I was.

Edie just glared at me and carried on throwing her clothes into her case. She didn't have much and I wondered where she would go. For all her fury she looked scared and she was biting her bottom lip as if to prevent herself from crying.

I swallowed hard – to get myself in control. 'Where will you go?' I asked.

'As if you cared! Mr L will give me a reference, though Mrs won't. There's a vacancy where my sister works, so don't waste any sympathy on me – save it for yourself – you're going to need it!' With that she put on her blue coat, the hat with a veil and her gloves. She fastened the small case and stormed out. I found that I was shaking; she had spoken with such venom. I checked the wardrobe and the drawers – I don't know – in case she'd taken anything or damaged anything, I suppose, though I was a bit ashamed of myself for thinking that about her. She wasn't that petty. I didn't know how the mistress had found out about me giving Edie the pills – no one knew but me and Edie, though I'm sure Johnny would have worked it out. Would he have got Edie sacked? I was trusting him to help me get out of this place and I didn't even know that.

I took Jessica's make-up out of the brown bag and then took out the gun. I wasn't sure how it worked – did I need to clean it? How many bullets were left? I had assumed it was loaded when Johnny gave it to me and it must have had at least one bullet in it. I remembered that noise and the recoil when the mirror had smashed. I opened it up carefully. The barrel flicked sideways – Jonno had a toy gun like it once and this worked exactly the same way. It took six rounds and five remained. I couldn't believe I was checking it, but Edie had frightened me. She had hinted that her family had dubious contacts – I hadn't taken much notice. I tried to remember what she had said, but so much of her conversation had washed over me – I'd understood a fraction of what she'd said. You had to be wary when people knew people, people more ruthless than themselves. I carefully replaced the chamber, put the gun back in the bag, and hid it under Jessica's underwear. Time for work, I told myself. I wasn't exactly popular with Mrs Lansdowne and I couldn't afford to piss her off any more than I had already, which meant that I couldn't afford to dwell on Edie.

I got changed quickly. My feet were a mess of blisters. I wondered if I dare ask Johnny where there might be some plasters. I straightened my hair and tried to put Edie from my mind. Today with Johnny's help I might contact Jessica. I had to focus on the positive, didn't I?

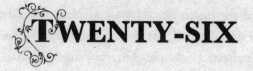

TWENTY-SIX

I avoided the kitchen on my way to the office. When the time came for elevenses, I was starving, but Cook did not produce her usual plate of cake or biscuits.

'No cake, Mrs M?' Johnny asked. 'And no Edie?'

'You can have cake if you must, Mr Roberts, but your friend there is no friend of mine – getting Edie sacked.' She followed this remark with a tirade in Punjabi. Johnny scowled in concentration, as if attempting to follow her outburst.

'I don't know what's gone on, Mrs Gowda,' he said at last, and I wondered if it were true. 'But I assure you Miss Allendon can have had nothing to do with Miss Grace's sacking as she has not been out of my sight for days. Mrs L did ask her a certain question, which she declined to answer, and I can vouch for her.' Cook snorted as if she, like Edie, thought there was something going on between us. She dumped a stale fruit cake on the table with the air of someone being more generous than she ought to be. The cake was very dry, the kind that sucks all the spit out of your mouth, but both Johnny and I ate it anyway: it had been a long time since breakfast.

I wondered, once I was back in the office, if it was a kind of tit-for-tat thing – James worked for Mrs Lansdowne, Edie worked for Mr Lansdowne. The Lansdownes had now lost one pawn each.

Coming back to Soho Square was like sinking into the mire again. Things had been clearer in Sheen; I'd felt like myself again. Dressed once more in my servant's clothes I felt trapped, forced into being Jessica.

I'd hoped that Johnny knowing would have made some immediate difference, but I felt just the same – lost and desperate.

I had been left a mountain of typing to do – all the previous day's work as well – and although I was getting better on the keyboard I couldn't claim to be accurate, but I held it together and kept plodding on, making slow but steady inroads through my in-tray.

Mr Lansdowne dropped in briefly in the afternoon to go over some papers with Johnny. We were down to two grey suits in the house and one outside, patrolling the external doors. The Constabulary officer seemed to have gone, but the grey suit kept looking at me, which I didn't like, but I couldn't do much about it. I wondered what would happen if they realised that I'd shot at one of them.

The worst thing of all, though, was the fact that Mr Lansdowne was using the Root, just feet away, and I couldn't get to it – that drove even my speculation about Edie from my mind. My hand almost itched with the need to get to that keyboard and make contact with the other Jessica.

I was startled when Johnny spoke to me. He rarely said much when we were working.

'I've had a telegram from Aunt Fitch – she has invited my mother to stay. She's going to pick her up in the cart later today.'

'That's good, isn't it?' I said, wondering why he wasn't more cheerful.

'Yes,' he said, 'but there have been rumours circulating. You haven't done anything else to make Mrs Lansdowne angry, have you?' I shook my head and lowered my voice to a whisper.

'I don't know that I've been doing such a good job as the other Jessica, though – my typing is a bit rubbish.' He raised an eyebrow at that, but said nothing more.

I suppose I ought to have been forewarned by what Johnny had said, but when Mrs Lansdowne asked me to step into her office I just thought she had additional work for me. She was wearing a tight grey skirt with some kind of bustle at the back and a salmon-pink cropped jacket. Beneath that she was wearing a pale grey cashmere sweater and a choker of pink, white and black pearls. I noticed all that before I noticed the crease of a frown on her face, or her pursed lips, painted the same pink as her jacket.

'Miss Allendon,' she began and perched on the very

edge of her red leather chair. She lit a cigarette, but did not bother with a holder. 'I am disturbed by what Edie has told me about your behaviour of late. Do you have anything to say for yourself?'

She seemed very agitated and got up to close the door so we could not be overheard – I didn't know if that was because she didn't want Johnny to hear us or if she was concerned about the grey suit.

'I don't know what Edie said about me,' I said carefully.

'She seemed to think that you were smoking opium and bringing my house into disrepute. Now I know that strictly speaking opium smoking is not illegal, but I made it clear when I employed you that I expected only the highest moral standards and, well, with this accusation and the incident with James, I don't feel that I can continue to employ you – the nature of my business here is sensitive. My work is desperately important to so many people and I thought you understood that I cannot see it compromised. Many of the women I strive to help through my charitable work are ones who have become addicted to the smoke and I must say that any one of them would be profoundly grateful for the kind of opportunities you have been granted . . .' She spoke to me as if she were a headmistress ticking off a naughty pupil; it didn't seem real.

'But Mrs Lansdowne, I have never smoked opium in

my life. Edie is wrong. She was probably angry because she thought I got her fired.' It seemed so clear to me that there had been some kind of misunderstanding.

'Why should she think that?'

I felt I had nothing more to lose, so I told the truth. 'Because the contraceptive pills were for her and she thought I told you that.'

'Edie was sacked because she had duplicated the keys to my office and was snooping round my papers on behalf of Mr Lansdowne – she knew that very well – and the reason I could not keep her had nothing to do with you. Moreover, she told Mr Lansdowne all about your opium habit and your affair with Mr Leonard and he believes her. You have to understand we are under siege here, Miss Allendon, with the Security Services breathing down our necks. Our household has to be clean as a whistle. Mr Lansdowne will see to it that Miss Grace is found suitable employment elsewhere, I am sure. I will see what I can do for you. I confess I can see some reduction in the quality of your work myself – sloppy spelling, careless errors. If you have not been at the smoke, then I cannot account for it.'

Perhaps it was to Mrs Lansdowne's credit that she looked increasingly uncomfortable through this entire speech. I do not think she wanted to sack me – at least not without giving me another chance – but, reading between the lines, it seemed as though her husband was insisting on it – perhaps in return for her sacking of Edie – that tit-for-tat thing again. It was hard to know. It didn't matter; her feelings of reluctance were no use to Jessica or to me. I began to panic. Where else would I find the internet access I needed?

I didn't ask her if I could sit down, just plonked myself on the other red leather chair. Mrs Lansdowne looked at me in surprise – I'm sure the other Jessica wouldn't have done that, but I was past caring. 'But you can't sack me! I haven't done anything wrong!' I said. I was outraged, frightened and angry all at once, and behind it all I had this terrible sinking feeling that it was all going wrong.

'I think you'll find that I can do whatever I want!' Mrs Lansdowne answered tartly. I tried a different approach.

'No, I mean – I've never taken opium and I'm sorry about the work, I'm trying as hard as I can. Please don't sack me. I have nowhere to go.'

I'd never have said that at home. I'd have walked out slamming the door or I might even have told her to stuff her job – or I'd like to think I would anyway – but here everything was different. I had never been really desperate at home – I had always got my mum behind me.

'As I've said, I will do what I can to help, Miss Allendon,' Mrs Lansdowne began. 'Now, I have made some enquiries and the secretarial school will be sending some candidates for the vacancy this afternoon so I would be grateful if you would move your things out of your room by then.' She examined her fingernails as she spoke; I wanted to slap her.

'I thought you were supposed to care about women's and workers' rights,' I said.

'Of course, I care,' she answered sharply, 'and I don't like your impertinent tone.'

'How can you care about workers' rights if you are prepared to ignore mine? I haven't done anything wrong – aren't you supposed to give me a warning or two weeks' notice or something? I have nowhere to go. My parents are dead. How can you support charities and not have any charity yourself?'

'That is quite enough, Miss Allendon,' she said. She was flushed and her eyes had a kind of hard glitter to them so that I supposed she really was angry. People like me did not talk to people like her in this way. She kept her voice low and controlled. 'I am sorry for your situation, Miss Allendon, but you have been given a great opportunity and you have chosen not to use it wisely. I do not run my home as a charity for any incompetent young woman of loose morals who can talk her way into a job.' Mrs Lansdowne's fingers trembled as she took a long drag from her cigarette. I was afraid I'd overstepped some invisible mark, but I had to do something to try to save Jessica's job. It occurred to me – too late – that a bit more humility might have gone further, but I had believed every word I said.

'I think you should go now,' she said in her clipped voice, like the Queen when she was a young woman. There was no hint of any possible change of mind in her tone.

I did not sob – I kept that much of my control, though maybe sobbing might have worked better with her. I got to my feet with as much dignity as I could manage – I'm not sure it was very much. I felt physically winded, as if I'd been punched in the stomach. I never thought it would go so far. Would I have to go to the workhouse now or was there some alternative?

'If I were you, Mrs Lansdowne, I would be ashamed of myself,' I said. OK, so it wasn't witty or clever, but I had to say something. I closed the door behind me and then looked round in desolation – what the hell did I do now?

TWENTY-SEVEN

Johnny was at his desk pretending to work, but somehow I knew by the way he held his back that he had known what was coming. 'I think it's your coffee break,' he said to the grey suit, who obligingly left his seat and appeared to be about to leave for the kitchen.

'She sacked me,' I said. Johnny nodded, tight-lipped.

'I should perhaps have spoken to her straight away. This is not an ideal approach, but it is the best I can do for now. I'll have to talk to her. You should come with me.'

'I think she's pretty angry with me,' I said, more reluctant to talk to Mrs Lansdowne than I was willing to admit. He gave me a thoughtful, appraising look, before saying firmly, 'No. You need to come too.' He took my elbow in that way he had and knocked on the door.

He pushed me into the room first when Mrs L told us to enter. She looked less than happy to see me, but whatever harsh words she was about to utter died unsaid when she saw Johnny.

'Mr Roberts, how can I help you?' Her smile was warmer than I'd ever seen it and broad enough to fold the corners of her eyes into a neat fan of creases.

'Miss Allendon has something to say to you which may cause you to reassess her position,' Johnny said. He looked at me and smiled encouragingly. 'Tell her,' he encouraged.

'Tell her what?'

'What you told me about where you come from.' I had not expected that and I reached out my hand to steady myself on his arm. Johnny glanced at Mrs Lansdowne.

'Miss Allendon, please sit down. You look unwell,' she said quickly and with more friendliness and concern than she'd ever shown me before. I sank gratefully into the red chair. Mrs Lansdowne indicated that Johnny should take the other chair and arranged herself on the cream chaise longue that was rarely used and almost hidden by the cream curtains at the window. It occurred to me for the first time that Mrs Lansdowne was putting on a show for Johnny. The thought made me uncomfortable.

'Pray tell me your story, Miss Allendon,' she said and her voice was softer, more girlish and less clipped than was usual for her. I *so* didn't want to tell her, for reasons I couldn't have explained – call it gut feeling if you like. Mrs Lansdowne looked at me with the alert interest of some kind of best-in-show Pekinese. She looked all glossy and groomed and tilted her head to one side just like Em's dog back at home. It was a look that did not inspire confidence, but Johnny was my only ally of any kind so I did what he wanted. Perhaps that was a mistake.

'Well, you see, Mrs Lansdowne, there has been some kind of event,' I began reluctantly. 'I don't know what else to call it and I'm not the same Jessica Allendon you employed. I have done the best that I can, but I am a stranger here. I come from another London . . .' Her expression altered and she glanced at Johnny.

'If this is some kind of joke . . .' she began. It did not seem that the Johnny I knew was very prone to making jokes, and he answered her gravely enough, without making any eye contact with me at all.

'It is nothing of the sort, I can assure you. I have told her nothing. I believe she is the real thing. Your Dunraven people did it! I think the actual exchange was mere happenstance but they did it and she is proof that all their suppositions were right.' I didn't like Johnny speaking about me in this way and I began to feel uneasy: what exactly was he talking about? Mrs Lansdowne's expression changed noticeably. She dropped her bright lapdog expression, which I suspected had been for Johnny's benefit anyway, then turned on some kind of radio or music-making device. I hadn't known there was one in the room, but it was hidden, as was everything else, so that technology did not interfere with the clean outlines of the furniture. She put it on at a low volume – presumably to make it more difficult for us to be overheard.

'Now then, Miss Allendon,' Mrs Lansdowne said with a smile that showed off her perfect white teeth. 'Why don't you begin at the beginning?'

I gave a simplified version of the tale I had told Johnny – missing out my feelings and the whole business with James and Edie. I didn't mention my Jonno either. I tried not to mention anything too personal – just the bare facts. The story sounded ludicrous to my ears; I would never have believed it. Mrs Lansdowne though was more credulous.

'And this happened last Sunday just before five o'clock?' she asked when I finished, excitement evident in her voice. I nodded. She leapt to her feet, or at least got up faster than I'd ever seen her move before, and made a phone call. She had one of those large phones with a dial, but it was made of crystal or glass – it was quite cool. She spoke to someone in a foreign language that I thought might be Welsh. When she finished and put the phone down, she was smiling – a rare, skin-wrinkling, genuine smile of what looked like triumph. 'The Professor said they activated the experimental machine – last Wednesday evening for a test run and on Sunday for an hour between four and five. This is very serious. Jessica obviously used the Root but how would she have known to use it at that time or to make an assignation at exactly the time the machine was utilised?'

'I don't know. That is the most mysterious aspect of the whole business,' Johnny said in a flat voice. He still hadn't met my eye – though I kept looking at him appealingly for some hint as to what he was playing at.

'When were you going to tell me?' Mrs Lansdowne demanded. At last Johnny glanced quickly in my direction.

'I had not quite finished conducting my preliminary enquiries,' he said.

'We will of course have to verify her story,' Mrs Lansdowne said. 'This has all to be properly evaluated, but I understand from what the Professor just said that he believes that both the breach and her presence here could be destabilising.' I had no idea what she was talking about and I wasn't wild about being spoken about as if I were invisible either.

'I'm sorry, what are you talking about?' I said, because the time for politeness was over.

Mrs Lansdowne favoured me with her most patronising tone – like I was really thick and the social equivalent of a worm.

'Miss Allendon, your story is so extraordinary it really has to be verified. There is a place I know – where your claims can be more fully investigated.'

Johnny had gone pale, and my stomach did a frightened little flip. 'I don't know that will be necessary, Mrs Lansdsowne. Could that not be done here?' Johnny said.

'That would be too risky. No. She can be taken to the facility at Dunraven.' I didn't like the sound of that at all.

I hated the sensation that everything was spinning out of control. If she was not going to help me get home or keep me on at my job, what was the point of my having told her? I looked at Johnny in desperation and, though this time he did meet my eyes, he kept his face smoothly expressionless. I had a horrible feeling in my twisting guts that he had just betrayed me.

'But, I want to go home,' I said and I know my voice sounded pathetic. They both ignored me. I fought down the rising panic and toyed briefly with the idea of running away. But where would I go? It seems a really stupid thing to think of, but I really wished for a pair of ruby slippers. I was suddenly very afraid.

TWENTY-EIGHT

Mrs Lansdowne made a number of rapid phone calls as Johnny left the room to get on with some other business. I think she spoke to Mr Lansdowne, but she spoke to him in German, correctly inferring that I did not speak that language. I sat in the red leather armchair like a kind of zombie. She ignored me completely.

I don't know how much time passed before Johnny returned. I was lost in some cold, hopeless place. I just sort of gazed out of the window, running through all the things I'd done since I'd arrived in the other Jessica's world and wondering what I could perhaps have done differently. When Johnny came in, I decided not to look at him – I couldn't. I really felt that he'd betrayed me. I heard him lock the office door behind him. I heard his footfall on the thick carpet and then his whisper as he said something to Mrs Lansdowne. I think I hated him at that moment.

'That is an excellent idea!' I heard Mrs Lansdowne say in the special voice she seemed to use for Johnny. I looked up in time to see her flicking her hair, like Shelley in my class, who flirted with anyone in trousers whether they were attractive or not. I thought she was a bit too old to be so girlish, but Johnny smiled back at her with one of his rare, precious, Jonno-like smiles. I did nearly cry then, which would have been stupid, so I'm glad I managed to hold it together.

'Miss Allendon,' Johnny said, speaking to me directly. 'Mrs Lansdowne is going to use the Root to try to find your doppelganger. Could you come here, please, to be sure we have the address right?'

Was this why he insisted I tell her? Maybe he hadn't betrayed me after all? I was at Mrs Lansdowne's desk in an instant. This was the first glimmer of hope there had been – my first chance of making contact with Jessica. I felt a wild surge of optimism.

I hadn't known Mrs Lansdowne had internet access in her office – I would have tried to get through to Jessica before if I'd known. I don't think Jessica had known either or she wouldn't have had to use Mr Lansdowne's terminal and brought the Security Services down on everyone's backs. Johnny had known though. I know he had – I could tell by the look on his face. I don't know what Mrs Lansdowne did – I suppose she must have pressed a button or pulled a lever or something because the smooth, apparently unbroken surface of her curved chrome desk opened and a monitor and keyboard rose silently from somewhere below like something from the launch sequence in *Thunderbirds*.

She typed in a string of numbers and letters – too quickly for me to see what they were. I presumed it must have been some kind of code. She then went through two or three security screens before typing in 'Googol' and an almost familiar logo appeared on screen – it was not in colour and it was in a plain font, but it was a search engine, that much I knew. I recognised even at that point that I could not have got that far on my own – I could never have got through the security screens without her passwords. I'm no hacker and my knowledge of computing was fairly basic (or 'crap' as Jonno would have described it).

Mrs Lansdowne slid gracefully out of her seat and let me have her chair. My hands when I typed in my name were shaking so much so that I mistyped it twice and Mrs Lansdowne suppressed a sigh at my cack-handedness. Eventually I got it right, but the message still came back 'Did you mean Jess Allen don?' – obviously I did not, so I tried again and again: 'No matches for Jessica Allendon were found.'

'That can't be right – there were loads at home.' I think I wailed like a toddler. 'You have to believe me!' I kept banging the keys, typing and retyping my name. Oh God! What had happened? Why wasn't she there? This time I did cry. I was racked with huge throat-ripping sobs, and great lumpish tears, bigger than raindrops in a storm, splashed on to the keyboard.

'Miss Allendon, please, not on the keyboard!' Mrs L said without any noticeable sympathy. Johnny helped me fairly forcibly from the chair and half carried me back towards the leather armchair. He put his arm round me and hugged me once and I felt his strength and, I thought, his sympathy before he pulled quickly away. I think he was about to say something to me, but Mrs Lansdowne gained his attention by saying loudly, 'So there are no Jessica Allendons on the unaugmented Root. I thought as much. No proof either way there then.' I looked up and she was doing whatever she had to do to make the screen and keyboard disappear into her desk again. Johnny patted me on my back, then gently squeezed my shoulder and left me to my grief. I felt – how can I explain it? I suppose I felt nothing less than total, hopeless despair. If I could not get in touch with Jessica, I could never get home. I would never see my mum or Jonno again and I was stuck here, in this awful world, until I died which, given the violence I had met everywhere, would probably be quite soon.

I didn't notice anything further until much later when Mr Green admitted two men into the room. They were not wearing suits, but were smartly dressed in dark jackets of some kind of thick linen with berets – like people in some old French film. They spoke to Mrs Lansdowne, but I took no notice. It would be wrong to say that I did not care what happened to me – obviously I cared a great deal, but I couldn't process any more bad news. I only became aware of what was going on at the point where Mrs Lansdowne instructed the men to take me. The first man was very short for a bloke – probably shorter than me – with pale skin and freckles, and what hair I could see was sandy. The taller of the two – a man with curly dark hair that grew almost to his shoulders – spoke to me in an odd metallic accent.

'Now then, Miss Allendon, isn't it? I am a doctor and my friend here and I are going to take you to Mrs Lansdowne's country house. It's a good long drive and you've obviously had a bit of an upset today so I'm going to give you something to help you sleep on the journey.' It was only then that I noticed that he had some kind of doctor's bag with him – the kind you see in illustrations of Doctor Dolittle. He took out some great big hypodermic syringe.

'I'm fine, thank you. I don't want to sleep,' I said and made a run for the door. Johnny was behind it and I ran straight into him. He caught me.

'Go with them, Jess – it's the only way,' he said in a low voice.

'I don't want to. I don't know who they are or where they're going to take me!' I was so frightened and bunged up from crying that the words came out as a breathless, half-swallowed squeak.

'Please, Jessica. Mrs Lansdowne is your best chance of getting away from here.' Once he said that, I don't think there was anything else I could do. Did I believe him? I didn't know what to believe but the little fight that was in me evaporated. Johnny held me while they gave me the injection of whatever it was and I have a hazy recollection of him helping me into the back of a car and covering me with a blanket. I only remember feeling horribly sick and woozy and mumbling something incoherent to him about Jonno. Johnny looked worried. I remember that. He was pale and he said something to me before he got out of the car, but by then I was fast losing consciousness and I did not know what it was.

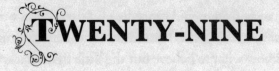

TWENTY-NINE

When I woke up, it was dark and I had been brought indoors and laid down on a kind of a day bed in a large high-ceilinged room. I had a banging headache and felt very groggy. I didn't know what they had given me, but I had only ever felt as bad after I had a minor operation that had needed an anaesthetic. There was no one around, but a fire blazed in a huge hearth and as I was cold I sort of staggered towards it. Perhaps they had some kind of CCTV in there because the moment I moved a woman came in and rushed to help me to my feet.

'You shouldn't get up yet,' she said. 'Let me get you some water. The grogginess will wear off in a while.'

I am embarrassed to say that my next question was completely predictable. 'Where am I? What time is it?'

'You're at Mrs Lansdowne's house, Dunraven Castle in Wales. It's ten o'clock in the evening. You've slept for rather a long time, I'm afraid. I'll get you that drink – I don't think you'd better eat anything – and then we'll examine you.' That sounded ominous and I shivered. The woman noticed. 'If you are who you say you are, Miss Allendon, you have nothing to worry about. We're just going to try to prove it, that's all.' She disappeared again and I think I must have dozed off because when she came back she had two men with her and I think they were speaking Welsh; I got the impression they had been waiting for me to wake up. The woman gave me the water, which I sipped cautiously – it tasted like water, so I gave it the benefit of any doubts I might have had. I was very thirsty. They all looked at me expectantly.

'Miss Allendon,' a man began – it was the one with curly hair who had identified himself as a doctor, 'I don't want you to be afraid. Nurse Jennings here is a medical nurse and we are going to give you a medical examination and then we will ask you some questions. There is nothing to be afraid of, but we live in dangerous times and we need to be sure that you are who you say you are. Is that all right?'

Of course it wasn't all right, but since I hadn't been able even to find Jessica's name on the Root I had felt numb. The after-effect of the shot they'd given me didn't help either. I didn't fight them when they escorted me to a small series of rooms, painted a hideous pale blue and furnished as some kind of surgery. Nurse Jennings began the examination. I submitted without complaint, made compliant by whatever sedation they had used earlier. My limbs felt heavy and my brain felt slow. I didn't say anything but it wouldn't be too melodramatic to say that inside I was screaming – for my mum.

You don't need to know the details – it was grim. She took stuff from my fingernails, my ears, my hair – everywhere. She said it was for analysis and they could tell all kinds of things from biological evidence. She paid particular attention to my teeth and she X-rayed them and poked around in my fillings. I'd had quite a lot of orthodontic work when I was younger so I was used to that kind of prodding, but it didn't mean I liked it. Nurse Jennings was perfectly nice to me. She was gentle and faintly apologetic, but it still felt like an invasion of my human rights to be examined by a perfect stranger, exposed and humiliated.

They took away Jessica's clothes and gave me something else to put on – kind of like pyjamas. That felt wrong too and unsettling. They gave me tea to drink, which made me sick, and then they took me into another room – a small sitting room, painted a pale and ugly grey. There was an electric fire, a table and three hard chairs. I was shown to one of them – the one nearest the fire. There were four of them: Nurse Jennings, who stood up by the door still wearing latex gloves, the sandy-haired man who'd brought me from Soho Square, the doctor, and a fourth man, with grey hair. He spoke with a German accent.

'Miss Allendon, I am Professor Meier and I thought it only fair to explain what you are doing here, before we begin. Dunraven Castle is a research facility owned by Mrs Lansdowne, dedicated to exploring the – let's say –

more unusual aspects of science. It has been a haven for those of us working on obscure projects, and one of those – the only one, that is to say, that need worry you – has been concerned with other-world theory. I won't bore you with the science, which in any case barely four people in the world today completely understand, but your claim to have come from another world is of great significance to us. If it is true, then you are the most dangerous and important person on the planet. If it is false, we need to know why you came to Mrs Lansdowne making that particular, very specific claim. How did you find out enough of what goes on here to make it? And what do you hope to gain from it?' He paused and took a sip of water. I wish I could say his speech made me feel better, but it didn't. I wasn't sure what he was saying, but I think he'd just accused me of being some kind of spy.

I didn't say anything for a moment and then asked, 'Why did you have to drug me and bring me so far away? Why have you taken away my clothes?'

'I can assure you the sedative was for your own benefit. Mrs Lansdowne was worried that you were hysterical and, as for your clothes, we will return them to you when we have checked them over. The Japanese and indeed the Americans have, we believe, devised a good many clever little gadgets that can be used for surveillance – it was important that we established that you were not wearing any of them.'

'What do you mean?' I asked. I couldn't remember if Johnny had mentioned the Japanese and the Americans when he had talked about this world's wars and I was confused.

'Surely, Miss Allendon – you are aware of the cold war?' Well, obviously I was – even though I only got a C minus for my essay on it – I wished I'd paid more attention.

'I don't understand why there's a cold war if you didn't have a First World War, or a second, and I didn't think Japan was involved,' I said, mumbling more to myself than to them. I still felt a bit weird thanks to the sedative. The Professor signalled and the sandy-haired man left the room to return some time later with a substantial-sized box, which he placed on the table. 'I didn't want to alarm you, my dear, but I think we need to record this conversation.' I thought at first the large box was some kind of tape recorder, which I think it was, but it recorded more than just my voice. 'Dr Ross, if you would do the honours.' He and the sandy-haired man then left and I heard them doing something in the corridor outside. I think they were lighting up because the smell of pipe smoke followed a moment later and made me cough. Dr Ross and Nurse Jennings started unwinding various bits of wire from the recording machine on the table and connecting them to me. They stuck the ends of the wire to my skin with tape and put them everywhere – even one at the corner of my eye.

'What are you doing?' I said. I was frightened then – what if they were going to give me electric shocks or something?

'Please don't worry, Miss Allendon – we just need to measure your body's reactions to our questions. Just tell us the truth and you will have nothing to worry about.' I felt like I was in a really bad horror movie. I had actually started to tremble with nerves and was afraid they would give me another sedative. In fact the doctor asked Professor Meier if he could, but the Professor said they wanted my mind to be clear; they'd be lucky. My mind was barely functioning. I'd seen so many war images of terrible interrogations I was imagining the very worst, and then it occurred to me that perhaps those things hadn't happened in this world. There had been no trenches, no Gestapo, no Auschwitz – would that make these people likely to treat me better or worse? I did not know.

The Professor puffed on his pipe for a moment. 'Are we all set?' he asked. 'I think some more tea would be good, Nurse Jennings.'

'I'll ring for some, sir, but I don't think it would be proper to leave Miss Allendon without a female chaperone.' I hadn't even thought to be worried about that.

'Quite so, nurse. The sooner we start the sooner we finish, Miss Allendon.'

There was a knock at the door and someone said, 'Mr

Lansdowne's men are here now, doctor, shall we send them through?'

'Yes, of course. Huw, could you organise more chairs.'

A few moments later two men in the grey suits of the Security Services walked into the room. That threw me. So Johnny was on their side. He'd set me up to tell the Security Services – the same Security Services who had apparently attacked his mother? It didn't matter. I was alone and friendless and I did not know who was good or bad. If these people could send me home, did it matter?

I think my confusion must have shown on my face because the doctor adopted his most reassuring tone. 'You mustn't be concerned about our visitors – they are here to observe only. You must realise that if your claim is true that fact has huge implications for national security. Now, I would like you to tell me about yourself – where you were born, your education, your parents. Imagine I am your favourite uncle and you are telling me the story of your life.'

I told him gladly – not because of the electrodes, or whatever they were, attached to me, but because I needed to remind myself of who I was. For a moment it felt like my real life was a distant dream, that I was in fact a madwoman in an asylum being cared for by doctors who were trying to expose the falsity of my remembered life. That idea freaked me out – so I was almost pleased to remember.

The Professor glanced at my face encouragingly from time to time, but was mostly just concerned with looking at the recording machine – it must have had some kind of read-out, I suppose. I was very conscious of the eyes of the others on me. As I talked they barely left my face even as they slurped their tea. At some point more chairs were brought. The Professor asked me about the war and seemed as much impressed by what I didn't know as by what I did. I think he felt that gave me more credibility because actually a lot of what I knew was incomplete and muddled. Doctor Ross asked me about medicine and the health service, the ginger man, who was called Huw, asked about mining – which I didn't know anything about – and Nurse Jennings asked me about women's rights and infant mortality. I answered everyone to the best of my ability. I didn't know if that was right or not. I didn't know who these people were or what they needed the information for. I did what I was asked and some-how, in talking about my real life, I got something of my confidence back. I think I even slipped into my usual way of speaking, where mostly I'd been making an effort to speak 'properly' and not use slang or say 'like' all the time. Many times they stopped me to clarify or to expose an inconsistency. A lot of the time, when I was talking about politics and science and stuff, I think I got it all wrong, but maybe the read-out was revealing that I believed what I was saying if nothing else.

I talked until it was light. Eventually, when I was hoarse, the Professor nodded and said, 'She believes what she's telling us – which is some way short of proving any of it to be true.' He turned to me and said, 'Thank you, Miss Allendon, for being so cooperative and entertaining. I think we will try to persuade Mrs Lansdowne to allow you to stay with us for a longer visit. For what it's worth, I believe you and I deeply regret that you must be exiled from the home that you speak of with such love. For now, I think it best if you return to Soho Square – your future is to some degree still in the hands of your employer, though I will do what I can to bring you here. It is beautiful – you will like it.' He pointed to the window where a spectacular sunrise was reflecting off the still surface of the sea.

'I will send for some food for you – would you like toast and perhaps some porridge or maybe an English breakfast?'

I ate hungrily of everything that was brought to me – eggs, bacon, sausages, porridge and toast. Nurse Jennings brought me Jessica's clothes – they had been washed and newly pressed, and her shoes polished. I don't know if they had been equipped with British listening devices – I thought it unlikely. She hung around after I'd changed – to keep me company I think. There was something that had been bothering me. 'Why does Mrs Lansdowne support the Professor's work?' I asked.

'She read about his theories and thought they might have practical application. The Professor thinks she wants to use the resources of another world to fund changes here. He thinks she thought she might be able to import commodities more cheaply. Most of the business in the colonies is tied up. He didn't think that what has happened to you was possible, though he never told Mrs Lansdowne that.'

This didn't make much sense to me. 'But she's rich already?'

'The Professor's work is costly. He is working at the very edge of scientific understanding. In successfully opening a way between worlds he has crossed beyond our under-standing.' She dropped her voice to a whisper. 'Now Mrs Lansdowne has involved the Security Services, and Mr Lansdowne and the government know, anything could happen.'

She seemed very nervous as though she feared we were overheard. She changed the subject and spoke in a more normal voice. 'Are there many women doctors in your world?' she asked.

'Yeah, loads – we even had a woman prime minister for a while. People complain that we don't always get equal pay and stuff and that not as many women get to the top as should do, but girls do better in tests and at university.'

'I'm glad. I studied medicine at Lady Margaret Hall,

but women are not awarded degrees and I cannot work as a doctor, only as a nurse under male supervision. I could probably get away with it if I went abroad – the colonies are more practical and open-minded, but I can't practise here.'

'In my world women fought hard for those rights – and I think women did lots of jobs in the war which helped. I'm sorry, I don't know as much history as I thought.'

'You're tired,' she said soothingly. 'I expect you'll sleep in the car. It has been a pleasure and a privilege to meet you, Miss Allendon. Good luck!' For some reason her eyes filled with tears as she shook my hand. I smiled at her because she hadn't hurt me, and because although she had invaded my privacy she had tried to be kind. I know that sounds warped, but I didn't blame her at all. When she had left, the Professor also came to shake my hand and to escort me to the car which would take me back to London.

'I hope we meet again, Miss Allendon, in the next world, if not in this one.'

I puzzled over that until I realised he meant heaven. I thought it was a really odd thing to say.

THIRTY

I think I may still have been feeling the after-effects of the sedative because I was so tired when I got into the car that I could not really think. I was no nearer home. I did not know if I had done the right thing in speaking to the Professor, but I had had no choice. The two unnamed men in the grey suits of the Security Services sat on either side of me, but I was too exhausted to be scared. I had never felt more ignorant or less in charge of my own destiny. There was a strange atmosphere in the car, I did notice that, and no one spoke. I did not know if that changed because the moment the car started to move I fell asleep and I only woke when the car pulled up outside 36 Soho Square. It must have been midmorning. My hair had fallen out of its bun and stray ends had stuck to my face and I hastily tried to tidy it up. There was a bitter taste in my mouth. I was a bit dazed to be honest.

Huw opened the car door for me and he and the Security men escorted me into the house through the front door. Mr Green gave me a welcoming smile, but my heart still sank a little as we were shown into the reception room outside Mr Lansdowne's office. It occurred to me that I was being treated like I was under arrest. I looked out for Johnny, but I could not see him.

I felt like I was waiting outside the head teacher's office for some unspecified punishment. To stop myself biting my nails, I put my hand in my pocket and my fingers closed around something that felt like a note. I didn't dare look at it while I was in the company of my escort and so I made the obvious reasonable excuse and ran upstairs to the servants' bathroom. I didn't see anyone – everyone was obviously busy. I locked the door of the bathroom and opened the note with trembling fingers – I don't know why – but I already sensed it was bad news. The note was brief and to the point. Carefully printed on a scrap of paper with a thick smudgy pencil, it said: 'The Security Services officers will kill you. You know that there are other ways to live, other forms of government. You are a danger to our political stability and some will say to God's natural order. Run. Hide. I will pray for you.' It was signed 'Elizabeth Jennings' – the nurse. She must have slipped the note in my pocket when she brought me my clothes. She had written next to her signature in brackets 'who will one day be a doctor'.

My heart immediately began to bang against my ribcage with so much violence that I actually began to wonder if I was having a heart attack. I believed her, my guts believed her and my mind followed soon after. Suddenly the Professor's last words to me made a kind of sense and I felt ice freeze my spine. I was from another London – a London where vagrants were not rounded up and killed, where workhouses were a thing of the past, where there was an NHS, however imperfect, and where women had rights. Maybe I *was* dangerous – it required little stretch of my imagination to believe that people wanted to kill me. Hadn't I been in some kind of danger since the second I arrived? I quickly washed my face and hands and ran into my bedroom. Jessica had a small amount of money there and I wanted to get my own things – my keys and phone were kind of talismans, and I didn't want anyone else to get them. I'm not sure I was thinking clearly. The thumping of my blood was like an urgent drumbeat telling me to run and my breathing sounded hoarse and loud. I was even clumsier than usual and dropped the key that opened the drawer. My fingers fumbled, fear had made them stiff and unresponsive. When I finally managed to overcome my clumsiness and get the drawer open, there was nothing there but Jessica's underwear – the gun, diary and my things were missing. Of course, I should have guessed that someone would have checked my room.

I looked in the other drawers, including Edie's, which opened with the same key. There was no doubt – I knew that my stuff had gone. I had wanted the gun – not to hurt anyone obviously, but as a deterrent – firing it even randomly had saved Anna. I checked the drawers once more, throwing things on to the floor in my usual messy panic. Jessica's money was still there in an envelope. I took a spare pair of pants, Jessica's toothbrush, comb, pen and the money and stuffed them into the pocket of Mrs Lansdowne's pink trench coat which I put on, along with a hat and a pair of gloves. I looked out of the window for a possible escape route but we were on the top floor, which must have been forty feet high; I wasn't great with heights and anyway a grey-suited man patrolled the pavement at the front of the house. I would have to get out through the door – the usual way. I would have to pretend I was on some errand. I checked my face in the mirror of the wardrobe – I looked as you'd expect to look after missing a night's sleep and being interrogated miles away. I applied some of Jessica's scarlet lipstick with a shaky hand – it looked like a bloody gash in my washed-out-looking face. I took a deep breath. I was gambling that the rest of the house would not know what had happened to me. I wasn't sure that was likely to be true, but Mr Green had smiled at me. Would he have smiled if he thought I'd been sacked or was under arrest? I had to gamble that word had not yet got out. I took another deep breath. My life might depend on my appearing normal. I needed to think. First, how could I get out? I could pretend I was on an errand for Mrs Lansdowne. Good. What errand? I grabbed the envelope that had held Jessica's wages and smoothed it out before writing an address in my best cursive script. I had to take my gloves off to do it and then put them on again when I'd finished. I wafted the envelope around and blew on it to dry the ink. The handwriting wasn't very good, but it would have to do. There was no one to say goodbye to. I didn't even know for sure if Johnny had betrayed me or not. I had been in Jessica's world a week and had learned so very little. I glanced round the room that had been my home. When I shut the door behind me, I felt like I was casting off into the totally unknown.

I walked slowly down the stairs. I was going to post something for Mrs Lansdowne – it was a normal part of Jessica's job, there was no reason to be stressed. I thought I heard someone outside the servants' entrance to the house – a grey suit? It seemed likely. I could not use the front door because the butler would see me so I tried to saunter through the kitchen as though I was meant to be there.

'You've missed coffee,' Cook said dourly when I came into the room. I nodded.

'Yes – a pity about that. I've got to go and post a letter,' I said. I thought my voice sounded strange, but Cook didn't look up from her pastry-making and if she thought it odd that I told her what I was doing, she gave no sign. I slipped out through the kitchen door and into the alleyway. I wanted to run, but I made myself walk. God, it was hard! There was a grey suit by the servants' entrance as I had suspected, but luckily for me he was lighting up a few yards away. He was the one who had winked at me. I smiled a wobbly smile and brandished the letter. He was cupping his hands around his cigarette because it was a windy day, and was so intent on the task that he merely nodded an acknowledgement. He had seen me leave – that wasn't good. But it wouldn't take a genius to work out that I'd left. I wondered how much time I had before anyone realised I was gone. What would happen then? One step at a time, I told myself, one step at a time.

I wanted to get on a tram – one in a busy place where I could blend with the crowd. The pink trench coat was probably too smart and too distinctive, but there wasn't much I could do about it. I would take it off later – perhaps if they had charity shops here I could swap it? My mind was racing ahead and my footsteps had got faster so I made myself slow down to nothing more than a purposeful, businesslike walk. One thing I did know is that women never ran. Several men raised their hats to me and I did my best to smile an acknowledgement. 'Lovely morning,' one said and I nodded a response. I found myself walking deeper into Soho – because I could guarantee there would be a crowd. I knew exactly two places I could go – the tea shop where the Indian girl helped me and Anna's house in Sheen. I was not at all sure I could find my way back to the tea shop without going along the alley by the WLUE building and I knew that would be full of Security men – so I discounted that thought quickly. That left only Anna's house in Sheen. Johnny might guess where I'd gone. Was that good or bad? I supposed there was a chance that Mrs Lansdowne might guess that was where I'd go too, but I was too afraid to risk finding somewhere safe by chance.

I knew that going to Sheen didn't qualify as much of a plan – but it was all I could think of to do. Now I can think of a hundred things which would have made more sense, but I was so afraid then it was all I could do to keep walking. I fumbled for some change in my pocket and got on the next tram I saw. It wasn't going anywhere near Waterloo, but it was taking me away from Soho Square. I wished that I still had the map of London and its environs with me – I did not much want to be lost in this strange, hostile version of London. I fought to control rising panic. One step at a time, I told myself, one step at a time.

I did not want to be anywhere in this city. I wanted to go home and I wanted not to be killed. At that moment it hit me with a kind of terrible clarity. I had to let go of one of those ambitions. I'd have to settle for not being killed.

THIRTY-ONE

I didn't look at anyone on the tram, but peered anxiously out of the window. Luckily I had noticed how much the fare had been when I'd travelled with Johnny so I didn't have to fumble too much with the unfamiliar coinage. I got out at some random stop. It would be harder for them to guess where I'd gone if even I did not know. I didn't recognise any of the street names. I felt a little conspicuous in the pink coat; I had to get rid of it.

This part of the city was dirtier: it stank of horse manure, bad eggs and boiled cabbage. I felt nervous and a couple of older women, dressed entirely in black, gave me hard looks. I passed a noisy pub and a grim brick building advertising itself as 'Westminster District Workhouse'. The shops were shabbier here and when there was a sudden gust of wind litter of all kinds was blown down the street. There was one shop with an odd sign outside – gold balls, which I remembered was a pawn shop. I'd heard of them but had never seen one. The door opened with the loud ringing of a mechanical bell. When I stepped inside, I was almost overwhelmed by a smell I'd not experienced before. It was rank – dirt, old sweat, mothballs and damp. It made me want to gag, but luckily I had more sense than to turn up my nose or pull a face. I wasn't sure what to do, but there was someone in front of me – a girl of my age with a couple of kids. The kids both had runny noses and a pinched, pale look – they were both crying. The woman turned and gave them a slap each, hard and sharp, that took my breath away and seemed to have the same effect on the children. I wanted to tell her that she couldn't do that, but I was too cowardly. She turned and glared at me anyway, as if she could sense my disapproval. The man behind the counter ignored her sudden violence, as though it was an everyday thing. The kids only briefly stopped crying.

'Mike out of work again?' the man behind the counter said in a bored voice.

'Ja – kids haven't eaten since yesterday. Same as usual – pick it up Thursday?' she said, handing over a brown paper parcel and taking some kind of ticket in return. Then I noticed that neither of the children were wearing shoes. I couldn't help but stare, but quickly pretended to be examining my own shoe when she caught me. She looked me up and down and sniffed. Her eyes were red-rimmed and she had a large bruise on her cheek – she looked as ill as the kids. I shuffled forwards to the counter, anxious to get away from her – I am a bit ashamed of that reaction now. I took off the coat and offered it to the man behind the counter.

'Two guineas,' he said.

'Come off it, Fred,' the woman butted in. I thought she'd left but she was hoiking one of the children on to her hip and trying to hold the other's hand while negotiating the door. 'Don't cheat the lady – it's worth at least four.' I looked back at her in surprise and she grinned – to reveal a big gap where one of her front teeth should have been. 'Don't let him take advantage, love,' she said. 'Men are all the same.' I smiled back and opened the door for her. 'Ask for four and settle for three and six – you can get smoked up or drunk enough on that,' she whispered and winked at me.

In the end that's what happened – I settled for three and six. The man behind the counter folded the coat inside out – I'd already carefully checked the pockets – and wrapped it in brown paper. He gave me a paper bag for my things, for which I was grateful. I'd managed to stick the underwear in the pocket of my dress along with the money, but I couldn't really carry my toothbrush and bits of make-up through London. I couldn't get out of there fast enough. Further down the same street I found a second-hand shop that looked clean and didn't smell too badly and bought a short black jacket that looked neat, respectable and not so noticeable.

'All our goods are treated for fleas and other undesir-ables,' the shop girl said in some heavy accent I didn't recognise. Great – I hadn't even thought about fleas. The coat had a slightly chemical smell, but I decided I would prefer that to fleas or tobacco. I bought a bag too – a small black leather shoulder bag. That too had been treated. I wondered about buying a purse before deciding that I didn't need one. At the rate I was going I would soon have no money left to put into it. I would have to get some kind of job. 'One step at a time,' I said to myself – I think I must have said it out loud because the shop girl gave me a strange look. I didn't see any of the grey suits in that part of town, though I caught sight of a few men in Constabulary uniform manhandling some poor unfortunate into a black van. I walked more quickly after that and caught the next tram out of there.

It was hard to work out where I was with so many familiar landmarks gone, but luckily the river was still the same, even though the bridges weren't. I recognised Waterloo Bridge only because Somerset House existed unchanged in this world and so I was able to find my way quite easily from there to the station. I got fewer raised hats in my second-hand coat. The smell of it was actually quite bad – like dry-cleaning fluid, only stronger. As I got hotter with the brisk walk, the smell got worse.

I walked past the front entrance of Waterloo long-ingly. I hovered for a moment at the place where I'd met Jessica, but all that happened was that a few well-dressed people gave me rather disapproving looks and one woman, in a hat which looked like a goose had died on it, wrinkled her nose as she got downwind of the coat. Time to move on, I thought.

I walked round the back of the building to the entrance to the second-class ticket hall. There were a couple of grey suits there, but I let my hair down so that it fell into my eyes and hid my face from view. I don't think they were looking for me. I had a little bit of trouble working out the fare. I think the man at the counter thought I was foreign because he spoke to me in German and then in something else – I didn't recognise the language but he directed me to the right platform in very slow, loud English, which was good – in a way – if embarrassing. I was ready for the crowds this time – the bikes and the dogs and smoke. I was nervous and kept looking over my shoulder. I thought for a moment I might have been followed by a very disreputable-looking man – not Security, something else – and was suddenly reminded that Edie's brother might be looking for me too. That made my already banging heart beat faster.

It was a relief to slink into the train, to sit down and take stock. I had exactly twenty-five pounds, four shillings and ninepence. I hadn't paid much attention to the cost of food, but I would have to buy something to eat. I could maybe get some bread and cheese at one of the small shops by Mortlake station. I thought that I could find my way to Johnny's house from there. I would have to break in. I tried to remember if Johnny had used his own key or if he'd found one under the mat or something. Mum and I had a system of hiding the house keys in one of four different places – I don't really know why. Maybe Anna had a spare key hidden somewhere?

As I sat there on the busy train making plans to stay alive in this place, I realised that in some part of myself I had accepted that I couldn't go home. I couldn't find the other Jessica on the web and what had the Professor said – something about being sorry that I could never go back? Was that because it was impossible or because they would kill me first? I didn't know and sitting there I felt a kind of desolation wash over me. I didn't want to die, but did I want to keep living in this strange world where I was so alone, and so lost? I don't think you can afford to think like that and even when you do, your body keeps demanding that you go on. My stomach rumbled again and I started to think about how Anna's stove worked and in that way I kind of found the will to get off the train at the right stop and to keep on going.

Vegetables were cheap. I didn't have any kind of shopping bag, but the lady at the grocer's lent me a couple of string bags, which I filled with beans and potatoes, apples, and tomatoes that smelled like the ones my grandfather had grown in his greenhouse. I had to fight back tears again when I thought of that. I bought cheese, milk and bread too. The whole lot came to ten shillings – which seemed cheap when I thought of it as fifty pence and very expensive when I thought of my store of money. The shopkeeper was very nice and reminded me of someone I knew – perhaps she was the double of someone who worked in my Sheen. I asked her if there was any work going and she did say that the doctor's receptionist at the surgery on Sheen Lane was about to leave her job to get married and that if my references were good it might be worth applying. I wondered briefly if I could forge some references – something I would never normally have considered. It doesn't take much to make anyone behave badly – just a degree of desperation, and I had desperation in spades.

I think it must have been about half past twelve then and I was really hungry. I ate an apple to keep me going and took off my jacket because the stench was getting to me. It was a half-hour's walk to Anna's, less if I hadn't been struggling with shopping, and it had turned into a really hot day. By the time I got there I felt faint, I was dripping with sweat and I'd knocked the scab off the blister on my heel and it was bleeding. I was so relieved when I found Anna's house. I left the shopping by the gate and went to look for the key. If it were my house, I'd have hidden the key somewhere out of sight, probably in the back garden. The garden gate creaked a little, which startled me. The key was under a large stone by a rose bush, and next to it was an envelope. Inside was a note in Johnny's handwriting. It said 'St Paul's. Tuesday. Midday.' That was all.

Was it intended for me or someone else? Did he mean the Cathedral? I put the envelope in my pocket, wishing Johnny had addressed it. I wasn't even sure what day it was. I was hazy about how long I'd been at the facility at Dunraven. Somehow I didn't think shops would be open on a Sunday. I knew that all the servants went to church on Sunday mornings because Cook had asked Mr Green which church he intended to attend. Yet he'd been on duty that morning. That suggested that I had lost a day somewhere along the line. I had been in Jessica's world for more than a week. It was Monday again, but I could not let that depress me.

I would have to try to meet Johnny the next day, assuming that the message was intended for me and that he meant St Paul's Cathedral – surely one of the few places he might guess I would know. But then I got to wondering how he would know that I would run away, or that I would run to Sheen? I was hot and tired and hungry and my brain refused to function so I picked up my shopping and opened the back door.

The house smelled of cigars, which was strange – it had not smelled that way before. I dumped the shopping on the work counter and then walked through into the sitting room. You know how you have a feeling when there is someone else in the house? I definitely felt that. I was trying to think of an explanation to give Anna, if perhaps Aunt Fitch hadn't managed to persuade her to leave. It was still a shock though when I walked into the room and discovered that the house wasn't empty.

A man in a grey suit was sitting on Anna's comfy chair – his hat and gloves were on the table next to him along with a revolver, a smoking cigar and, of course, a cup of tea. 'Aha!' he said. 'Just the person I was hoping to see.'

THIRTY-TWO

I stood there like an idiot and looked at him. I didn't recognise him but I had a strong feeling that he was the man I'd startled and sent hurtling out of Anna's bedroom window. That meant he was dangerous – of course he was dangerous – he had a gun and I was alone with him in an otherwise empty house. How stupid was I?

'H-How did you know I'd come here?' I stuttered. He looked surprised.

'We had a tip-off, didn't we? We've been watching the house on suspicion that it would be used for terrorist activity. My colleague is looking for evidence upstairs.' He raised his voice and shouted up the stairs. 'Hey, James – look what we've caught!' There was the thump of heavy feet running down Anna's narrow staircase and a second man strode into the room. I recognised him at once. It was James, the former butler, my enemy, the man I'd got fired.

He looked stunned to see me. So I gathered neither of them were actively looking for me. That was good, I thought. James being there was quite definitely bad, but the fact that they did not know that their colleagues wanted to kill me made the situation less bad than it might have been.

I recovered from the shock of seeing James quite quickly.

'Hello, James,' I said, doing my best to smile. My lips sort of wobbled with nerves. 'Mrs Lansdowne sacked me too. She found out about the pills. I thought I might be able to stay here with Anna. I'm sure you're wrong about Johnny . . .'

I did my best to sound unthreatening and confused; it wasn't difficult.

James scowled. 'You little bitch,' he said. 'Dropped me right in it. We've got a right one here, Fred, a poppy poppet who might be on the game too. Not a very respectable friend for Mr Lansdowne's personal secretary. Is she the one who fired at you?'

'Very likely, I'd say,' the man James called 'Fred' answered, looking me up and down in the way the men of this world had: a week was not long enough to get used to it.

'What should we do then – take her in?'

'Why not?' James answered. 'I'll sort her out and you hang on here in case anyone else turns up. No point in both of us going into town.'

I felt a chill in my veins when he said that. I did not like to think what James might mean by 'sorting her out'.

'That's jolly decent of you,' Fred said, puffing at his cigar. 'I must say I've got rather comfortable here and our orders were to keep the house under surveillance. Here, catch!' He threw a set of car keys in James's general direction and James plucked them from the air with nonchalant ease.

'Good catch! You might be useful in the divisional cricket team. Standard's quite good actually.'

James nodded. 'I enjoy the odd game,' he said. 'I'll see you in a couple of hours.'

Fred waved his cigar expansively in the air. 'In your own time,' he said. 'There's no rush, if you were to find it necessary to investigate this young lady further. Just make sure she doesn't enjoy it. She tried to kill me, you know. Toodle pip, poppet,' he said and he flashed me a vicious grin, his teeth bared like some predatory animal. I shivered and it wasn't with cold. There was nowhere to run.

James grabbed me quite roughly by the arm and led me to the waiting car. I couldn't think of anything to say. I wanted to beg him not to hurt me, but I think he was the type who would have enjoyed that. I wished I still had Johnny's gun.

'So,' James said conversationally. 'You're Johnny's poppet now, are you? You get around a bit – for a secretary.' He pushed me into the passenger seat and kissed me hard on the lips. I wanted to gag. He pulled away. 'We'll find somewhere a little more private, shall we? We don't want old Fred watching, do we?'

He got in the driver's side and slammed the door. I didn't think my door was locked. I should have run then, but Fred was watching us – I saw Anna's curtains twitch. I wasn't sure I'd have the courage to jump out when the car was moving, but that was probably going to be my best chance.

Either way I didn't take it. James pulled out of Anna's street and drove along almost familiar roads – in the wrong direction, away from Central London.

'Where are you taking me? I thought you were taking me to London,' I said.

He grinned at me. 'I want to have some fun first. I've wanted some fun with you, Jessica Allendon, since I first set eyes on you. You're the prettiest poppet I've seen for a long while.'

By then we were going too fast for me to jump out of the car. The door handle, cool and chrome, lay beneath my fingers, but I couldn't make myself do it.

Then I heard a man's voice and I jumped – actually physically jumped. James laughed. 'It's just the radio.' The voice spoke gibberish. I didn't understand a syllable – it was all code words.

Whatever was said, it was sufficient to make James pull over suddenly with a screech of brakes.

'My gaffer there says you are a threat to civilisation. London's most wanted. To be taken to Paddington

Green at once if apprehended. Why would that be then? You don't look very dangerous to me.' He had moved very close and his hand was on my thigh – under my skirt. Then unaccountably he pulled away.

'Has Johnny been helping you?' he asked and I didn't know what to say. I think he saw the answer on my face. 'What are you into, Miss Allendon, that threatens civilisation?' I shrugged. The Security Services already knew who I was but I didn't want to tell James.

'Miss Allendon, I am all that stands between you and Paddington Green – I could be in a position to help you. Start talking. Why are you a risk to civilisation?'

His hand moved further up my leg and I pushed him away. 'I'm from another world,' I said – to distract him as much as anything else.

I would have expected him to have laughed, or maybe to have got angry – I would have done in his shoes, but instead he went very still. After a long pause he asked, 'Does Johnny know this?' I didn't answer.

'Miss Allendon, this is very important – does Johnny know this?' He pulled out a gun and pointed it casually in my direction. I think my brain stopped working then.

'Yes or no? Does Johnny know this?'

I didn't want to get Johnny into trouble. He might have been on my side – I still wasn't sure – but I didn't want James to shoot me. Was that cowardly? I think it probably was. I nodded. He let the gun drop and let out a kind of a sigh. Then he began undoing his trousers and loosening his tie. Did I have time to get away? The gun was barely an inch away from his hand. Could I grab it first?

'This is what you are going to do,' he said in a businesslike tone he'd not used with me before, 'in a minute I'm going to give you my gun and I want you to hit me with it as hard as you can across my face – then I want you to run. Do you understand me?'

I didn't. I think I must have looked at him dumbly. James was on my side. It made no sense.

He continued, 'Twickenham is about half a mile down the road. Get on a train there and go anywhere, it doesn't matter, but get out of London. If you can change your appearance, do it. Keep moving – call yourself,' he paused, 'Jennifer Richards. Someone will find you. The code word to let you know they are to be trusted will be "cuckoo".'

He gave me the gun. 'Hit me with it as hard as you can. I'll make it easy for you.'

He made a lunge towards me, grabbing for my breasts, and I swung the gun so that the butt of it hit him hard on the skin above the eye.

'Harder!' I did it again and blood suddenly spurted from somewhere. I think I got him across the nose. He pulled his trousers down so that they became entangled with his feet.

'Run!'

I had to fight with the door handle and grab my bag with my money in it and then I sort of stumbled into the road and started running. My knees were wobbly and I was shaking all over with shock, but I ran. James followed me out of the car shouting and swearing and tripped awkwardly over his trousers so that he lay sprawled on the ground beside the car. He made it look real.

So James was an ally of Johnny's? Why hadn't Johnny told me? Nothing made sense.

THIRTY-THREE

I ran until I couldn't run any more. I stopped just before the road narrowed through the main shopping street of Twickenham. I was struggling to breathe. I hid James's gun in the bottom of my bag; it was still smeared with his blood. I straightened my clothes and caught my breath. I didn't want to look like a fugitive. As it happened, my efforts were wasted. I turned the corner into the High Street to find three grey-suited Security men waiting for me.

I had neither the pace nor the energy to outrun them.

One of them, the one from Anna's house called Fred, searched me roughly – finding both the gun and money in my handbag.

They shared Jessica's hard-earned money out between them, calling it a finder's fee. They laughed about me getting away from James, but appeared to believe he was a fool for 'pretty poppet' rather than a traitor. I supposed that was a good thing.

I stopped listening to their banter; the boys in my class weren't so childish about girls. I had never heard so many pathetic jokes and I imagined James was going to have to put up with a lot of stick for a while. I couldn't feel too sorry for him. I still couldn't quite believe he was on the same side as Johnny – my side, if I had understood him right.

I knew I couldn't escape these men. I allowed them to bundle me into the car. I was scared – of course I was – but I was so shocked by everything that had happened to me I was almost insulated from my own fear somehow.

I watched the miles of unfamiliar cityscape speed past. I tried not to think about what was to come or what I'd lost. I think for a little while I gave up hope.

Paddington Green police station was modern as in 'modern for alternative London'. It didn't look like anything I'd seen before – with a curved facade, like a frozen wave of Portland stone and glass. There were none of the large expanses of plate glass common at home. Instead the windows, which spanned several floors, were long and narrow and angled to catch the light. The door was a huge studded thing like something from a castle, only of some light-coloured wood, reinforced with bronze. The senior grey suit put handcuffs on me to take me inside and covered my head with a blanket; there were photographers and journalists outside – I hadn't somehow expected that.

'Rest assured, Miss Allendon, that from now on it is going to get pretty unpleasant,' the Security man said. I didn't reply as I was doing an impression of the Elephant

Man at the time, but my stomach flipped over when he said that – and not in a good way.

When we got inside, Fred took the blanket from my head and led me through a rather beautiful marble reception area into the cells behind. I think they were part of an older building. They smelled of bleach, vomit and urine overlaid with tobacco smoke. Men and women were held separately. Fred gently moved a stray hair from my eyes.

'They'll book you in here – this officer will search your bag and your personal possessions and bring you through for charging and questioning.' He looked grave.

'May God be merciful, Miss Allendon. You are such a pretty little thing. I recommend that you tell them everything you know straight away. There are no laws protecting terrorists or traitors against the Crown and you can expect brutal treatment otherwise.' I don't know if he said this to terrify me as part of some 'good cop, bad cop' routine or if he was trying to warn me and was merely being helpful. I'd like to think it was the latter. He undid the handcuffs and patted me on the back. I don't know why. He seemed uncomfortable about leaving me there. He handed me over to a woman in a blue uniform who looked like a cross between Mrs Trunchbull and the old bag who taught me gym in year seven. She didn't say much – just asked me to empty my pockets and took my handbag. She wrinkled her nose at the smell, which surprised me as it was nowhere near as bad as the stench wafting in from the cells. She pulled a disgusting-looking comb through my hair, as if I was going to hide anything in that and patted me down – like they do at airports. She smelled of fried onions and nicotine. She didn't strip-search me or anything, although she made me take off my shoes and checked them over before returning them to me. She handcuffed me to her and escorted me to a dingy little room containing only a wooden table, covered in graffiti like an old school desk, and two much-stained grey canvas-backed chairs. I sat on one of them reluctantly and the scary woman gaoler then called for two male officers to guard me while she undid her end of the cuff and then handcuffed me to the chair: closer inspection revealed that the chair was bolted to the concrete floor. Then the woman left without a word and the male officers stood guard at the door like sixteen-year-old Jessica Allendon from Sheen, South West London, was so dangerous she had to be locked up and guarded by two adult men. It ought to have made me laugh or cry, which is my preferred method of dealing with a crisis – this time I didn't do either.

If this had happened to me at the beginning of my visit to Jessica's world, I would have been a gibbering wreck, but, you know, when a lot of bad things happen to you, you do change and I wasn't the same person I had been a week ago. I won't say I was stronger because in most ways I was a lot more fragile. Fred's response to the situation had woken me up. Adrenalin was pumping and I was more frightened and more desperate than I'd ever been. After a while the two officers also went out, locking the door behind them, and I was left alone.

I don't know how long I was there for – there was no clock on the wall and I still hadn't acquired a wrist-watch. I had a lot to think about. Mostly I worried about my mum. It was Monday – eight days since I'd left my world. By now even Jonno's ingenuity must have failed and he wouldn't have been able to keep Jessica from her. She would be grieving for me as badly as I was grieving for her. I wished I could hug her or somehow let her know that I was safe, admittedly some fairly broad and idiosyncratic definition of safe. She would be wild with worry if she knew what I was going through. I thought of Jessica sleeping in my bed, having supper with Mum, going into Richmond with Jonno, hanging out with my friends and I felt this overwhelming sense of loss; I'd definitely drawn the short straw in this exchange.

I knew the Security people, police – whatever they were – had left me alone so that I could reflect on what they could do to me, so that I would be terrified and tell them everything. The thing was I had nothing to tell besides my true story, which they'd already heard.

They were going to kill me, if not in this room, then somewhere. I believed Nurse Jennings. A bit of me wanted to get it over with, another part wanted to stay alive as long as possible. Most of me was too scared to think at all. I was so jittery I had to try to calm myself down. It seems stupid looking back on it, but for some reason I made myself remember everyone in my year at school – their names and what they looked like so that I could mentally say goodbye to them. I thought about Em and her panic attacks and almost laughed out loud: she didn't know what panic was.

When I'd remembered everyone I could, I started on the year below – which was harder. You would think that this dwelling on what was lost might have made me sad and feebler even than usual but, though it did make me sad, it sort of helped too and the effort of it took me away from where I was. I was not a terrorist, but I wasn't just Jessica Allendon from Sheen any more either. I was someone that bit tougher, someone who had already lost everything.

THIRTY-FOUR

After what I think might have been a long time, I heard a fumbling at the door and a man in a dark suit walked through the door flanked by two uniformed officers and a woman I thought I recognised. She was carrying what could have been either torture equipment or some kind of recording device; I hoped it was the latter.

I felt curiously calm again, like you do sometimes when an exam you've been dreading actually starts and all you can do is endure it. I don't know what the man in the dark suit expected, but I got the impression it wasn't me.

'So, Miss Allendon, you're a pretty little thing, aren't you? An unlikely threat to civilisation – very clever.' I was a bit taken aback. The last thing I'd expected was a kind of a compliment – even if it was a rather condescending one. I didn't say anything. I just waited for whatever was going to happen next to happen. I sat with my hands in my lap and looked at him. It wasn't my truculent 'I don't want to be in this class' look – I know when I'm doing that. It was an 'OK, I'm ready for whatever you're going to throw at me' look. Obviously it was a bluff, but it seemed to surprise the dark suit. The woman, who was a good-looking blonde in her early twenties, started arranging her equipment on the desk. I think a tiny bit of my tension eased when I recognised that one of the pieces of equipment was a microphone. She turned it on – or I think that's what she did – and also got out a pad and pencil – I think she was going to take down anything I said in shorthand. Our eyes met and then I remembered her – my chaperone from my interview with the Security man in the house at Soho Square. I knew she recognised me too. Dark-suit cleared his throat.

'Is the recorder on?' She nodded.

'This is Commander Doyle at 20:00 hours, present for the interrogation of the suspect Miss Jessica Allendon, currently of 36 Soho Square, London. Also present Officers Rendall and Christian and Miss Shadrake.' He looked at me again and I maintained my carefully blank expression.

'I haven't been told what I am suspected of,' I said, trying not to sound petulant. I had been here before – in a room with some guy and his henchmen about to question me. 'Aren't you supposed to read me my rights?'

'What rights would they be then, Miss Allendon?' I felt a little quiver of fear then, right down in the pit of my stomach.

'Don't I get some kind of lawyer?'

'Not unless you're Lady Allendon and I've made some kind of mistake, which, I assure you, I don't do very often.' He flashed his teeth in what he seemed to think was a smile – he had gold caps on all his back teeth which isn't what I expected. He wasn't that old – perhaps the same age my father would have been if he'd lived.

'Now perhaps you can tell me who you work for?' I could do that one.

'Mrs Lansdowne of Soho Square,' I answered.

'Yes. Very good. You ought to know that we have footage of you leaving the scene of an IBI bombing. You have clearly been very active in undermining authority. Who is the leader of your terrorist cell?'

'I'm not in a terrorist cell, unless you count this room,' I said, probably more boldly than was wise. Commander Doyle nodded at one of the officers, who then marched round to my side of the table and hit me with the flat of his meaty palm. My mouth suddenly filled with blood and I felt my head snap backwards with the force of the blow. The force knocked me sideways off my chair and only the cuff stopped me from falling on the floor. My whole face stung. Oh, God! This was it. They were going to beat me up and then kill me.

'Now, Miss Allendon,' the Commander continued amiably, 'Officer Rendall here hit you with the flat of his hand without even trying, trust me when I say he can pull you apart, cute little limb from limb – like snapping a chicken carcass. You won't look so pretty then and I'm sure Mr Roberts will be a good deal less interested in you.' He did that thing with his face again that was supposed to be a smile, but he looked a little blurry through all the water that was in my eyes: they were not tears. It was simply the force of the blow that had brought them to my eyes. I thought that Miss Shadrake tensed perceptibly as Johnny's name was mentioned.

I felt experimentally inside my mouth with my tongue to check that Rendall had not dislodged a tooth.

'Let's take the handcuffs off, shall we? That way Rendall can throw you against our nice hard walls.' Rendall leaned forward and undid my handcuff and then returned to his previous position. Even after such a short time in cuffs my wrist was chafed and sore.

'Now where were we?'

'Miss Allendon was just leaving,' said a cool female voice and everyone turned in surprise to look at Miss Shadrake, who was holding her pen as if it were a gun.

'This is a detonator,' she said, 'a new Nip model. Once it has been set, as it has been, it will cause the tape recorder to explode, taking you, me and the station with it, unless I keep my finger on this button. You could probably overpower me, but it probably isn't a risk you're going to take. What you're going to do is handcuff Rendall to Christian, if you wouldn't mind, Commander.' Her voice was almost conversational, but authoritative. 'Miss Allendon, it would help if you came to stand here next to me. Don't bang the table if you can avoid it, the explosives are not that stable.' She was very calm. The Commander seemed to consider knocking her over and then thought better of it. Rather to my surprise he did as he was told. The two large officers permitted themselves to be handcuffed together without resistance. I skirted the table to stand by her side. When I was closer to her I could see that, in spite of her apparent self-possession her knees were trembling – they were almost literally knocking, but she kept the pen detonator and her voice steady. She was amazing.

'Now Commander, we three are going to walk out of the building. You are going to have to come up with some excuse – but remember this will detonate the moment I take the pressure off.'

'You wouldn't dare . . .' the Commander began, but whatever he saw in Miss Shadrake's eyes apparently caused him to reconsider.

'Oh, I think you know I would, sir,' she said. I believed her. I didn't know why she was helping me, but I believed her.

The Commander opened the door and was about to take me by the arm, but Miss Shadrake intervened. 'Don't touch her. Just walk.'

She took my arm, a gentle pressure just above my elbow – a guiding hand and maybe something more, something for her to hold on to. Her hands were damp with sweat. I didn't speak. I didn't want to distract her and at least if I kept my mouth shut I couldn't arouse suspicion.

The Commander led us out of the building. Several officers saluted him but none questioned him. For a high-security police station they were pretty lax. When we got outside he said, 'Now what?' His face was red and shiny with sweat.

'We are going to walk away down this street. If you raise the alarm while we are still in view, I blow the whole place up.'

'What is to stop you blowing the whole place up anyway, now that you're no longer in it?'

'My honour and my humanity,' she said with a taut smile.

Still holding my arm we walked away. After twenty paces, she whispered, 'For God's sake run!' and we did, faster than I thought I had the strength for.

I had no idea where we were going; I hoped she knew. Passers-by got out of the way and stared at the unusual sight of two women running for their lives. I had heels on, but I would have run in skis to get away from the station. She pulled me into a side street and bundled me into the back alley of some shops. She was bent double and gasping for breath.

'I just need a second,' she said. 'Oh, God, oh, God,' she rasped, 'I never thought I'd get away with that.'

'Who are you?' I panted. I felt dizzy, my lungs felt like they'd been seared and I had a stitch in my side. 'Thank you.'

'I'm Miranda Weiss, of the IBI. Pleased I could help.' She held her hand out for me to shake it. She was still breathless and her blonde hair had fallen out of its fastening and was getting into her eyes. 'Sorry there isn't time to talk – we have to get away from here. Follow me!' After what she'd just done for me, I'd have followed her anywhere. I did not see what she had done with the detonator.

# THIRTY-FIVE

She knocked on the back door of what I presumed was a shop. It was a dark green wooden door, which, in spite of its peeling paint, looked solid enough to me. There were no handles on the outside, just a brass-mounted spyhole. There was a pause and then the door swung open and my saviour said something – it sounded like 'Lighten my darkness, for God's sake!' – and then pulled me by the hand up a steep stairway. There was a lot of shouting and banging downstairs, which Miranda ignored. At the top of the stairs there was a series of doors. A stepladder lay propped up against the wall. She opened it and, breathing heavily, climbed up it, then, pressing hard on the ceiling, pushed open an attic entrance that had been almost invisible beforehand. 'Come on,' she said and, taking my hand again, pulled me into the darkness above.

There was a light, though it took her a moment to find it. She kicked the ladder over and pulled up the door. 'We haven't got much time. Are you all right?'

'Yes. I don't know how to thank you.'

In the dim light she smiled. 'I wouldn't have done

anything if it hadn't got so ugly. It was a bit more dramatic than I'd planned.'

'What about the detonator?'

'Oh, this?' She pulled what looked like a stainless steel ballpoint pen from her pocket. 'I am really astonished that they fell for that.'

'It was a bluff?' I felt giddy at the thought of the nerve of it. Miranda laughed.

'Oh, in my business we consider trying to build such weapons from time to time. It probably wouldn't be that hard, but you'd have to be genuinely prepared to kill a lot of people. I prefer the threat over the actuality.' She paused. 'Yes, it was a bluff. I thought they were going to hurt you.'

'They could have shot you.'

She thought for a moment, 'Yes, I suppose they could have, but I didn't think they would and I was right. The good thing is they'll be horribly distracted for a while making safe the non-existent bomb. I should have thought of that one before.'

I wanted to hug her, but we'd only just been introduced and Jessica's London wasn't the sort of place where people did that.

'Come on – we have to keep moving. Keep to the joists – they're the thick pieces of wood that hold the roof up. Don't stand on any boards – they're all rotten and the shop people below won't take kindly to you falling through the ceiling.' I followed her as she crouched forwards, agile as some kind of circus performer, balancing on the beams. Normally I would have been terrified, but Miranda did not give me time. The attic seemed to link a long street of buildings. As we moved away from our starting point, the only light came from chinks in the roof construction. I did not dare think about what I was doing. I just followed Miranda's dark form and concentrated on keeping up.

Eventually she stopped when we came to a boarded loft space and found a light. 'These boards are safe,' she said. I sat down on them with relief. Miranda was still busy though. There was a chest in the eaves which she opened and I suppose there must have been a phone in there or something because I heard her say, 'I've got her. She's safe, but I'll never work at Paddington Green again. You owe me three or four deadly, life-threatening jobs in return.' Then she laughed as if, now that it was over, it had all been a huge joke.

I had never met anyone like her.

A short while later there were five taps on what I supposed was the hatch door, a pause, then three taps, a pause and then another one. Miranda pulled open the hatch door in the floor and Johnny's head appeared.

He nodded towards Miranda and then ran towards me and hugged me, enveloping me in his arms. 'Jess! Thank God you're safe. I thought they might have killed you.'

I didn't know which 'they' he meant as there were

quite a few candidates. I also found that my heart was pounding and not just from the danger of my escape. Johnny had his arms around me: I was overwhelmed.

'Miss Weiss was amazing,' I said shakily. 'She pretended there was a bomb and . . .' My voice petered out. 'I was scared. I don't think I would have survived if Miranda hadn't rescued me.' The rest came out as a whisper. Johnny did not take his arms away.

'I'm sorry I wasn't there when you came back from Dunraven.'

'Johnny had to leave Soho Square in a bit of a hurry before you got back from Dunraven. Long story. I'd left a note for you at his mother's house. Huw was supposed to drive you to a safe house, but that all went awry when Mrs Lansdowne got her husband and the Security Services involved. I'm afraid that caught us napping. We should have guessed she wouldn't have kept something that big from him. Anyway we lost you until James rang in an emergency report, but we always knew that the minute you left Soho Square the Security Services would get you and you would end up at Paddington Green. I have worked there intermittently for a few years, helping our people in small ways and debriefing them when there was nothing that could be done, so it was easy enough to arrange for the regular secretary to be – erm, indisposed and to take her place.'

'But you won't be able to do that again?'

'No.' Miranda smiled. 'But no cover lasts for ever. Johnny was already compromised – his time at Soho Square was almost over even before you got there.'

'Why are you helping me?' I said at last. Johnny's closeness made it difficult for me to think. I had sunk into the circle of his arms almost without meaning to. I wanted to trust him, I wanted to feel safe with him but I was still unsure, or at least my head was. The rest of me was treacherous to the last – however much I doubted Johnny, my body relaxed into his embrace.

'How many people from other worlds do you think there are around here?' Miranda asked, and for a second I thought it was a real question – there could have been others – and then I understood what she meant.

'I talked to the people at Dunraven,' I said, anxious in case that was the wrong thing to do.

'We know,' Miranda said calmly. 'Huw is one of ours – he recorded the interview. You see we do have some gadgets – it's not all bluff and bravado. Johnny thought Huw would take care of you – but Huw is our under-cover boffin, not a real action man. He wasn't quick enough. He's going to be very glad you're safe despite his incompetence.'

'What happens now?'

'We have to stop Mrs Lansdowne and the Professor from killing you – they think you're going to destroy our universe. We have to stop the Security Services capturing you, torturing you and killing you – they think your knowledge and other-worldly experience could destroy our civilisation – and we have to find a way of getting you back in touch with our Jessica and getting you home.' She smiled as she said it and instead of making me feel hopeless, because it was such a tall order, I felt flooded with sudden optimism. If Miranda was helping me, maybe it wasn't impossible. Actually, if I'm honest it wasn't just Miranda – I think Johnny's arms around me made a difference too. 'I'm going to make some calls now. Perhaps you can tell Johnny exactly what happened as it will be useful to us.'

Miranda turned her back to do something and Johnny didn't move. His expression was as unreadable as ever. The light was poor, which was no bad thing because I think I was blushing. I told him about the Professor and the note from the nurse and Anna's house. He pulled a face when I said how the Security Services had been watching it for a while, though he smiled when I told him that it was James who had been searching for incriminating information in the house.

'We knew that while Mr Lansdowne trusted me, I had a measure of protection – and there was no hard evidence against me.'

'I wouldn't have thought that would worry them much.'

'It's about influence, Jess, about money and power and

some people being worth more than others. While I was under Mr L's protection, I was somebody to respect. That's why I'm in the Brotherhood – to fight all that so that everyone matters, not just the rich white men.' He sounded passionate – fired up as I hadn't heard him before. 'Jessica Allendon is nobody – she's an orphan without connections, apart from me, which hardly counts. She's not an aristocrat, nor the daughter of an industrialist. She owns no property, is female and under thirty. She has no vote. She has no union contacts, no sugar daddy, no voice and no one who will fight for her but me and "the General" – that's what we call Miranda. We're trying to fight for all the Jessicas, by getting all adults a vote, by changing the way government works so the people can choose their own leaders, so that everyone has a voice.'

'So what is the Brotherhood?'

'The IBI – the International Brotherhood for Independence – but we're allied with a lot of other organisations too. Miranda is in charge of the UK organisation and I've been one of her officers – since Dad died.'

'But you'll have to give it up now.'

'It was getting too risky anyway. Before James was sacked we arranged for him to frame me so that the Security Services would trust him, in spite of the various rumours flying around about his background. My cover was nearly blown anyway. That's why he gave me that package to take to Sheen.'

I didn't ask him why he hadn't told me – he didn't tell anyone anything unless he had to. 'So you and James were both – what? Double agents?' It seemed like something from a not very convincing spy film.

'Yes, I was always working for Miranda and trying to find out as much about Mr Lansdowne's department as I could from the inside. My dad being a hero in the army helped. Mr Lansdowne is very pro military. Mrs Lansdowne is on a side of her own. I know that I should have expected her to involve the Security Services at Dunraven. I'm really sorry I underestimated her conservatism. I think she must have panicked when she realised the Professor's experiment had brought more than just unspeakable pornography into her house. I suppose that was something too big to keep from her husband.'

I thought about that, my brain whirring, trying to fit everything together. There were still things about my time in Jessica's world that I just couldn't understand. 'Why did we get attacked that day, by the WLUE building?'

'The men were guarding the IBI, they thought I worked for Mr Lansdowne and although one of them knew I was the General's man – I had to act as though I was Lansdowne's.' I thought I got it – but I still didn't ask him about the bombings – I didn't want to know if he were truly a terrorist.

He asked me about my capture and interrogation.

Even in the dim light I saw the muscles of his jaw tense when I told him about how they'd hit me – so I quickly moved on to Miranda's bluff. He was impressed – how could anyone not be? But the anger was still there. I could feel it, in the way he held me – in the tension of his muscles and in the darkness in his eyes. Johnny was dangerous all right – I was just glad he was on my side.

THIRTY-SIX

I found it surprising that Johnny continued to hold me while Miranda explained the next stage of our escape. I'm not saying I didn't like it. It just wasn't what I'd expected a man like Johnny to do in Jessica's London. I couldn't move away – I liked the heavy pressure of his arm and his closeness. It made me want to be alone with him and it also made it hard for me to concentrate on what Miranda was saying. The basic point was that we had to get out of there – move to a safe house if necessary until we could make contact with Jessica.

'But she wasn't on the Root.'

'No, because the Professor's machine was not activated when you looked. You two Jessica Allendons meeting on the Root and in real life on the only two occasions the machine was activated was a miracle or a massive cosmic accident – depending on your point of view. The breach between worlds has to be effected for our Root to connect with your world. According to Huw, the Professor did not expect the Root to mesh with your – what did you call it? internet? He didn't expect any other world to have attained our degree of sophistication. He was looking for radio broadcasts – that kind of thing. When he found your internet – well, that raised a number of issues. What was seen of your world,' Miranda pulled a face, 'well, it was rather unsavoury. Mrs Lansdowne was horrified. She wished to shut the programme down immediately but the Professor wanted to try it one more time to see if he could find another world which might be more suitable for their purposes.

I thought about what she said for a moment. 'So how come we physically swapped places at Waterloo?'

'Waterloo seems to be a weak spot in the fabric of this world – or some such thing. It may be that Jessica overheard Mrs Lansdowne talking to the Professor about the possibility of using the machine again at 5.00 p.m. that Sunday. Huw thinks the Professor told her that the breach between universes would be centred on Waterloo and that Jessica must have overheard – otherwise it was an extraordinary coincidence that Jessica met you there at that time. I think she had to have overheard the conversation and misunderstood it, believing it had something to do with the IBI. As we know, she was desperate to find a pack and, poor innocent, blundered into this whole business.'

Miranda paused for breath and to rub her eyes. I thought that she seemed suddenly very weary. The last few hours must have been stressful even for someone like her. She carried on with her explanation: 'The experiment was deemed a scientific success but a practical failure – your world a hell to be avoided. The Professor closed the breach by dismantling the equipment. He never intended anything other than the free flow of information between worlds in the first instance. I don't know what Mrs Lansdowne hoped to get from it. Anyway, the thing is the Professor believes your physical existence here risks the stability of our world. Huw, who is brighter than he looks and a far better physicist than he is bodyguard – thank the Lord – also wants you out of here, back home and our Jessica back here, and then he'll destroy the equipment that created this "accidental breach". It's a kind of a hole which allows an exchange of matter between universes. It was all a bit beyond me to be honest, but the gist is there is a risk that you may accidentally destroy the known universe the longer you remain here. Dead or alive you're not of our universe, so killing you doesn't actually solve anything – we have to get you home.' I was glad to hear it, and I knew that behind her flippant delivery Miranda was as worried as a person like her gets. I knew too that she would have killed me without batting a long, attractively curled eyelash, if it was what she believed was right. She spoke lightly, but her body language did not match her tone of voice.

I suddenly understood why she'd taken the risk she had to get me out of Paddington Green Station. Perhaps

I really was worth blowing her cover for. I began to wish, not for the first time, that I hadn't googled my name, that I hadn't tried to meet my namesake. It didn't seem fair that the whole universe could be at risk because Jessica Allendon was nosy, egotistical and stupid. I think I said something to that effect but Johnny squeezed my hand and said that I wasn't the one messing with the laws of nature and trying to build a breach between worlds out of nosiness, egotism and stupidity. I think that perhaps he had a point.

Miranda was pacing around the loft space like some kind of caged beast – a lioness maybe – disguised as a rather cute fluffy kitten.

'I think maybe we should take Jessica to the women's hospital – with the nuns.'

'On Soho Square?' Johnny asked, incredulous.

'I'd hide her inside thirty-six, if I could get away with it – under people's noses is often the best place to hide.'

I remembered the women's hospital, but had seen no nuns there, only young girls in nurse's uniform. I thought for a moment. 'Would I have to be separated from you and Johnny?'

Miranda nodded. 'Then I don't want to go.' I think I might have sounded a little more overwrought than I'd wanted to. Miranda looked at me thoughtfully.

'All right, that's fair enough. We'll all go to Harry's together.'

'Is that a good idea?' Johnny asked.

'No, it's a terrible idea, very risky, quite insanitary, but if you can think of anything better I'd like to hear about it.' Johnny shook his head.

'I suppose it would be better to have Jessica close so that as soon as we've made the connection on the Root, we can arrange a meeting with the other Jessica,' he said. Miranda seemed to have already come to that conclusion and was moving on.

'We'll need some boys' clothes for us and something unremarkable for you – no large hats and grand collars. I think something to eat would be good too. Can you organise it, Johnny?'

He unwound his arm from my shoulders, leaving me suddenly cold and bereft. The look he gave me made my heart do something strange. 'I won't be long. You'll be safe with the General,' he said and I smiled – more because I wanted to be nice than because I believed him. The General could not stop me from accidentally destroying the universe and she knew it.

'Who or what is Harry's?' I asked, when Johnny had gone.

'Harry is Huw's twin brother. He's a recluse and lives in a cellar below a brothel in King's Cross. The owner sits in the House of Lords and so it's rarely raided: it's much safer than you'd imagine. Harry doesn't wash much though so it's not very fragrant. He's connected to the

Root via an unlicensed computer. He and Huw between them will get you home, if it's possible. If it's not possible, then God help us all. This puts even universal adult suffrage into perspective.' She pulled a face.

'I'm so sorry – I've caused all this.'

'You didn't – you got caught up in something, that's all. It happens!'

I suddenly had a terrible thought. 'My stuff – I brought some stuff with me, clothes and my phone – they came from another universe too . . .'

'Don't worry – your knight in shining armour got them.' I think I looked blank. 'Johnny went to your room as soon as the alarm was raised. He brought everything he thought might be yours to me. I'm sorry, I read your diary.'

I felt myself colour. 'Did Johnny?'

She shrugged. 'I don't know – maybe. You'll have to ask him. I wanted to be sure, you see, that I believed you.'

'Do you?'

'Oh yes, but mainly because of the way you spoke to the Commander as much as anything else. You're not from here – that's clear.'

'Do you really think I'm a danger to everything?' I asked.

She sighed. 'Well to me it would have made some kind of sense if the two universes had been destroyed the moment there was some kind of exchange. If it was going to happen, surely it would have happened by now? But I freely admit that science is not my thing, and Harry and Huw are real boffins – Nobel Prize kind of boffins – the very best kind. I don't know, Miss Allendon, but in my world you take responsibility for problems you see. I have been made to see this one and so it's my problem.' She smiled again as if her face had a kind of physiological need to smile at regular intervals. 'But you are not the problem, dear Miss Allendon – you're a very plucky young woman and one I'd be proud to have in the organisation if things were different.'

I was well pleased with that, I can tell you, coming from her. I knew how scared I'd been all the time since I'd arrived at Waterloo and, although I could wish that I'd not burst into tears quite so often, I wasn't ashamed of too much that I'd done. There were lots of things I wanted to ask her, but she sat down on the boards and leaned back against the bare brick wall, then shut her eyes and in a moment she was snoring.

I'd never seen anyone fall asleep just like that. I suspected that Miranda had missed a lot of sleep one way or another and knew how to take advantage of any small bit of down time. I couldn't sleep for thinking about Johnny and how it had felt to be close to him and how he seemed to really care for me. Maybe I managed a light doze, I don't know, because it didn't seem very long before I heard that distinctive knocking on the door again and Johnny was back. Miranda was instantly awake and alert. Johnny said something in Welsh, which seemed to be the language of the Brotherhood and its allies, and then she let him in. He'd brought not sandwiches as I'd half expected, but a large pot of some kind of broth as well as bowls, spoons and napkins.

'He has his airs and graces,' said Miranda with another of her smiles, 'but Johnny can always be relied on to find some good comestibles.' It felt like a thousand years since my last meal. There was bread too, as well as stew, and tea in a flask, all of which he pulled out from his army-type rucksack like a magician pulling a rabbit from a hat.

When we'd finished, he produced clothes from the bottom of his bag – which had something of a Mary Poppins quality to it, as it didn't look big enough to hold all that he'd managed to stuff in it. He left to get rid of the plates, while Miranda and I changed into the boys' clothes he'd brought us. They didn't seem strange to me at all – trousers, flat shoes, a shirt and jacket – stuff that I could imagine wearing at home had they been a slightly different cut. I'm not a voluptuous type and I'd lost weight, so that what meagre curves I'd had were gone. While I'm on the small side at home, here my size and slight build seemed normal. Many of the men I'd seen on the street were of a similar height. It was probably something to do with diet, though Johnny seemed if anything bigger than Jonno. Whatever, I felt that I could make a convincing boy. I would have cut my hair but Miranda looked horrified.

'Oh dear, no – quite unnecessary – you'll be fine as you are. Just put a smudge of dirt on your upper lip and a bit on your chin and you'll be wonderful.'

Miranda was more womanly-looking than me, but even she seemed convincing enough in her male work clothes. 'People don't expect to see women in trousers and they rarely see what they don't expect, even when it's right in front of them. I gather you're quite used to walking in flat shoes.' I nodded – the ones Johnny had got for me were a bit big but blissfully comfortable compared to Jessica's ladylike heels.

'All right, don't talk, don't look up, keep your hands in your pockets and if absolutely necessary grunt. You're perfect!' she laughed, as if we were going on a picnic. I wondered if she did that more when she was afraid. 'Come on, let's go,' she said and led the way down through the attic hatch.

THIRTY-SEVEN

I was lost and nervous and I wanted to take Johnny's arm and remembered only just in time that I was supposed to be a boy. I had a strong feeling that kind of thing would not go down well in Jessica's London. I kept my head down and kept walking. We avoided the smarter streets and walked through the poorer areas. I felt that it was only Johnny's bulk and air of menace that kept us safe. There were a lot of pawn shops and workhouses and narrow stinking streets, and a lot of kids without shoes. We didn't stop and I didn't look round much, but I knew that while there was poverty at home it was of a different order here and I wondered if Miranda had brought me this way on purpose so that maybe I would understand what Johnny had been talking about – on the other hand it might have been the safest route to our destination. The streets got seedier and seedier and that smell was everywhere – the Soho smell – I think it must have been opium.

At last we came to a rundown series of large houses all with broken panes and boarded windows. Rubbish over-flowed in the street and even in the coolness of evening the stench of rotting food and horses was overpowering. A few horses – in terrible condition, their bones showing through their dusty coats – were tethered against a wrought-iron railing. We passed a couple of young girls hanging round outside one of the houses – they looked about fourteen and called out something to me that I didn't understand. By Johnny's reaction I guessed it was slang and probably obscene – I kept forgetting I was supposed to be a boy.

Miranda walked over to the girls and put a hand on each of their shoulders. She said something to them and they scuttled away in apparent terror.

Johnny stationed himself in the street and I followed Miranda down the slime-covered steps which led to the basement door of the house. There was some kind of leak from a pipe so that the stairs were slick and wet and in the fading light I clung cautiously to the rickety iron rail for fear of falling. Miranda gave me a stern look and I realised that was rather a girly thing to do. She marched down the stairs as if the thought of falling never entered her head, but then she was in charge of a large revolutionary group and I wasn't.

I definitely saw the long naked tail of a rat disappear up and over the wall as we got to the bottom of the stairs. Here the predominant stink was of urine and stagnant water. There was a pool of something nasty at the foot of the stairs. I tried not to shudder – sometimes I really do need to get over myself. There was a door into the basement – it was so covered in graffiti and torn posters that I couldn't see even see what colour it was. There was one narrow bay window with a rotting sill, which was boarded and covered in a rusting iron lattice-work grille. It looked like the kind of place you ran from not to.

Miranda hammered on the door, which sounded as if it was made of metal. I think there may have been some rhythm to the knock – like it was secret code. Underneath the overgrowth of Russian vine and ivy that hung over the entrance I'm sure I saw a glint of light on glass or on a camera lens.

The door creaked open and I saw that it was about fifteen centimetres thick and made of steel. I didn't see who opened the door, but followed Miranda into the stark corridor, and into the overwhelming fug of pipe smoke and the stench of old curry and stale beer. I couldn't stop coughing. Nice. Johnny followed us inside a moment later.

The narrow corridor opened into a room that looked like a *Doctor Who* set – full of screens and thick spaghetti loops of different coloured wires. Most of the light came from the screens and the orange glow of a noxious-smelling gas fire. It was hard to breathe.

A tall, thin man with thick, jam-jar bottom glasses disentangled himself from his work station and loomed above me. He must have been at least six foot six and way skinnier than any man I'd ever seen – this was Harry. I don't know what I'd been expecting exactly but not this – Huw, his twin, was shorter than me. Apparently he didn't speak much English or if he did he refused to speak anything but Welsh so, after wishing me good day in English, he proceeded to talk very rapidly to Miranda and Johnny.

There was nowhere obvious to sit and the floor was concrete, painted in a dark red and a bit sticky looking – so I stood there like a spare part for a bit. It was too hot in the low-ceilinged room, the computers and their associated bits and pieces were noisy – I was finding breathing difficult. Every wall was full of electronic gear and I didn't dare lean against anything. When I started to sway, Johnny grabbed me and got me a seat – something rickety with a broken back, but better than nothing.

'I'm sorry,' I said. 'It's so hot in here.'

'It's all right. I'm sorry we ignored you, but there was a lot to catch up on. Huw has gone back to Wales and will try and rebuild the machine as soon as possible. He's hoping to get the first stage under way by early tomorrow so with any luck we'll make contact with Jessica then. One of our men has gone to kidnap the Professor to get him out of the way. Without him there will be no more project.' I didn't know what to say to that. I was feeling overwhelmed again.

'It will be all right, Jessica. With the General on the case your chances are good. There's no one like her.'

'I know, she's amazing,' I said.

'Jess – I want you to know – I read your diary, partly because it was my job and partly because I wanted to know . . .' He looked embarrassed. 'I want you to know that there wasn't anything between the other Jessica and me and I never wanted there to be. I felt differently when you came. I felt . . . well, I knew something was different and that confused me. I want you to know that when she gets back I'll look after her, but she is very different from you and it won't be the same.'

'And what if you don't get her back? What if it's still me, what then?' I don't know why I asked him – we weren't alone – Miranda was still talking with Harry not three metres away. I didn't think she was listening though – her mind was on the serious business of saving the universe and I have to admit that at that moment mine wasn't. When Johnny stood close to me, I couldn't think of anything else.

'You know that's different, Jess, but you shouldn't be here.' I could feel the sweat trickling down my shirt, my hair clung to my face – he gently pushed it away.

'There's nothing to be done. You have to go, I have to stay.' I nodded – tearful again.

Of course I wanted to go home – I was desperate to get

home to my mum, to my friends and to Jonno, but there was something about Johnny, something that I hadn't felt before. I caught his hand as he moved to wipe away my hair.

'Don't!' I said. 'I can't bear you to touch me. I . . .' He nodded and didn't take offence.

'I know,' he said, 'but we don't have much time.'

'You're so sure it will work?' I asked, trying to steer us to safer ground. I wanted to be alone with Johnny and I was scared of how he made me feel. I didn't feel in charge of myself any more. He could ask me to do anything – anything at all and I'd have done it. I think he knew that and he let me change the subject. Maybe he was scared too. I still had my hand on his arm even though I'd asked him not to touch me. I couldn't let that contact go.

'Our under-cover Huw is a genius – like the General said. The Professor has no idea of what his sandy-haired henchman can do. I think he'll get you home, Jess. I thought that's what you wanted.' I nodded – I couldn't meet his eyes. I couldn't look at him at all. Of course going home was what I wanted. Oh, God! What kind of girl falls properly in love for the first time with a man from another universe?

THIRTY-EIGHT

It was a good thing that Miranda stopped her lengthy talk with Harry and started to issue orders, in the nicest possible way of course, mobilising her ubiquitous smile to deflect any resentment. The basement had a second room where Harry slept – Johnny and I were to do what we could to make enough space for us all to sleep there and to rig up a screen separating the 'ladies' from the 'gentlemen'. However radical Miranda's politics were, she was a woman of her world and would not even consider sharing a room with men if it was avoidable.

The bedroom was every bit as bad as you would expect it to be and then some. If my mum had been there, she'd have scooped everything up and binned or burnt it, but we did not have that option. Johnny and I looked at each other dubiously. In my real life I'm not neat, but Jessica's neurotic tidiness had got to me and I was appalled by the state of Harry's room. Dirty underwear lay everywhere and his bedding – his foul, filthy sheets – lay in a tangle half on and off the bed. There were a lot of half-empty cups of tea lying around, biscuit crumbs, pipe ash, mouse droppings and a number of cups that were apparently empty but were host to some amazing fungal growths. The filthy carpet was of an indeterminate browny-green but was more or less hidden under the detritus. There was only one mattress and no clean bedding. I don't think either of us wanted to stay there. There was an outhouse with a sink and WC – I think a rat lived there, or so Johnny said anyway, when he went to check it out. I don't think he was winding me up. There was also a tiny kitchen which had hot water and to my surprise some kind of washing-up liquid.

After we'd washed up the mugs and the other stuff in the sink and then cleaned the kitchen, I washed the sheets in the sink. Johnny found a washing line and somehow rigged it up in the bedroom and then we wrung out the sheets. I hadn't done that since I was a little kid – our washing machine had a spin dryer and the only things I ever hand washed were jumpers of 'the dry flat and don't even think about wringing or we'll never give you your money back when it falls apart' variety. It was fun, or at least it was fun with Johnny. We each took an end of the sheet and he twisted his end one way and I twisted mine the other until the sheet twisted up and brought us together. We soaked ourselves and much of the floor in the process. There wasn't much room in the kitchen and . . . oh well – it's hard to explain – you probably had to be there. It was funny and it was good to laugh. After a bit, we hung the sheets on the makeshift line so that they acted like a rather damp room divider. There was a dustpan and brush with a few bristles so I attempted to clean the floor while Johnny picked up the rank underwear and stowed it in the paper bag he'd used to keep our shoes from dirtying our good clothes: I felt better once it was out of the room. The mattress was on an iron bedstead – the kind with springs – between us we managed to turn it, but even doing that made us laugh as I couldn't get the right kind of grip on it and nearly fell over, both sides were horribly stained: I did not want to sleep there. By the time the light faded, the room was clean-ish and Johnny and I were still laughing at nothing very much. I know it was stupid, but it was really good to see Johnny relax. His laugh was like Jonno's but different and though he laughed at exactly the same things it wasn't at all like being with Jonno. I think I was quite close to hysteria.

The General had obviously been doing some arranging in between trying save the universe. At some point during our attempt at cleaning up, three camp beds arrived along with sleeping sacks – sort of sheets sewn together to make a kind of sleeping bag – a few clean blankets and pillows arrived too. The General insisted we all had a hot drink and some toast before going to bed – because 'you never know,' she said enigmatically. I suppose she meant that when you are in constant danger you eat, drink and rest when you get the chance – that's what I took it to mean anyway.

Locking up was a bit of a performance – they had bolts on everything and a number of alarms which Harry set with enormous care. Johnny kept guard while I used the outhouse – I wouldn't have gone otherwise, I'm really afraid of rats. I regretted losing my bag with Jessica's toothbrush in it, but managed a quick wash in the sink. I know it's stupid of me, but I don't like being dirty.

Miranda and I took the half of the room which did not contain the sordid bed. I chose the bed nearest the divide and so did Johnny, as Harry obviously slept in his own bed – he was so tall I couldn't imagine it was very comfortable. Miranda's gentle snoring and Harry's smoker's wheeze might have been loud enough to keep me awake were I in any danger of falling asleep, which I wasn't. I was too aware of Johnny lying just the other side of the thin sheet, his presence made it impossible to sleep. I could hear his breathing, his every movement as the camp bed creaked under his turning weight: he was very restless too.

I lay awake thinking about home and about this man that I would never see again, if all went according to plan. The still-damp barrier between us trembled briefly and Johnny's strong hand found mine in the darkness. I gripped it tightly, interlocking my fingers with his. It was something – less than we wanted, but something, a touch, a bond, a communication. It was impossible to do more: Miranda woke at the slightest noise and every time her snoring stopped I was afraid she'd wake up and somehow stop us from holding hands. I don't know whether she would have or not, but I was very reluctant to find out. We both slept as close to the sheet as we possibly could – insofar as we slept at all. We dared not speak and barely dared move, but I knew he was awake and was aware of me as I was awake and aware of him. It wasn't restful, not by any measure, but it was – I don't know, somehow important and meaningful – a kind of a vigil in the soft darkness, a secret, silent, seal of our connection.

I was startled to rather sweaty full wakefulness by the sound of an alarm. I think I had dozed off, my hand curled within the curve of Johnny's palm. Miranda was up in an instant, clambering into her dress and running into the main room. Johnny squeezed my hand in a gesture that seemed to my overwrought senses to be part reassurance and part promise – he only squeezed my hand for God's sake! – and then leapt from his camp bed and was not far behind Miranda, pulling on his shirt as he went. I could not see much in the darkness but I felt around, found my own clothes and followed after them.

'What is it?' I asked blearily. I doubt I'd had above an hour's sleep all night.

'I think that buzzer means that we have access to your internet,' Johnny said encouragingly.

'Well, as it happens that's true,' Miranda said, bending over the mass of keyboards and screens. 'But that particular alarm was to let us know that our security has been breached. Someone was here and tried to get in.'

'Drunks? Thieves?' Johnny asked. In the light of the screens he was little more than a dark, powerful silhouette – but I saw that he had a gun in his hand. There was a kind of holster under his arm – I could see its shadowy form under his open shirt.

Miranda got to work trying to replay images from the CCTV camera above the entrance. It was obviously not a very simple process; I saw her scowling in the reflected blue light of the screen. She was pinched and pale with weariness. 'There, got it!' she said, tapping away. 'It looks like it's the Security Services.'

I felt the cold chill of fear. Johnny stood behind me and put a hand on my shoulder and I held it gratefully.

'What do we do now?' I said, my voice sounding small and feeble much to my disgust.

'We contact our Jessica Allendon and get you out, of course,' Miranda said tersely. 'I'm not so worried about the kit. We can rebuild all this again – though it takes money and time. The main thing is to get personnel away. Johnny, wake up Harry – he has to be moved to another safe house. You have to go now – both of you.

We can't afford to have him captured. I can handle what we need to get Jessica out of here – you don't mind if I call you Jessica, do you, Miss Allendon?' Her sudden polite question took me by surprise. Her mind was already leaping ahead, planning, deciding in all that I was amazed she remembered such trivia as the correct form of my name. I shook my head. Johnny was already in the other room, I could hear him trying to rouse Harry, who had slept through both the alarm and our panic. Miranda was typing and fiddling with knobs and buttons on the complex system Harry had installed. Harry objected when he saw her messing with his equipment, but she spoke to him in rapid Welsh and he shrugged.

'All right, this is what is going to happen. Johnny, you see Harry safely to Mad Marcus's in Hampstead. I've sent a few messages on the Root, which ought to distract Security for an hour or so to give you a clear run. Jessica and I will make contact with our Miss Allendon and arrange a time to meet – I'd like it to be in the next twenty-four hours. I have the codes to destroy anything that could be useful here, which I'll do before leaving and then Jessica and I will head for Karim's. Johnny, you collect Jessica's stuff from my safe and then we'll meet at Karim's to go to Waterloo for the meeting. The ideal time would be early evening so Jessica can wear her unsuitable clothes without drawing too much attention to herself.' She pulled a face. 'Ugly, ugly clothes, Jessica – whatever were you thinking of when you chose those?' She smiled her all-purpose smile again. 'Got it?' she asked and Johnny nodded, as did Harry who appeared to have no trouble following her clipped, quick-fire English.

Harry shook my hand and mumbled something that sounded like 'Good luck and God speed.' Johnny just hugged me.

'I'll see you,' he said. There was a radio somewhere in the room and Miranda turned it on. Johnny and Harry both paused to listen before leaving. I didn't listen at first. I was trying to deal with the mixture of emotions Miranda's quick briefing had engendered and then I heard Miranda chuckle. I started listening then and just managed to make sense of the end of a news report about a vital terrorist arms cache that the Security Services had just discovered in Bermondsey. There had been a tip-off apparently and there would be some disruption to London that day due to operations under way as a result of information received.

Johnny looked horrified. 'You told them about the arms?' He was incredulous. Miranda grinned again, this time rather savagely.

'A sprat to catch a mackerel or more accurately the sacrifice of a sprat to save a mackerel. I'd rather loose a few guns than what we've got here. Move it, Johnny – I haven't bought us long and what little time I *have* bought us has cost us very dearly, so be sure to use it well.' She was ruthless – I could see that – constantly calculating costs and benefits. She didn't look up as the two men left. She was busy again totally focused on the equipment – dealing with the next issue. She was relentless – a woman at war.

'All right, Jessica,' she said, without taking her eyes off the screen, 'let's "google"!'

THIRTY-NINE

I sat down in the chair that Miranda had just vacated – Harry's chair, which was so high my feet didn't touch the ground. I typed my name into the Root and immediately saw several references to Jessica Allendon – there were pages of them; we were through.

'Can I just email her?' I asked and Miranda's fingers flew over the keys.

'Yes, of course, there, type in Jessica's address – make it brief. I don't know how long we'll have the connection for.'

The layout of the email was not quite as it would have been at home but I typed in my home email address and wrote: 'Hi, meet again. 17.00 same place? Hope you're OK. Complications here – talk to Johnny Roberts. Jess.'

It seemed very inadequate – there was so much we could have talked about. I wanted to ask about Mum and Jonno and I wanted to say sorry for screwing up her life and making it impossible for her to return to her job. What was she going to do now that I'd wrecked every-thing for her? I don't know if Miranda understood any of that, but she smiled at me encouragingly. I wanted to cry.

I could see Mum again! I could go back to school, get on with my life. It seemed so unlikely – I'm not sure until that moment I'd believed it could really happen.

'Now we wait for Miss Allendon to get this and reply, and the second that happens I destroy everything of any value here and we get out. Now, why don't you get yourself ready to leave? And put the kettle on – a cup of tea would be lovely.'

It was gradually getting lighter. Though little daylight managed to leak through the shuttered window, there was enough to show that in spite of her bright, decisive manner Miranda was grey with exhaustion. Her hair had tangled and had taken on the appearance of a kind of crazy bird's nest and she'd put her dress on inside out.

I washed as well as I could in the kitchen, dressed in my boys' clothes as they made me feel more like myself than the dark dress of my namesake, and carefully made tea and some toast with the remaining bread. Miranda was still typing maniacally, her eyes never leaving the array before her. 'Thank you very much indeed – if you wouldn't mind just putting it there. Oh, and toast too, bless you.' She glanced up then and seemed surprised to see me in boys' clothes. 'It may not be a bad idea, I suppose,' she said speculatively.

I perched on the rickety chair behind her and drank my tea. A loud ping alerted her to the fact that she had mail. I nearly spilled my tea my hands were shaking so much. It was Jessica: 'Yes – meeting wld b gd. All well.' I smiled – she'd obviously had some practice texting. I wondered who she'd been texting and what phone she'd used as mine was with me. I think I felt a pang of jealousy. I typed in 'OK CU' over Miranda's shoulder. The minute she sent the message, Miranda was on her feet, still typing furiously. She pulled out a fat disc thing that looked a bit like the cartridges some people used instead of cassettes when my mum was young. She pushed it into a slot in a box hidden behind a jungle of cable and typed a rapid string of numbers, letters and symbols followed by 'END'.

'Right, we have five minutes to get out of here,' she said. She pulled a couple of levers and then raced into the bedroom from which she emerged a minute later with her hair redone and her dress the right way round. Somehow she had also found time to apply a coat of pale lipstick. 'You take Johnny's backpack and walk behind me as if you're with me. Stay close. Do not allow us to be separated. Oh, and here.'

She gave me the gun – the same one that I'd used before. I took it but had no idea where to put it. She was throwing various pieces of equipment into the rucksack. 'I don't think there's anything here that Harry can't live without,' she said, glancing round. 'Put the gun where you can get it easily.' She helped me to put the rucksack on my back – it was unexpectedly heavy. There was an outside pocket on the rucksack that I could reach relatively easily when it was on my back and she stowed the gun for me there. 'Whatever you do, don't shoot yourself in the back or we'll never get you to Waterloo,' she said, her smile this time swift and cursory: the strain was beginning to show. 'Ready?' she said crisply, looking for all the world like the archetypal neat and reliable secretary. 'Tuck your hair up under your cap and let's do this!'

I did as I was told, stuffing my hair into the flat cap I'd worn before. As a disguise I thought it pretty poor but once more it satisfied Miranda, who had a better idea than I did of what worked and what didn't.

We left the basement as smoke was beginning to pour from the abandoned machinery.

Was the whole thing going to explode? What about the people in the house above?

I didn't ask, but as soon as we got outside Miranda ran up the stairs to the main building, and rang the bell. Once the door was opened she shouted, 'Fire! Fire!' and within seconds people in various states of undress began to emerge running from the house. Someone had hit a mechanical firebell too – or at least some kind of alarm – it was loud, discordant and effective. Miranda turned to me. 'When the fire starts, we run, we don't look back. Are you ready, Miss Allendon?'

By now the stream of people exiting the house had

grown to a flood. There were many young girls in a variety of peculiar costumes – some in dressing-gowns and some merely wrapped hastily in blankets. In the main the men were older and trying hard not to be seen. It was perhaps a minute and a half before there was the sound of exploding glass and tongues of flame started dancing out of the window. Someone screamed, 'It's for real – Nellie – get the hell out!' A second later a young girl painted gold with a headdress of plastic grapes came racing from the building closely followed by a young man also painted gold and wearing nothing but a loin cloth. There were a few jeers and catcalls and then suddenly all the windows blew out with a bang – panic set in and people began to run in earnest. 'Now!' Miranda said and started to run herself.

I hefted Johnny's rucksack on to my back and ran after her, grateful that I was wearing the boy's shoes Johnny had brought me. The thing is Johnny is six foot three or four – I don't know – huge and strong and I'm not huge, though I don't like to think of myself as a weakling, so by the time we had gone a hundred or so metres I was really struggling with the weight, particularly since, as I've already explained, I'm nowhere near as fit as I ought to be. Fear had a part to play in my ability to run at all; after a while even the adrenalin ran out. 'Miss!' I called out after Miranda, pleased that I did at least have the wit not to call out her name, 'Miss! Can you wait a minute?'

Miranda stopped to allow me to catch up. 'I'm really sorry, the bag is too heavy for me to run,' I panted.

'All right – we'll get a tram.'

I followed her on to the next tram and kept my head down when she paid rather grandly for 'her man'.

'A poor excuse for a boy,' the conductor said with a sniff, but did not appear to mean anything more than that I didn't look like much of a man to him. I was so busy trying to appear as un-girl-like as possible that I honestly couldn't tell you where the tram went or in what part of London we got off. I followed Miranda without looking up as she had originally instructed me.

Karim's turned out to be a rather extensive Indian curry house. We entered through the back door – as ever – and were quickly ushered down into yet another basement, though one that was a good deal cleaner than Harry's place.

'You might as well sleep,' Miranda said, 'I've got a lot to sort out. I suggest that when Johnny comes you fill in the diary with any information you think will help the other Jessica Allendon and get changed into your own clothes – take off everything that is from this world, including your underwear, and put on everything that you brought with you from the other world. This is vital – do you understand me? I don't know about microbes and all that other stuff – we'll have to hope it isn't significant because I have no way of cleansing you of everything from this place. She paused to draw breath and to wipe a bead of sweat from her brow. 'Now, listen carefully. This is a safe house, but nowhere is really safe, not for me and not for you while you're with me, so you must always be prepared.' She smiled her plucky-woman smile yet again. 'It takes a bit of getting used to, but after a while it becomes second nature. Keep your gun near you and if I whistle like this –' She put her fingers in her mouth and produced the most ear-shattering whistle I've ever heard. She grinned at my expression. 'My brother taught me when we were kids – isn't it delightfully unladylike. Anyway, when you hear that sound – you take what is yours, you get out and you make a run for Waterloo on your own. Is that clear?' I nodded. 'Brave girl. If all goes well, I'll take you to Waterloo myself, otherwise God speed.' She hugged me swiftly and I was surprised at how slight she felt.

'Thank you,' I said, overcome by unhelpful emotions as ever. She was gone almost before I'd finished speaking – without a backward glance.

The basement had a number of mattresses on the floor, as if it had often been used as a dormitory. The sheets looked clean and I'm not sure I'd have cared if they weren't. I lay down – worn out with everything – and I think I must have fallen straight to sleep.

FORTY

I woke with a start when I felt a man's hand touch my face.

'Hush, Jess – don't worry, it's only me, Johnny. I brought your things,' he said. On seeing him, I smiled and stretched.

'Thank you,' I said. 'What time is it?'

'About three o'clock in the afternoon.' His hand stayed near my face and I kissed it.

'Jess . . .' He began moving his hand away. 'I don't think . . . We shouldn't . . . I think I should go and find out if Miranda wants me.'

'I want you too, Johnny,' I said. 'I'll have to go soon and we'll never see each other again. Miranda can wait a few minutes.' I don't know what made me so bold. I'm not like that usually. I suppose it was the gut-level realisation that what I knew I felt for Johnny was precious and special and that we didn't have months to get to know each other, to hedge round each other – there was no time left to play games. He seemed to agree, or at least he didn't argue. In fact he didn't *say* anything.

It was a good while later that he went to get his orders from Miranda. I got dressed in my old clothes, which felt strange and alien now. There was no mirror but it didn't matter. I was embarrassed by the shortness of my T-shirt and the way it revealed my stomach, but so happy to put my favourite trainers back on. There was still no signal on my phone, but I stuffed it and my keys in my pockets – I found five pounds too.

I filled in Jessica's diary. I wrote as neatly as I could and was careful to be honest about what had happened, not making excuses for myself but explaining everything that went wrong as well as I could. I didn't know what to say about Johnny. I couldn't say nothing, so after a lot of pen chewing I finally wrote it down. 'I fell in love with Jonathan Roberts.' It wasn't really enough on its own, so I added, 'He fell in love with me too.' The rest she would have to work out for herself.

I was sitting down to wait for Johnny to come back when I suddenly heard Miranda's piercing whistle. Oh shit, what did I do now? I ran for the back door only to see two grey-suited men coming towards me. I slammed the door shut and bolted it. My heart was pounding wildly. I ran back into the room and floundered about until I managed to get the gun out of the pocket of the rucksack. I could hear the men banging at the door. There was a stairway, which I supposed must lead to the restaurant. I stuffed the diary in the back of my jeans –

which were 'boy cut' and not tight at all by my normal standards – then I legged it up the stairs. I ran straight through the kitchen, through the empty dining hall. Someone was after me! I didn't care about the shrieks of the clientele when they saw the gun. I didn't care about anything but getting away. I was much faster in my trainers and I was very scared. I pushed past a couple trying to get into the restaurant without really seeing them. There were grey suits outside – there were bound to be – but which way did I go? The person chasing me was gaining on me, but I didn't stop. I put my head down and ran, faster I think than I'd ever done in my life, because I knew this time that my life depended on it. I could hear heavy footfalls behind me. My lungs were bursting and my mouth dry. My hair was in my eyes, making it difficult to see, but my vision was blurred anyway so I'm not sure I'd have been able to see where I was going even if I'd had any idea of where that should be. Somebody grabbed my arm. Oh, God no! Not when I was so close to getting away.

'Down this way,' he said, manhandling me down a side street. I struggled in his grip and then saw that it was Johnny.

'I thought you were after me!' I gasped.

'I was – I was afraid you'd run the wrong way. And, and I can't let you go without saying goodbye.'

I was sweating badly. There was a storm feeling in the air

– hot with the promise of thunder and a strange sulphurous smell. I thought I saw lightning. Johnny guided me down a quieter tree-lined road and then I had to stop because I'd a stitch in my side. I wanted to retch.

'I – I – don't think I can run any further,' I gasped. He patted me comfortingly on the back.

'You don't have to. We chose Karim's because it's so close. It's nearly time. Look – Waterloo is just there!' Straightening up, I could see that he was right. We were more or less opposite the main entrance. We hovered behind one of the few parked cars in the area – a gleaming scarlet Achilles-Benz. I could see a group of men in suits and bowler hats heading for the doors of the first class concourse. I was trembling, with fear I suppose.

'Were we followed?'

'I don't know, but give me the gun and the diary. Have you anything else from here?'

I shook my head. 'What time is it?' It was hard to sound even slightly normal with the great tide of emotions that was surging through me. I felt like I was being flattened inside every few seconds, as a new tidal thought overwhelmed me: the meeting wouldn't work and I'd never get home; it would work and I'd never see Johnny again.

'Two minutes to five,' Johnny said, evenly.

I clutched his hand. 'Johnny . . .' I began.

He put his finger on my lips. 'There's nothing more to

say, Jessica. Nothing. We both know all that we ever need to know.' He smiled that rare smile that lit me up inside just as much as it lit up his face. 'I'll do everything I can for the other Jessica – you have my solemn word of honour. You can be certain that every moment I'm with her I'll be thinking of you – wishing she were you.' I nodded, too full of tears and too battered by my emotions to be able to speak. He pulled me towards him and kissed me, right there in the street – I can't tell you how very un-Johnny-like that was: he was so proper in public. I can't tell you either how hard it was to break away from him when somewhere a clock struck five.

I saw her then. She stood ramrod straight, as smartly dressed as when I'd first met her – Jessica! She was standing on the steps of the main station. I think she saw me at the same moment as I spotted her. She waved a black-gloved hand.

'Go home, Jess,' Johnny said gently, and pushed me towards her. I ran then, unable to look back. I didn't know what she was thinking – I couldn't guess. I'd walked in her shoes and she'd walked in mine – she was closer than a sister and still a total stranger. As I got nearer to her, I could see that she was crying and so was I – hot tears were streaming down my face and I couldn't stop them. She held out her arms to me and I didn't know if she was making a plea for help or a gesture of welcome, but I opened my arms too and we ran towards each other. People were staring, shouting, but my eyes were fixed on her eyes, my doppelganger, another me, my twin. I felt her embrace for less than an instant, her sob and her tears as our cheeks touched. 'Jessica!' I said, and then it happened again, just like before. The world disintegrated and was remade.

I thought for an unmeasurable space of time that perhaps both universes and all in them might have died or be about to die. There was an explosion, a roaring in my ears, an unbearably bright light and then I was sitting on the steps and a man ran past me almost trampling over me – he was wearing dirty trainers and ragged jeans. I got shakily to my feet to avoid the rest of the milling, thoughtless rush-hour crowd. I looked around wildly. He must be here. And then I saw him, my friend, Jonno, white with anxiety and wearing Johnny's face. I launched myself at him, sobbing, and he held me tight. His skin even smelled like Johnny's skin.

'Is Mum OK?' I gasped as soon as I could speak. I think Jonno was crying too.

'It's been really hard, Jess, but she's OK. Call her.'

I groped in my back pocket for my phone, which astonishingly sprang into life at my touch. It rang and I heard her voice, the voice I thought I'd never hear again. It was difficult to say anything through my sobs but I managed to get something out.

'Mum? Mum, it's me, Jess. I'm home!'

EPILOGUE

I was lucky – I know that; I got home alive – a bit shaken up but all in one piece, apart from my heart that is, but you can't have everything.

It was so good to see Mum again and Jonno – the days that followed were constantly punctuated by hugs and tears. Mum looked like she'd aged ten years – she had realised the second she saw Jessica that something was very wrong, even though Jonno had helped Jessica to dress like me.

Jessica had kept a careful diary and through that I was able to piece together a story of a difficult and confusing few days of culture shock and fear, but I'll say this for her, she was pretty adaptable and I think she did quite a good job of being me. She'd offended loads of my friends, obviously, and school was a bit difficult for a while, but compared to being shot at, bombed and questioned by brutal Security Service thugs, it was all great. Jessica rather impressed my Maths teacher and my English teacher, but it took a long time for my history teacher to forgive me for the detailed, complex and as far as he was concerned totally fabricated essay on the origins and consequences of the cold war.

I never found out how she got on with Jonno; he was curiously evasive about it and her diary was silent on the subject.

About a week after I got back I received an email.

'All well. The General has arranged for Jessie and myself to work in the colonies for the Brotherhood – Australia probably. Hope you are "OK". Love, always, Johnny.'

And that, I suppose, is the end. I take politics and social issues a lot more seriously now, and I am a lot more grateful for the chance to stay on at school and to get a degree. I can't help thinking of Elizabeth Jennings. Maybe I'll become a doctor too – who knows? One thing I do know is that one way or another I'll be looking for Johnny for the rest of my life. What is the quote? Something like: 'It is better to have loved and lost than never to have loved at all.' Yeah. Right.